THE BIRD OF TIME

Gavan Bromilow

Valentine Press

First published by Valentine Press in 2014

Valentine Press
P.O. Box 527,
Bellingen NSW 2454
www.valentinepress.com.au

National Library of Australia Cataloguing-in-Publication entry:

Creator:	Bromilow, Gavan, author
Title:	The bird of time / Gavan Bromilow
ISBN:	9780987506368 (paperback)
Subjects:	Survival--Fiction
Dewey Number:	A823.4

Printed and bound in Australia by Lightning Source Australia

When you have finished reading *The Bird of Time*, Valentine Press and Gavan Bromilow would appreciate your feedback. There is a Reader's Comments page on the Valentine Press website: **http://valentinepress.com.au/?page_id=1439**

Come, fill the cup, and in the fire of spring,
The winter garment of repentance fling:
The bird of time has but a little way to fly and lo!
The bird is on the wing.

The Rubaiyat of Omar Khayyam

Contents

Chapter 1: Burning cold

He didn't know what it was that woke him, but as soon as his eyes were open he knew that something terrible, something almost too frightening to think about, was happening. It was bitterly cold. So cold it might have been the start of the end of the world. It was winter and he and his partner Rohini had two Indian padded, cotton quilts on their bed. These were warm enough for any winter night they had ever had there on the Deccan plateau where temperatures could drop at night to near freezing. But this cold was coming through the quilts and eating his body warmth like nothing he had ever known and they had often camped in the high Himalayas. He could hear the wind howling around the house like the jackals that often visited the farm. They always slept with the windows open. The wind was whistling through the mosquito mesh and hitting the skin of his face and shoulders like a shower of acid. They usually slept nude all year round although Rohini sometimes pulled on a pair of trekking socks. Griff gave her a nudge.

"What, what? What is it?" she said, sitting up.

"There's something bad happening. Very bad. So bad I don't know what to think."

"Oh god, what is it? Is it the dogs, a rabid dog, bandits, have the animals got loose? God, it's cold, has the roof gone or something?"

"Worse than that."

"Worse? How could it be worse?"

"There's worse, believe me. We don't get cold like this in this part of India. It's not possible. You know when we camp in the mountains in autumn or in Ladakh and there is an early snow storm, it's not as bad as this. If we don't do something we'll freeze to death by morning. We have to get up now."

They rolled out of bed and the cold was burning. It was getting colder by the minute. They had a large teak chest at the foot of the bed with winter clothes and some trekking gear. They dragged gear out and put it on, including boots.

"Whatever could be doing this?" Rohini said, just as Griff was trying to sort out the possibilities in his own head.

"It's hard to say but it's got to be one of the following. The world has flipped out of orbit, or been knocked out of it and is hurtling into space away from the sun. That's probably the worst option and means we'll be dead within twenty-four hours. Or there has been a huge volcanic eruption that has put a blanket of ash between the sun and the earth, or it could be a large asteroid impact that has done that or even a nuclear war. But I don't think it's any of those. We almost certainly would have felt the impact. There is another possibility and, because of the wind, I think that must be the most likely one."

"Oh hell, what is it?"

"I think the earth has wobbled on its axis and we are now at the North Pole or very near it. Somewhere in the Arctic zone at least."

"That's wonderful. We haven't got any skis or sleds and only two ill-matched mongrel dogs." She laughed. "Do we need to get out fast?"

Griff looked out the window as he closed it and could see that snow was starting to fall thickly and build up on the window sills. "No. I think there will be a massive and murderous rush to get away. The roads will be choked. There will be accidents everywhere. People will be freezing to death in cars and on motorbikes. There'll be robbery and murder. People killing people to get their cars, their fuel, food and clothing."

"Yes. I expect you are right. It will be mayhem. But can we afford to wait?"

"Yes, I think we can and we will survive if we act now. The good thing is that a large part of the world, most of the world, will still be functioning fairly normally and they will get rescue operations in hand. We need to survive until the great stampede is over. Could be a month or two. There should be news bulletins on TV and radio. We'll have power from our solar panel inverter battery for a few hours at least if not from the government grid."

Rohini went upstairs to switch the inverter on so they could turn on the television and Griff went downstairs to the sitting room to get the fire going. They had a slow combustion wood burning stove that would keep the whole house warm if they kept it going day and night. There were still some embers there and Griff added kindling and small pieces of wood and fanned them into flames.

Rohini came downstairs and turned on the TV. It usually took a minute or so to warm up and get the satellite picture.

"I've put water on to make coffee," Griff said. "We'll have to keep the stove going twenty-four hours a day. Next to food it's our most important thing to do. If it goes out we die."

"Well, at least we've got plenty of good dry hardwood to keep it going for months. Okay, here it is. I've got the news," Roh said. She turned up the volume so they could hear it above the wind. "You were right, Griff."

A panel of earth scientists and geographers on BBC-TV were exercising their hobby-horses. The earth had changed its axis. India and China had moved close to the North Pole. The US, Europe and Australia had moved closer to the tropics. Gigantic storms were raging on land and sea everywhere with massive flooding and damage, and that would hamper rescue operations. The United Nations Security Council was holding an emergency meeting to decide on how to cope with the cataclysm. Panic migration was expected. Fleets of large ships were being mobilised to take refugees from India and China and nearby nations to safe havens. Scientists were not agreed on what had caused it. Some said it was just a natural event that could happen at any time and had happened before.

Others said it had happened now because the ice caps were melting due to global warming. It might flip back to the old position soon or it mightn't. No way to tell. Others were saying that the gradual movement of the tectonic plates over millions of years had altered the gyroscopic balance of the earth and it had flipped to the new perfect pole position. We were lucky the earth hadn't wobbled. Hadn't flipped back and forth creating even greater chaos than had already occurred. The Archbishop of Canterbury and the Pope were saying the clean jump from one axis to another showed the hand of god. He was still looking after us.

"Ah, Dr Pangloss isn't dead after all and I bet the nuts who talk to god are saying it has been caused by the growing weight of sin,"Griff said.

"Well, the old ice cap may be melting but we've got another one forming here right now, so we had better get to work." Griff got one of the kerosene storm lanterns from the pantry, lit it and hung it in the sitting room.

"Let's sit down with our coffee," Rohini said, "and do a quick list of priority jobs."

"Ooooh, nooo," she cried, "the dogs, the poor dogs. We have to get them inside." She rushed for the front door. The dogs slept in big woven bamboo baskets lined with hessian bags on the front veranda.

"We'd better get Namji, Wasanta and Seema and Suman while we are at it," Griff added.

Namji, the nickname for Namdeo, was the night-watchman and Wasanta was the dairy hand. Seema was his wife. Wasanta and Seema had a room in one of the farm outhouses. Suman, their widowed, elderly housekeeper cook, lived in a room adjoining Wasanta and Seema. Namji had a house and small farm on their road half a kilometre away, but at nights he slept on a charpoy, a bed frame strung with twine, under the awning of the old house and storerooms that now formed part of the farm outhouses and cattleshed.

The dogs stumbled shivering out of their baskets as they got to them. They gave them a quick pat and rub and then ran across the farm yard or wasti to the outhouse area adjoining the dairy. The wind was whipping snow into their eyes and stinging the skin like wasps. There was a light in Wasanta and Seema's room and they banged on the door. The four of them, wrapped in blankets, were huddled around the small metal shegdi, a portable wood or charcoal fired cooking stove.

"Bai, Saheb, what is happening? We are so cold?" Wasanta cried.

Rohini told them there was a serious weather problem and they would have to come into the house straight away bringing their food and clothing. She would explain the weather problem in detail in the

4

house. Everyone grabbed something, cooking pots, kerosene, utensils, bedding and bags of grain. By the time they got to the house they were close to numb with the cold. They settled them around the stove to warm up and gave them a coffee each with a tot of rum. The dogs, Rani, a medium sized black and white mongrel bitch and Digger, a big pai dog, were standing and looking a bit lost. Roh and Griff brought their baskets in and settled them near the stove with a biscuit each. They were happy.

Namji was an ex-soldier who had been discharged after being shot in the knee and had a limp, but was young and fit, well-built and strong. A very handy man. He could read and write, take orders and handle weapons which Griff thought might be needed before their uncertain situation was resolved. Wasanta and Seema were illiterate but far from stupid. They were smart and strong, hard-working and loyal, as was Namji. As soon as they had recovered from the shock of the sudden cold, they were plying Rohini with questions. Griff's Marathi was okay for basic things but Roh was a linguist. She explained in simple non-scientific terms that the earth had tilted on its axis, an event which had happened in prehistoric times and could probably occur at almost any time, and that India was now near the North Pole which was an icy wilderness continent. That meant that where they were on the western side of the Deccan Plateau, along with all of India and most of China, would slowly turn into a new icy continent and what was left of the former North Pole would melt completely. Meanwhile they would experience massive freezing storms as the cold air moved in from the old pole. They would be without sunlight for many months, then they would have six months of light and weak sunshine. She explained that they would have to try to survive until they could be rescued but that it would be very dangerous. They would all have to work very hard to make themselves secure and that they might be attacked by people wanting to take their food and fuel and clothing. She said that most of the world would be operating normally, although they would also be affected by climate change that would cause storms and flooding and that rescuers would come looking for them sooner or later. They needed to keep their heads, work together and survive until then. Roh asked if Griff wanted to add anything. She would translate. He said that he would post Namji as watchman on the front door with a shotgun and that all the other doors must be kept locked at all times. No-one was to go out without telling Namji and another person where they were going, and how long they would be. Namji would write that in a log and they might soon start having daily passwords so that Namji would know when someone who was not one of their group was approaching. Because of the dark it would be difficult working and keeping the place secure. They would have a lot of work to do immediately and they would be given jobs shortly, when Roh and he had worked out a list of things to be done. He said that Rohini and he wanted them to stay with them for safety and they were sure they could survive. Griff knew that the most pressing topic on their minds was the fate of their relatives. He told them that if they wished to go to their relatives or friends in the village that they could do so, but to try to go any further than that would be suicide. They could not bring their relatives back to the house, except that Namji could bring his wife, Laxmi, and teenage daughter, Jyoti. There would be people maddened by fear who would do anything to get food, firewood or fuel, warm clothing and shelter.They would probably have a few more joining them. Perhaps the supervisor and his deputy from Roh's other farm, Kamala farm, nearby and that would make ten people counting Namji, Wasanta, Seema and Suman.

Griff said he thought they could not go beyond ten people in the house along with food and fuel, including livestock which they would need to have in the house, because it might be three months or more before rescuers came along. Wasanta and Seema seemed satisfied with that and said that they wanted to stay with Bai and Saheb. They had no close relatives in the nearby village. Their relatives lived five or six kilometres away. Namji said he would leave straight away to get his wife and daughter, Jyoti. Suman had many relatives living near the village but she realised they were too numerous to be accommodated in the house. They would have to do the best they could, she said.

Griff told Namji to take the one-bullock cart and be back within an hour and to bring what clothing, grain and other food, cooking pots, kerosene and useful items they could carry and to try to get an

6

idea of what, if anything, was happening along the road. Griff gave him an old pair of his boots and a couple of pairs of thick socks as well as a heavy jacket and a pair of leather gloves and told him that he would have to bind Laxmi and Jyoti's feet with cloth, pull plastic bags over them and then tie a piece of bagging around the feet to give grip on the snow. Griff realised that he would have to do something quickly about footwear because the men would all have to go out into the snow almost straight away to bring in tools, grain, logs and equipment. The locals often went barefoot and at best wore sandals. Plastic bags wouldn't be adequate. They would only do for a very short trip. But he knew they had old car tubes and tyres in one of the godowns. He would cut lengths of tubes that would reach up to the knees and seal them at the toe end with a wire twist. He could then cut half shoes from old tyres to go under the foot and be tied on over the instep so that they could walk without slipping. They would have to wrap cloth around their feet before pulling on the rubber boots. But before then Roh and he needed to do the priority job list.

"Griff, I have to try to speak to my parents. The phones may be jammed but I have to try," she said, and headed up the stairs to the roof to use her mobile phone.

"Go. I'll start drafting jobs."

Rohini's parents lived in Pune, one hundred and twenty kilometres from the farm. Her father was a manufacturer of agricultural equipment and her mother an English lecturer at the university. They were well off and well connected and had links with the US as well as with Australia. Griff guessed they would be already making plans to fly out to the US where Rohini's brother and sister lived. All Griff's relatives were in Australia. He called out to Rohini to try to get through to his brother in Perth to let him know that they were fine. His brother would spread the word through his family.

Griff loaded up the fire with fresh logs and brought another two armfuls in from the front veranda where he always stacked wood during the winter months. He let Namji out, bolted the door and sat down with his coffee and a notepad to make a list of urgent jobs. The two most pressing needs were food and firewood and in that they were very lucky. They had at least one hundred and fifty bags of wheat, millet, sorghum, maize and chick pea in the godowns for seed and sale use and many tonnes of dry firewood. Rohini grew grain crops on the farm and ran a small timber business from eucalypt plantations that took up about half of her forty-acre home farm. On the other family farm, Kamala, half a kilometre away, she raised sheep as well as fodder crops. There were more than three hundred ewes and two hundred half-grown lambs there and if they could bring some across to the main homestead they would be in a fairly secure situation for several months. They had two huge haystacks on the home farm and another three at Kamala that would keep the livestock going if they could shelter them from the cold.

However, the first job was to get the shotgun out, check it and load it. Namji would be door watchman with the gun. They had one whistle which they would give him to use in the case of the need to alert them all to danger. Next, Griff would need to get the old tubes and tyres from the godowns, a hundred metres away, to make snow boots so that they could work outside carrying grain, stockfeed, tools and fuel and other useful items to the house. They would need to stack furniture in the study and sitting room against the windows to make them secure and to clear space in the middle for grain and timber storage and livestock. Meanwhile, Wasanta and Namji would go to Kamala farm, with two bullock carts to bring Subhash and Ramesh, the supervisor and his deputy, along with grain, kerosene, clothing, bedding and lambs. Reinforcing the front and back doors with teak planks was about the next priority. Griff figured it would take several days at least before the surviving hard people from the local area, the ones who would stop at nothing to get what they wanted, would come calling and it would take a couple of days to get the top priority jobs done.

Rohini came down from the roof terrace after trying to get the calls out to her family. "I couldn't get through to my parents. They weren't answering. I reached your brother. They were worried, but I told them if anyone could survive it's you and me. I said we would be staying on here for a while. They sent their love and said they would tell the hotline the Australian Government had set up in Canberra, where we were and that we needed rescuing," she said. Griff could see she was upset.

"Thanks for that, my love. I am sorry about your folks, but I reckon they would be safe. They are probably at the airport waiting for a flight out. We know they don't use mobile phones and getting hold of a public phone to call you would be hard if not impossible."

She came over and gave Griff a hug and started to cry softly into his shoulder. She was the youngest of her parents' children and very close to them. Griff had been a little surprised initially that she hadn't wanted to rush to Pune to help them but she was clever and he knew she would know that she would never make it.

"They are old but I don't want them to die. I want to see them again."

"You will, Roh, you will. They will get out to the US and we will survive here. You'll be able to meet them after we get rescued from here."

"How can you be sure of that?"

"Trust me. I know we can do it. We've got the supplies, the fuel, the help, a house we can make into a fortress and, most of all, we've got brains and grit."

Griff didn't tell Roh that he'd had a moment of despair and near panic when he considered the endless list of things he would have to do and organise to set them up and keep them safe. But he had pulled out of it. He knew he was the only one of the group who had the know-how and the vision to get them through this crisis. Roh was brilliant in her field but she had never lived in snow country and had never been a skier. He had at least had been a cross-country skier when he lived in Canberra and had lived in the snow country for days at a time. The closest the others had been to snow and cold was an ice-cream and they'd had very few of those. They'd lived their lives dressed in nothing heavier than a pair of sandals and light cotton gear or rags. They knew nothing of the dangers of frostbite and hypothermia and how quickly they could reduce a person to a useless deadweight. He would have to think for them and make them do things they probably would have little understanding of. He would drive them relentlessly through the days and weeks of work needed to

9

set them all up securely. He was determined to survive himself and he would make them survive too.

Griff told Roh the priorities he had jotted down and asked her how many lambs she thought they could put in the study and how many on the roof terrace. He said he thought ten for each space.

"Oh, hell, do we have to have them in the house? My beautiful house. They will make such a mess and a stink. We'll never get the stench out."

"Well, the sad truth, Roh, is that this house is a goner anyway. What we are doing now is a temporary survival strategy. In a couple of years this place will be under a hundred metres of ice and snow. In 10,000 years, if the planet survives, archaeologists will drill down through a mile of ice, discover it and have some interesting questions to solve."

"Yes, I guess you're right. We just have to do everything we can now to survive until we are rescued. So you may as well double those figures for the lambs. We've got the fodder. Greater numbers will help keep them warm and some will probably die anyway, so we need extras. But how will they survive on the roof terrace? The sides are open to the weather."

"We'll stack bales of straw to the roof around the walls on the weather sides and just a foot short on the other side for air. We have plenty of plastic tarps which we can put on the inside to protect the straw from the sheep as well as the outside to stop snow from blowing in."

"What should we do with the first floor terrace outside our bedroom?"

"Since it is open to the sky, I thought it would be a good place to stack hay fodder. The fodder is the most space-consuming stuff we have. It will act as an insulation for our bedroom and the house generally. We can stack it with an outward slope and cover it with plastic so that the snow slides off. In that location it will be easy to get at from our bedroom."

"That sounds good and we could do the same with the downstairs kitchen terrace and the open part of the roof terrace," Roh said.

"Yes. And I want to stack some sawn dry logs for the stove under the straw in both places as well as the unroofed top terrace. We have to make sure we have plenty of timber for the stove in the house or close to it because I suspect that within a day or two people will be scavenging for timber as well as other things and, as you well know, desperate people around here will steal anything they can lay their hands on."

"What do you think we should do with the dry wood already cut for sale? I would feel bad if we just kept everything and didn't help the village people desperate for heating," Roh said.

"Give it away. There will be people screaming at the gates at 6 am wanting wood and we should let them have some. But we should ration it at 40 kg to a family otherwise the greedy will try to hog it. There's quite a few tonnes there and if we ration it out it will give us time to cut and get in all the big stuff we need to survive. And we can give away the partly seasoned poles too if anyone wants them. Okay. What next, Roh?"

"What were you planning for the cattle?"

"We need to keep the female buffalo for the milk and we can keep the buffalo heifer for the time being too. I think we should butcher the male buffalo and one of the three draft oxen fairly soon. They eat a lot of fodder and they take a lot of space to stall."

"But where will we store so much meat? They are huge."

"We will only do one at a time and if we haul the carcass high up into the rain tree and anchor it to the ground with a chain and padlock, this weather will keep it refrigerated. I'll drive a large steel stake into the ground to chain it to. One carcass will keep us going for weeks. We need to keep the draft oxen for dragging in stores and fuel and in a few days to go on scavenging hunts ourselves."

"So that leaves us with three draft oxen, a milking buffalo and a heifer buffalo. Where did you think to put them?"

"In the guest suite along with a lot of fuel wood and most of the grain. The buffalo and her heifer can go in the guest bathroom. We can forget about using the bathrooms and toilet for the usual things because the drains and the septic system will be frozen solid. We will be crapping in buckets and having armpit and crutch baths with a wet

11

towel from now on. We'll have plenty of water from melted snow and we will need to have daily sewage runs to take out the dirty water and dump it away from the house."

"The guest suite runs off the sitting room. The smell will be terrible," Roh said.

"Yeah, that's true, but if we clean the area where we have the cattle and also the sheep rooms everyday, it won't be too bad and their body heat will help to keep the house warm. We have plenty of hands to do the work and it will keep people occupied and not sitting around worrying about their relatives dying from cold and starvation."

"Yes, that's the last thing we want."

"Are we being a little bit ironical, Roh, my love?"

"Perhaps. You seem to be so clinical about it all. You don't have any relatives in India or in danger of dying of cold and starvation, do you. You almost seem to be enjoying this."

"Yes, I am. I'm not going to sit in a corner wrapped in a blanket and wait for death. Life is a struggle and that is what makes life interesting and worth living. People who have everything handed to them on a plate get fat, lazy and unable to survive when the challenge comes."

"Yes, I do agree, Griff. I am just upset about my parents and I can't help thinking about all the people in my country who will die miserably while we have so much. This will be the end of India, won't it?"

"Death by cold is fairly quick and painless. You just feel cold a short while and then go off to sleep and anyway, it won't be the end of Indians or Indian culture. Hundreds of thousands of Indians, even millions, will survive by escaping in planes and boats and Indian culture will survive to enrich the cultures of other countries. That's been the way of things since the beginnings of human culture."

"Do you really think hundreds of thousands will survive this?"

"Yes, I reckon millions will survive. Indians are survivors and we are going to survive too, if we move quickly. Scores of people, desperate to survive, will be screaming at the gates in an hour or two. What do you want to do with the ewes and lambs we cannot use from Kamala farm?"

"Well, we cannot take all the Kamala farm workers here and most wouldn't want to come anyway. We can only take Subhash and Ramesh. So we can let the rest go to their families in the village and they can split the lambs and sheep we don't want among themselves, and give some to the village people as well."

"That's good, Roh. Most of the people won't have enough fodder to keep even three sheep for more than a few days, so the village people will all be well fed for a while. And they will have fuel wood from here to cook the meat.

"I'll try to get Subhash on the phone, and tell him what to do. As soon as Namji gets back he and Wasanta can take the two bullocks' carts to Kamala farm and get them and their gear and bring the forty best lambs across. That means I will have to make rubber boots for Namji and Wasanta and Subhash and Ramesh right now. Let's get across to the workshop and godowns now to get tools, tubes and tyres and bring them here where I can work on them. Wasanta, you will have to stay here and guard the door." Griff gave him the whistle and a torch and told him to lock the door from inside and only to open it when they came back. He should blow two blasts if people came and started to cause trouble.

Roh and Griff put on heavy jackets, woollen hats and gloves, took their torches and headed for the wasti – the farmyard godown area. Outside it was wild. The wind was tearing the leaves from the trees and buffeting them about. The snow was already six inches to a foot thick. Here and there dead birds lay in the snow, frozen stiff amid leaves and branches blown from the stripped trees.

"Griff, I am really worried about the cattle. We will have to get them into the house quickly. They won't survive this cold for long. Let's put them into one of the godowns now to get them out of the wind and snow and if they are all in together their own heat will help to protect them until we can clear the room in the house and move them across."

They untied the animals. They were all standing and bellowing from time to time. They led them across into one of the empty godowns, threw armfuls of straw in for them, and closed the door.

13

From the main equipment godown they collected half a dozen car tubes, enough to make six pairs of long boots and two car tyres which would make the shoes to give grip in the snow. They took them across to the house and then went back to the workshop to get tools including binding wire, bolt-cutters, hacksaws and a couple of bags of other tools and bits and pieces Griff thought he could use, including ropes and twine, punches, screws, nails and bolts. Lumping the stuff back to the house through the increasingly thick snow and battling against the wind was tiring them quickly. Griff knew he would have to find some way of getting gear across to the house more quickly and easily and it came to him. He took an old axe and a hacksaw and five metres of rope and went around to the back of the wasti area where there was an old car. There were four pillars plus the areas on each side of the rear window holding the roof to the body of the car. Griff chopped into the pillars in front first and was pleased to see that the axe worked well on them. He used the hacksaw to finish off the remaining strands that the axe was not effective on. The two side pillars went quickly but the rear pillars were close to half a metre wide. Surprisingly, the axe bit into them well and the hacksaw finished them off. Griff tied the rope onto one of the pillars and pulled the roof clear of the body and flipped it over. With a rope tied around each of the two front pillars, it formed a sled that moved easily across the snow. He went back to the godowns with it and loaded it up with all sorts of gear they would need, from plastic tarpaulins and rope to lengths of teak that he would use to reinforce doors and make other improvisations. Roh and he pulled the sled over the snow to the edge of the patio to unload it. Wasanta came out to help. As they were moving the gear inside, Namji arrived back with Laxmi and Jyoti and they got them into the house and by the stove quickly to warm up. Suman had made tea for everyone and they needed it. Snow had formed clumps on their hats and shoulders.

"We'll have to do something to keep the draft oxen warm, Griff. I just had a quick look at the one that Namji took and it looks to me as though it is suffering badly from the cold."

"The only thing I can think of is that we use our carpets to make coats for them. Would that be enough do you think?"

14

"Yes, that should do well."

Griff finished his tea and went to the guest room and the upstairs bedroom and brought out several of their precious old, hand-woven tribal carpets, Persian and Afghani, which they had collected over the years. It broke his heart but as he had said to Roh earlier, all this would soon be gone forever. When they left they would go with what they stood up in. He brought the bullock Namji had used onto the sheltered veranda and threw a rug over him, with the wool side close to the hide. He was the youngest and slimmest of their three draft oxen. The carpet covered him from the neck to the rump. Wasanta held the rug in place under the bullock's neck and Griff pushed an awl through and then threaded rope through the holes: two ties under the neck, one under the chest and one just before the hind legs and then a rope running from under the neck to the rear to hold it in place. That left him free to pee and crap without soiling the rug. Wasanta suggested another short tie under the tail to make sure the rug didn't slip around. Wasanta harnessed him back into the cart.

The next job had to be making rubber boots and car-tyre overshoes for Namji and Wasanta, so they could go across to Kamala to get Subhash and Ramesh and the lambs, and two more rug coats for the two oxen to pull the big cart across to the Kamala farm.

It didn't take Griff long to do a pair of "car-boots". He cut a tube into two pieces, put a binding wire twist on one end to seal off the toe and cut a twenty-five-centimetre length of tyre to form the boot. The farm workers were smaller-boned with smaller, narrower feet generally than westerners. In the front part of the boot he put a permanent wire tie to hold it together and two holes on each side towards the rear to enable a piece of rope to be threaded through to go around the ankle to hold the boot in place. They weren't beautiful but this was no setting for a fashion show. Footwear was a bit of a novelty to these farm people. Most of them at best wore leather chappals or rubber thongs, and socks were affectations of city slickers. Most of the time the locals preferred to go barefoot and the soles of their feet were as tough as shoe leather. Griff showed Namji how to bind his feet with a piece of old towelling and then slip the rubber tube over the top and tie the tyre-boot on. The others all watched. When Namji had both feet

15

done he stood up and did a test walk and then a little dance. Griff realised that he would have to make several pairs of gloves straight away for the men going outside. He made them from woollen socks. While doing that he realised he had an old leather jacket and a pair of leather rigger's gloves that he could use as a pattern. Later he would cut gloves from the leather jacket. Namji, who would be the watchman and a couple of the other men would need gloves that would enable them to fit their fingers into the trigger guard of the shotgun. He would have to modify the trigger guard so that a leather-gloved finger could fit into it. He finished the gloves and boots and called the other men. "Teek, hey, let's go out and try them in the snow," Griff said.

Roh and Griff and Wasanta went out with him and he tramped around for a while. A different walking style was needed but he was certainly stable and in no danger of slipping. The tyre-boot had plenty of grip. They went back into the house and Roh quizzed Namji closely about how warm his feet had kept and if the boots had chafed or caused any pain. No pain, he said, but he showed them that the tubes had slipped down his leg a little. Griff fixed that with a couple of holes and a piece of twine to tie snugly around his leg above the calf muscle. That seemed to solve the warm dry footwear problem. He set to work to make a pair each for Wasanta, Subhash and Ramesh, so Namji and Wasanta could leave for Kamala farm. Roh told them to have a look at what was happening in the village on the way through and to get back as quickly as they could, hopefully within one hour. She told them to tell Subhash to share the unwanted sheep among the other Kamala farm workers who lived on the farm and that they could drive the remaining sheep into the village to be taken by whoever wanted them. She also told them to make sure that their gloves were kept dry and warm. Frost-bitten hands and feet could render a person useless and nothing more than a mouth to feed, she said.

Griff looked at the time. It was now 4.30 am. It was 2 am when they had woken and he was worrying about getting a lot of the high priority jobs done before 6.30 am, when he reckoned people would be clamouring for firewood. They still had so much to do. Griff put his arm around Roh and gave her a hug and a kiss on the cheek. Kissing on the lips was something you didn't do in front of other people unless you were a Bollywood film star. Neither of them were that. Roh was beautiful enough to be a Bollywood actress but that would be the last thing in the world she would want to be. She had been an outstanding student who had done medicine and then decided she would much rather work with animals than people. She had become a veterinarian and a farmer and, because of her brains and drive and long hours of work, she was very successful. She served on several government advisory bodies and published papers that were widely quoted internationally. She was lean and wiry but shapely. Griff often told her she had the most beautiful backside in the world. Her face had chiselled lines with wide-set eyes, full lips and clear skin. She had a wonderful spontaneous laugh and an equally explosive temper if things were not done according to instructions. Griff thought she worked too hard. Driven. Her family were Chitpawan Brahmins from Konkan, the south west coastal plains of India, and they had been pioneers in education and social development in India for several generations. They were sophisticated and cosmopolitan people who were devoted to helping India struggle free of poverty, ignorance and religious superstition. The women in her family were independent and free-spirited. They made their own decisions about lifestyle and marriage. There was a belief among many Indians that the Chitpawan Brahmins were descended from the crew of one of Alexander's ships that was blown out of history by a massive storm that swept the Gulf of Cambay when his navy with half his army was trying to make its way back to Greece after the Indian campaign. The ship is said to have landed in Konkan and its crew settled there, intermarrying with the locals. They were, according to the British in the days of the Raj, scholarly and innovative in agriculture among other things. Rohini had travelled abroad with her family since her teenage years and had studied in the UK and Australia, but she was never going to emigrate.

She and Griff had a shared interest in natural history and had met during a natural history trek in the mountains of the Western Ghats. The attraction was immediate. They kept in touch by letter and telephone almost daily while Griff made arrangements back in Australia to be able to move to India to spend a sabbatical year with Rohini. He was lecturing in Australian history in Canberra and had

17

been in India lecturing on the social and historical background to the works of Patrick White when they met. Griff lived on a small, hobby farm on the rural fringe of Canberra. He had grown up working on farms in Western Australia as a boy in his school holidays and had never lost his love of country life. The skills he had picked up on farms, working with his hands and improvising, served him well at Rohini's place. He collected and restored antique teak furniture and used old teak to build new pieces and built additions to the house. Gradually, as his Marathi improved, he took over much of the running of the timber business while Rohini concentrated on her veterinary clinic work and research. He had rented out his property and decided to live in India for the foreseeable future. Since then they had been together for eight years and felt very happy with their situation. They had no children and no plans to have any. Rohini believed India already had more than enough people and Griff had no urge to argue with her about that. They lived a very comfortable life with a large stone house of three stories, their own clean water bores, and grew much of their food from grain, to fruit and poultry. They had close to an acre of garden with large flowering trees, shrubs and ferns around the house and it was a beautiful place to be. The birds loved it as much as they did. It was an oasis of greenery, shade and shelter in farming countryside in which most of the trees had been cut down. The local farmers didn't want trees. Any patches of shade reduced the productivity of their crops. Griff and Roh new all the birds that came to their garden. Some stayed all the year and others came only in the winter to escape the cold of northern India. They had magnificent white paradise flycatchers with flowing thirty-centimetre tails, and a host of other flycatchers, magpie robins, golden orioles, hair-crested drongos, crow pheasants, partridges and jewel-like sunbirds, many of whom were almost tame. Sunbirds, finches, bulbuls and tailor birds nested in the shrubs on the front patio. They had a large paved front patio adjoining the veranda surrounded by ferns and beyond that an equally large paved barbecue area overhung by giant gulmohur trees and scented neems and bordered by ferns and the sweetly perfumed ratrani, 'queen of the night' creepers. Often, as many as six golden orioles would gather in the trees around the house and sing their beautiful fluting calls. The hair-crested drongo, a winter visitor, would mimic sounds from inside the house. Roh and Griff were amazed to hear it imitating the rusty squeak of the sprocket on their indoor clothes line when Suman hoisted it up and down. Soon it would all disappear forever beneath an ice continent. Perhaps in twenty million years it would re-emerge, thrusting upwards to the light as part of a new mountain range. Griff didn't want his or Rohini's bones to be among the fossilised relics emerging then. He wanted to postpone the dispersal of their molecules back into the building blocks of the universe for quite some decades yet. But most of their beloved birds were already dead, frozen stiff and blasted out of the trees.

Roh's parents had built the house when Roh was a teenager. It was strong and roomy with a reinforced concrete frame and floors, and basalt walls. It was robust enough to resist storms and earthquakes. Roh and her parents had planted lots of trees and when Griff came he added the patios and established the garden with the help of the farm workers. They planted lawns using couch grass collected from wild patches around the farm; poached clippings and seedlings of shrubs from friends and gathered ferns from around waterfalls in the hills. Griff planned a reticulation system for the garden and Sonba, the farm mechanic and driver, built it out of old water pipes. It was fed by a new bore they had sunk near the house. A veranda ran all the way across the front of the house leading into a spacious sittingroom-diningroom with the slow combustion wood stove Griff had imported from Australia. Off that, to the left, was a guest suite of bedroom and bathroom with lavatory. Beyond the sitting room was a very big kitchen with marble top benches around two sides and a pantry beneath the stairs which led to the second floor. Off the kitchen to the left was an open terrace about seven metres square, where Suman dried bananas and ground grain daily on a small basalt grindstone to make their chapattis. In the corner close to the back doors was a chip-wood shower water heater. All the ceilings were twelve feet high for cooling in the summers, when the temperatures rose to the mid-forties centigrade.

The first floor held a large bedroom with built-in cupboards all around between the windows, a large bathroom with shower and lavatory and a study as big as the bedroom. Leading through French windows to the left from the bedroom was an unroofed terrace with a one and a half metre high parapet around it. The stairs continued up to the loft that led to the roof terraces of which there were three. It was a flat-roofed house with reinforced concrete skeleton and slab ceilings. Griff had roofed the terrace at the front of the house overlooking the patio and the main part of the garden to reduce the heat of their bedroom in the summer and to prevent pooling of water when the monsoon rains hammered down in October and November. Before, they had to sleep out on the terrace in summer under mosquito nets because the room was like a sauna. Flat roofs are a taunt to nature and nature nearly always wins. Inevitably water would find a way through minuscule hairlike cracks in the roof to drip into their bedroom. But now no longer. There was another equally large unroofed terrace on the other side of the house and between the two, leading straight out from the door, a smaller terrace where they kept the rain gauge, now unneeded. There was another small terrace above the loft which held their water tank, filled daily by pumping water up from the main bore. It was a big, comfortable and strong rather than beautiful, house and before the trees had grown up all around they could see for miles from the roof terrace. Griff had built a large table from an old teak farmhouse door for the roofed terrace and a dresser for essentials and they had put cane furniture there. It was something like seven metres above the ground and all year round it was a delightful place to be among the tree tops with the birds. They often had breakfast, lunch and drinks while watching the sun set on days that were not so busy. Their house guests spent a good part of their days up there reading and writing. Would the archaeologists who rediscovered the place in the far distant future when the ice cap shifted once again be able to tell what a peaceful and pleasant life they had lived there before the ice storm, Griff mused. Historians say the Carthaginians would sit out on their roof terraces and sip a fermented drink in the evenings in the time before the Roman horde swept down and wiped out their city. Everything dies and rots or crumbles, Griff said to himself, and despite his mother's assurances that the bad always get their comeuppance and the good survive, he knew that the good and the beautiful perished along with the bad and the ugly when nature decided to flex her muscles. All life was a struggle, he believed, and when you stopped struggling, exploring, fucking and fighting for what you believed, you started to die. It was a rule of nature. He felt a sort of exhilaration about the struggle to survive that now faced them. It was a chance to stretch the mind, to dig into the lode of knowledge acquired over decades, to try out ideas, to pit himself against the elements, work with people he loved and to fight off those people who would try to pull him down and take what he had. Griff was only of medium height but he was well-muscled, fit and agile mentally and physically and confident about solving problems. He had clever hands. He knew that he and Roh and their small tribe were going to fight and with a little luck get through to peaceful times on the other side of this calamity. Live to a hundred years or die in the attempt was Griff's mantra. Griff and Roh didn't bother with gods and, so far as they could tell, gods didn't bother with them. This disaster that had engulfed them wasn't personal. There was no malice in it. It was simply nature doing what it had to do to keep going and they would do what they had to do, to accommodate it.

Chapter 2: Stocking a safe haven

"What task do you think we should tackle now, Griff? Get the rooms ready for the lambs?"

"Yes, that's timely, Roh. Let's do the study first because we can put most of the lambs in there initially while we get the roofed terrace fixed up for them."

There was one grand desk in the study that Roh had inherited from her grandfather's estate and two other smaller desks. Luckily, the big one broke into three parts. They lifted the desk top off and put it aside to be used later and carried the two side supports, essentially two small cupboards with drawers, into their bedroom. There were three smallish bookcases around the walls and one big glass-fronted one. They left the latter in place and were able to fit the smaller bookcases into the window openings. They sat there by themselves which was handy because they needed to block most of the window spaces against possible intruders and cold, although in the case of the study it would be a lot more difficult for any would-be intruder to tackle than the ground floor windows. Griff said he would fix the bookshelves in place with timber cross pieces later on. They dismantled the teak table from the roof terrace and brought the top downstairs to be used to reinforce the front door. The frame was dismantled and taken downstairs to use for reinforcing work eventually. When Wasanta, Namji, Subhash and Ramesh got back they would haul hay to the roof with ropes to provide the sheltering walls which would have plastic tarps on the outer side to protect them from the weather and on the inner, from the sheep.

Next they moved to the guest bedroom where Griff sawed the tops off the four legs of the big teak bed. It was a huge bed over two metres long and wide. They had some friends who were more than two metres tall and Griff had built the bed with them in mind. Having done that they tipped it on its side and pushed it against the front window that opened on to the veranda. They would soon stack bags of grain against it to hold it in place, but for the time being, they leaned the heavy kapok mattress against it. They would have to put twenty of the lambs in there until they had the roof terrace ready. There was a fine big antique wardrobe and roll-top desk, a small writing table and another large corner cupboard in the room. They would have to leave them for the time being. Griff took the teak door off the bedroom and stood it on its side. It would form the half door to close off the bedroom from the bathroom and Griff then removed the bathroom door to form the half door to close off the small alcove in front of the two rooms from the sitting room.

Just as they were about to head out to the haystack they could hear the four men returning from Kamala farm. The lambs were bleating with despair at being separated from the rest of the flock and probably with some fright caused by the drastic wind-whipped snow and the cold which they had never before experienced. Roh led them into the house, channelled about half into the guest bedroom and got the rest up the stairs to the study. These sheep had always had shepherds looking after them and they followed where the shepherds led them, so it wasn't hard to get them up the stairs even though they slipped a bit on the polished teak.

Roh told the four they would have to bring a couple of cartloads of hay across to the house straight away, as soon as the carts had been unloaded onto the veranda. They carried the goods off the veranda into the kitchen and stacked them on the floor. Already the ground floor was beginning to look like an over packed warehouse and it would probably become more so before they were completely organised.

One of the big haystacks was only twenty metres from the house so the men were soon back with the hay which they carried to the study and the guest bedroom. The men were suffering with the cold and needed to have a spell inside to warm up and have a hot drink. Suman had an urn of tea already made and they sat near the stove with mugs of tea warming their hands.

Subhash told Roh the other Kamala farm staff were pleased to have the sheep. He had also given them as much grain as each of them could carry from his stores and brought the rest here. He said that there were villagers up and about who quickly took sheep into their houses as soon as they heard them bleating. He confirmed that the villagers he saw were really suffering and some were even running about in the snow in chappals and thongs. Griff didn't say anything to that but he knew that they would soon have frostbite so badly that they would be immobilised and without medical attention, death would follow fairly soon after. Many of the villagers asked if they could come and get firewood and Namji and Wasanta had told them they could come at 7 am. Subhash said the village people were burning furniture to keep their houses warm. Subhash and Ramesh had brought ten bags of maize and ten bags of the high protein pellets used as a supplement to the lamb fodder. There were another twenty bags of pellets still there. Roh said they would go and get them when they had got other, more urgent tasks out of the way.

"Something bad in the village, Bai, Saheb," Subhash said. The farm staff all called Griff Saheb, which was the equivalent of sir. He had tried initially to get them to call him Griff but it was too much for them. They all called Rohini, Bai, which was madam. That was their culture. Griff accepted it.

"Ho, kai Subhash?" Roh asked.

"There are bodies outside some of the houses. People have already died. They have wrapped them in sheets and put them outside their doors."

"Well, that is sensible if sad, but nothing less than we would expect in this cold," Griff said, but he could see that Roh was upset that people were dying so quickly. Apart from people in the village who admired and respected her, there were others who were envious and malicious if an opportunity arose. She had loyal friends there, mainly poor struggling women and their children whom she had helped. Unfortunately, they were usually the least powerful people in the village. The poor and the old die first. It happened there in ordinary winters let alone something like this.

Wasanta and Namji said the rugs had worked well at keeping the bullocks warm and dry and they had pulled well with plenty of energy through the snow. That was good. They also said that the

24

rubber boots had worked well. Their feet were dry and warm, but their hands had got very cold and their eyes became sore from the whipping snow. Roh checked but there was no sign of frostbite. Griff realised he would have to try to make some rubber mittens out of motor cycle tubes and goggles too. The goggles would need some more thought. He put it aside for later consideration.

Roh told Suman to get started on making breakfast. She could set up two of the shegdis on the kitchen floor for cooking. Omelettes with onion and chopped veg and chicken would do, along with chapattis. It was then that Griff remembered the poultry. They had about twenty deshi, local hens, and a couple of roosters. The fowls had a shed for roosting at night so he guessed they would have survived the snow storm. He mentioned them to Roh and she suggested that they could go into one of the godowns on the wasti. If they were out of the wind they could probably survive. He agreed. They would put them into one of the empty godown rooms with some roosts and a kero lantern. One of them would have to go across each morning to light a kerosene lantern for the fowls and then return at night to turn it off. If they didn't do that the chooks wouldn't lay and would just go into a state close to hibernation and die of starvation. Their eggs would be a vital source of nutrients. Griff sat at the dining table and put his head in his hands. There were so many things to do and he needed a moment to clear his head and work out the right order. Roh came over and put her hand on his shoulder.

"You alright, Griff?"

"Yes, my love, just clearing my head. We've got to get hay baled and up to the roof to make the walls for the twenty lambs and while we are on that, we need to haul up the hay to make the stacks on the first floor terrace and the top unroofed terrace. With so many people here and mouths to feed we will have to kill and dress a couple of lambs early today. We've got to get the grain from the wasti into the house and we've got to cut big dry logs into short lengths and get them onto the kitchen terrace and also into the house."

"That's about two days' work," Roh said.

25

"Yes, I know, but I want it done today. If I kill two lambs and string them up on the peepul tree by the back of the house will you skin and dress them?"

"Count it as done."

"Good. We need to save the skins. Later I'll make mittens and jackets out of them. Two pairs of mittens from each lamb. Four skins to make a jacket."

"Okay, well let's get Subhash and Ramesh and Wasanta to start baling the hay and getting it up to the roof."

As they spoke there was a call from the front door. It was Sonba, their farm mechanic and sometime driver. He was a very handy man who could fix anything electrical and mechanical. They called him in and he broke down weeping. He knew something bad was happening when he woke in the middle of the night, he said, and told his wife and sons that he needed to come and check on Bai and Saheb. His wife who was prone to anger turned on him and said that if he left he needn't come back. He was useless and lazy and she and the two grown sons and their wives would look after themselves. That was cruel and untrue because Sonba was a good provider although his sons were profligate with his money on hopeless schemes.

"Now I have no home, Bai. I will just have to go out and die in the snow." Sonba had a dose of the melodramatic in his personality. He was a recovered alcoholic, largely due to the work, help and encouragement that Roh had given him, but not beyond a lapse in moments of stress.

"You will always have a home with us, Sonba," Roh said. He burst into a bout of grateful weeping. His clothes were wet with snow as well as tears and they saw that he was barefoot, having left his chappals outside the front door. Despite his rich brown skin his feet were pale and greenish with the cold. He had ridden his motor scooter that Roh had helped him to buy. They got him into warm clothes and sat him by the fire. Griff quickly made up another set of boots and over-boots for him. He told them that cars had broken down on the main road between his place and the farmhouse with people huddling in them and that there were dead people in the snow. Roh gave him hot tea and briefed him on the jobs they had to do. She put him in

26

charge of getting the hay stacks to the terraces and rigging the canvas coverings. Griff told him about the car-roof sled that could be used to haul hay bales to the house.

Roh briefed Suman on using buckets to meet the calls of nature and that for the time being they could keep the buckets in the guest lavatory. Namji would be in charge of giving out the firewood when the village people came. They could have it for free but only forty kilos to a family and twenty kilos to an individual. They set about the work, stopping at 7 am for breakfast. Usually when the farmhands worked by themselves it was a pretty leisurely pace. But with Roh and Griff supervising, the work was done fast. By breakfast they had moved a lot of hay to the house, done the lambs and two roosters to make a big pot of stew, moved the poultry and chain-sawed a few tonnes of dry wood and dragged it to the house using the bullocks. They had plenty of meat and grain.

"What we need is some sort of green veg in our diet," Griff mentioned to Roh at breakfast.

"Do you think we could grow sprouts?" she said.

"You are brilliant, my love. No doubt about it. We have grain and I am fairly certain we will be able to get sprouts growing in the house," he said, leaning over to give her a kiss and a squeeze. She added that they could also send a couple of the workers to the guava orchard to gather the last of the fruit from the season. Suman could stew and bottle a lot of them and in that way they would last for weeks.

"We can make up a soil mixture using sawdust, sheep dung and straw to grow the sprouts. The only problem is that they need to be in the house for warmth and things are starting to get very crowded. I can make up some plastic sheet lined trays to grow the sprouts and I suppose I could make a stand to sit in a corner of the kitchen so they can be stacked. That will have to wait for a few days until we are secure," Griff said.

After breakfast they went out to get to work again. There was a crowd at the wasti gate waiting for wood. Namji let them in and told them the wood was free but twenty kilos for an individual and forty kilos, which was a maund, pronounced "munn"by the locals, for a family or a vehicle was the limit. Most were happy with that but a few wanted to argue and started shouting that she was condemning them to death. Roh pointed out that if they were greedy and took too much, they were condemning other people to death. They wanted to argue, but Roh told them they could take it or leave it. Namji was carrying the shotgun and looking grim. They got the message. Most of them had wheeled their push bikes from the village because the snow was too deep and the wind too strong for them to be able to ride, but they could load the wood on their bikes, tie it on and wheel it home, which was what they usually did. The number of people coming for firewood increased rapidly and the process of weighing out half a maund was too slow in this cold so Namji said two big armfuls. The wood was Australian eucalypt, mainly red gum and blue gum, so it gave good heat. Australian missionaries had brought eucalypts and a range of other trees and shrubs including bottlebrush and casuarina into India around the 1850s and planted them in the Nilgiri Hills in south central India. From there they had spread throughout the length and breadth of India. The eucalypts were commonly called nilgiri because of that. Roh had about half of her forty acres under eucalypt plantations and selling poles for building and fencing was a major part of the farm business. The trees were cut about sixty centimetres above the ground and within two years or so were ready to be harvested again.

They worked on until noon when they were all exhausted in spite of a short break each hour for a cup of chicken soup. They gathered in the sitting room which was really cosy to warm their hands by the fire. Griff could see that the men needed warmer clothing for the outside work. Their jackets were not warm enough for the cold which was increasing by the hour. He knew they had some old blankets used for camping in one of the cupboards. Later, in the evening he would cut ponchos for them from the blankets and over coverings of plastic sheeting, and Namji's daughter could stitch the plastic sheeting on to the ponchos to make them water and wind-proof. A rope belt around the middle would stop them from blowing open and letting cold in. He realised then that he would have to make a set of outdoor gear for all the women as well as the men.

After lunch they needed to rest for a couple of hours at least. They'd been at it since 2.30 am and they were knocked out. Roh and Griff went up to their bedroom, closed the door and collapsed on the bed. Roh said she was shocked at the state of the village people who had come to buy wood. They had jackets and pullovers but they were not heavy enough for this weather and their trousers were thin cotton or jeans. Some were wearing hessian bags with sheets of plastic over them. Very few had gloves. Many of them were in chappals and others in joggers that quickly became soaked from the snow. Some had tied numerous plastic bags over their footwear with hessian or rag over that to give them grip on the snow.

"They won't last long. I feel so bad that we have so much and a hope of surviving and they have virtually no chance," she said. She sobbed quietly. Griff put his arm around her. "I know, my love, and it distresses me too, but if we are to have a chance of surviving we can't take them all in or give away our food stocks. We are giving them free wood and you have given them free food in the form of the sheep as well as grain. That is a lot. I doubt if any of the other well-off people in the village are sharing anything but the odd meal. We are busy saving our small tribe of eleven who would otherwise perish without us."

"Yes, I can see that and I am grateful that you are working so hard to give us a chance, Griff." She turned and kissed him passionately.

"Let's make love."

Griff was about to answer when Namji began shouting from near the veranda.

"Saheb, please come. There is a saheb here who wants seven munn for his mother's cremation. He is saying he will take it if we don't give it to him."

"I will come down." Griff told Roh to stay and rest.

Namji was standing by the veranda with the shotgun in one hand and his hurricane lantern in the other.

"He is being very rude, Saheb, and waving his fist at me."

Griff took the gun from him and checked that it was loaded. It was a twelve-gauge single-shot piece. They walked over to the wood area. The usual practice in these rural areas was for a body that had not been murdered, as well as quite a few that had, to be cremated almost immediately after death. It was a quick way to get rid of the evidence of internecine foul play, of which there was not a little, usually over land and money. They often had calls at nine or ten o'clock at night or at first light in the morning to sell seven to nine maund for a cremation. Virtually all the villagers for miles around bought their wood from them. Their prices were the lowest in the district.

Griff could see there was a group of four, headed by a thickly clad local bigwig whom he recognised and three of his not so heavily wrapped followers and a few other poorer, lightly clad, shivering villagers standing by and watching.

"Ah, the foreigner," the big man said, as they approached.

"Yes Saheb," Griff said. "How can I help?"

"We are wanting seven munn of logs for the cremation of my mummy who has just died."

"I am sorry, Saheb, but we do not have enough dry wood left to be able to provide wood for cremations. As you can see, this is a great disaster we are experiencing and many people will die but in this weather the bodies will not decay. If you wrap them in a sheet and keep them in a safe place outside the house they will freeze and be preserved until the crisis passes. At the moment we must try to keep as many people warm and supplied with heating and cooking fuel as we can."

"It is our religion and our custom that our dead people's bodies must be cremated straight away so that their spirits can go to their heavenly abode. God tells us that we have to do it."

"Is that so? I've never been able to have a conversation with him. Saheb, your mother, sadly, is already dead and I feel quite sure that her soul is already in heaven."

"What do you know about our heaven and our religion? You are a foreigner." The big man was used to throwing his weight around and getting what he wanted. He was angry.

"Well, I know that your religion doesn't strictly specify any time in which the body is to be cremated, merely that it should be as soon as possible. If it has to wait, it has to wait."

"I don't want to talk to you, gora. Call Bai. I want to speak to her. She is an Indian." Gora means white and is a mildly derisive term for a

30

white person. It's a bit of a joke really because most Indians envy white skin. The marriage ads are full of references to pale skin or 'wheatish skin', but the chip of colonial oppression still sits heavily on the shoulder of many even after fifty years of independence.

"She is very tired after working long hours but she will say the same. She just told me before I came down. No wood for cremations."

"You damn foreigners. You are both foreigners. She is not of this village. We know you. You are godless people. You never go to marriages or to the temple. You live without getting married. You are a criminal Australian. You have a criminal nation. You have no god," he shouted.

"Yes, we have given up calling on god for anything. He doesn't seem to bother with us so we don't bother with him. We work to help people have better lives. We find it's more effective. They respond more."

"There you are blaspheming. Who are you to be telling me what wood I can or cannot have? This is Indian wood, it is not Australian wood, and I am going to take it."

"If you do that, Saheb, you will be committing a worse crime than most of the people who were sent to Australia from England as criminals two hundred years ago. Anyone who committed a bad crime in those days was hanged. The various parliaments of your country are packed with people who have committed far worse crimes than the people sent to Australia as convicts. They were mainly poor, hungry rural people and farm hands like the ones standing behind you."

"Yes, they are all thieves too," he interjected.

"Well, I will do this for you. You can take one maund now for the cremation and one maund for your family needs and if you come back each day for a week you can get another eight more for your mother and you will then have enough for the cremation."

Griff knew as he said this that the bigwig would probably be standing over the village people down near the main road and buying their wood from them or even just taking it. But he and Roh had to be seen to be sticking by their ruling as well as being fair. One rule for all, not one for the rich and powerful and another for the poor and weak which was the usual way in India. And anyway, it was just plain common sense to save wood for heating and cooking.

"You damn bloody Australian. I will see that you pay for this. This is India, you don't run our country with your drunken habits and prostitute women who wear hardly any clothes and your criminal arrogance and race prejudice."

"Okay, do your worst, but you take only one maund a day for the cremation. So take your two maund now and go and, by the way, I have seen more people lying drunk in public here than I have ever seen in Australia. And please tell your cronies to stop spitting on our farm. It spreads diseases."

The bigwig turned and stormed off to his expensive, warm, four-wheel drive vehicle leaving his minions to carry the wood to their tractor trailer waiting at the wasti gate. Griff told Namji to measure out two maund on the weighing scales. Not a kilo extra. The cronies by now greenish with the cold carried the wood away. Griff told Namji to go in and have lunch while he supervised the giving out of the wood to the waiting people, grown now to a small crowd. The wind was still howling around them and Griff propped up with poles one of the half forty-four gallon drums, cut lengthways, that were used as fodder troughs with its back to the wind to shelter the hurricane lantern which kept threatening to blow out. Now that Sonba was with them, Griff hoped to use his skills to set up a generator to keep them in electricity. They could use his 350 cc Bullet motorcycle, he thought, to charge a bank of batteries. The bike had a generator for its lights and Sonba could use the inverter from the now useless solar power generators. The problem would be to get enough petrol to keep the bike engine going but Griff reckoned they should be able to gather enough petrol from abandoned cars along the main road to keep the bike going. They would collect batteries as well as petrol from the abandoned cars and trucks to create the large bank of cells that could be charged each day by running the bike engine for half an hour or so. As soon as they had finished the tasks of hauling in the grain and fuel wood and getting the house secure he'd get Sonba onto that job. Having plenty of electric power might mean also that they could receive television news from their satellite dish. Although reception was often interrupted during storms they might be able to get reception from time to time and that would be a great boost for their morale. Their morale had been high so far, with plenty of work to keep them busy and little time to dwell on the grimness of their situation, but Griff knew that when they had all the systems in place and the novelty had worn off and the work schedule was not so onerous, some of them could become very morose if rescue were delayed.

By the time the farmworkers came out after lunch, at about 2 pm, the wood buyers were coming only intermittently and Griff went in for a cup of hot chicken soup and a warm-up by the fire. Roh came down the stairs to join him and asked about the fuss with the local big-shot. He told her and they had a laugh about it. She told him her grandfather had come to the village sixty years or so ago and bought some swampy wasteland from the local temple that no one wanted. He had drained and cleared it and turned it into the most prosperous farm in the district. Now the local mythology was that the family had come and swindled the unsuspecting locals out of their best land and waxed fat on it. They had a laugh too about their godlessness, which had served the villagers well at times in the recent past. It was the habit in the distant past, hundreds of years ago, to make an offering to the gods of a prime bull by giving it to the temple. This, in effect, meant turning it free because that is what the temple trustees did. It served a purpose then of impregnating village cows. These days it was no longer needed because many if not most of the locals were now using European breed crosses that gave bigger yields. But just recently a village man had turned a cow loose and it had become a plague on the other village farmers, cutting a swathe through their crops and causing considerable loss of crop yield, fodder and income. No one dared trap it because it supposedly belonged to the gods and a dire fate must therefore befall anyone who constrained it. One farmer, who became a frequent victim of the marauding cow, captured it and kept it in his cowshed. Not long after, his wife died and he was diagnosed with HIV. The villagers were convinced that the death of the wife and the HIV were the punishment of the gods for the wrong of capturing the cow. The farmer released the beast to continue its depredations and it was by then eating for two. It seems that the cow got pregnant

33

while incarcerated and not long after gave birth to a male calf. The two of them continued to ravage the farmers' crops. However, a year or two back, Rohini was known to have captured a male buffalo and a bull that she had found creating havoc in her crops and used them as draught animals. So the villagers turned to her and pleaded with her to capture the cow and calf which had become quite aggressive. The idea was popular in the village even among the pious and the envious, since it offered the possibility of getting rid of the marauding animals and her in one stroke, if the gods took punitive action. She said she would, but when she mentioned it to her own farm staff, they said they wouldn't do it because of fear of divine retribution such as had befallen the farmer and his wife who had previously caught the cow. Rohini appeased them by telling them that she would tell the gods that she was the sole person to be held responsible for capturing the cow and calf and that they were not to be held blameworthy. While they were contemplating that, Rohini suggested to the temple trust that they do something about the cow and bull, or let her capture them. The trust said they would sell her the cow and calf for Rs100,000 but she would have to capture them. She declined the offer. A short while after, she noticed the cow and bull in the maize crop of one of her neighbours who was a member of the still-powerful royal family that had once ruled the district. She rang him and asked him if he knew that the cow and bull were getting into his crop. No, he didn't and he became quite agitated. What should he do, he asked. Rohini explained the whole story and said she was prepared to catch the animals but the temple trust was creating difficulties. "Don't worry, I will fix that," he said, knowing, as Rohini did, that the members of his family ran the trust. When Rohini told her gadees that she had the all-clear to capture the animals, they said that they had decided they would only take part if she guaranteed to pay for any injuries they suffered during the capture and any illnesses they might suffer in the ensuing years, that would result from divine punishment. She said that she would pay for treatment for any injuries suffered during the capture, which she normally did anyway, as she had them all insured against work injury. That was where the matter rested now. Her gadees were still debating among themselves about whether to risk the retribution of the gods in the form of late-developing illness.

"Well, that is all settled now. God has intervened," Roh said.

"Yes, but why should the innocents be punished as well as us?" They laughed together.

They worked on until 6 pm, by which time Griff had sawn many of the big dry logs into smaller pieces easily carried into the house or hauled by rope up to the terraces for storage and the men building the hay stacks were just about finished too. Tomorrow they would finish those tasks early and then set about strengthening doors. Griff would put the sedan car from the carport beside the house into the cattle shed and cover it with a tarp and use the carport as a wood store.

That night they were all so tired that during dinner they sat hardly talking. After dinner they rigged up some plastic sheeting in one corner of the sitting room for the women to change, sponge themselves and use their toilet bucket. They moved and stacked furniture to make spaces and to create sleeping areas with mattresses. Namji's family and Wasanta and Seema would sleep in the sitting room, Sonba on the stair landing below the loft where Suman would sleep. Subhash and Ramesh would sleep in the kitchen and Roh and Griff in their usual place. Before adjourning for bed, Griff and Roh got the world globe out and had a look at it to try to work out how the poles and the tropics would now be aligned. They figured that much of Europe would now be a Mediterranean climate, North America, Australia and New Zealand would be tropical and sub-tropical and Africa would have rotated so that the equator would now run through the Sahara desert. Most of South America would be the new Antarctic. Russia would be roughly where the US had been. It wasn't hard to conclude then that there would be massive migration from India, China and South America to the US, Australia, New Zealand, Europe and Africa. But the good thing was that the developed, rich nations that had the equipment and the wherewithal to carry out rescue work with ships, planes and helicopters had survived the worst and would be able to help save people from the calamity. Of course, the raging storms would make it difficult for them initially and, in addition, governments would be flat out creating camp cities and organising the

35

massive inflow of refugees able to get away from the disaster areas under their own steam. It wouldn't be good to be in those early outpourings. The death toll would be savage with people fighting and killing for places on boats and disease scything through them. Wise to be right out of that turmoil until the dust settled.

Subhash asked if they could put on the TV or the radio to hear what was happening in India and other countries. Rohini told them it was not possible because the solar-powered inverter battery was now flat and there was no other electricity to run the TV. She told them she had tried the radio but there was too much interference from the blizzard. They were cut off until they could get some source of electricity. Griff told them then about his plan to use the motorbike to charge a bank of batteries to keep the house in power all the time and that they might then be able to get TV from time to time.

There were two final jobs Griff wanted to get done before hitting the sack. The first was to cut ponchos for all of the women from old blankets and sheets of plastic. Roh and he cut them while the women sewed them. Tied with a length of rope around the waist, they were warm and would keep people dry. Roh and Griff wore their best, expensive Italian greatcoats. They made plastic ponchos to go over the top of them. Griff also cut some lengths from motor cycle tubes that could be pulled over the hands and lower arms to act as a sort of mitten. They gave each of the five men thick socks to put on their hands and then slid the tubes over the top of them. They could do a lot of work with the hands covered like that, but for anything requiring manipulation or strong gripping they would have to roll the tubes back. They made sheepskin mittens for the women from one of Roh's old leather jackets. Griff had a talk then with Sonba about rigging up the motorcycle to charge the battery bank. Sonba was excited about the idea and was sure he could do it. He would start as soon as Griff gave him the go-ahead. The last job Griff tackled was snow glasses. From a truck tube, he cut a four-centimetre band big enough to be pulled over the head to cover the eyes with a flap hanging down to cover the nose and upper cheeks. In the place where the eyes were he cut two holes the size of spectacle lenses and on the outside, glued with super-glue two pieces of clear thick plastic cut from a large

36

plastic bottle. He tried it on and it worked well for him and Roh, so he made a set for each of the men. That was it. Roh and Griff were too tired to even bathe or make love. They just fell into bed, locked together like two spoons in a draw and were asleep in minutes. They didn't have to set an alarm clock. They were both early risers and would wake naturally around 6 am dark or not.

Griff woke at 5 am, with an urgent desire to re-consummate his love for the beautiful Rohini and with a full bladder, as usual. He'd read somewhere that waking with a rager was a sign of a healthy, fit man, so he was pleased about that, but it posed the problem of how to piss into a bucket with a dick that was pointing at the sky. He would have to work on that problem but meanwhile he held a cup over the head of his dick and pissed into that while standing over the bucket. He went downstairs and put a couple of hefty logs in the stove. He could see that Namji or Wasanta had been feeding it during the night as instructed and he went back to bed, careful to keep his hands to himself until they warmed and then gently massaged some life into Roh.

"I'm all yours Griff," she murmured, still half asleep.

He entered slowly from behind but in less than a half a minute she broke away, rolled and pushed him on to his back and slid on top. In a couple of minutes she was done and collapsed on to his chest breathing heavily and muttered: "Oh god, here I am completely fucked and the day's work hasn't yet begun."

"Not completely yet, my love," Griff said, rolling her on to her back and hovering over her like a bird of prey above a fresh kill. It always amazed him how young and innocent she looked lying on her back, legs apart and impaled as he took his pleasure to its peak and, groaning, gave up what passed for his seed these days since he'd had a vasectomy at the time they began living together. He fell to the side of her and they kissed and snuggled and uttered mooing sounds of contentment. Shortly before 6 am, Rohini whispered that this was all very well but they needed to get on with their gardening. They rolled out, made the bed, padded to the bathroom to sponge themselves down. The water was too damned cold.

"Wait a mo," Griff said, and went downstairs to the kitchen to get a dipper and a bucket and then to the stove on which there was always a large pot of water to humidify the air. He put a couple of dipperfuls into the bucket, went upstairs with it and gave it to Roh. They both hated the cold but she more than he. European genes he assumed. Thick blood and probably thick skin too. After all, his ancestors had lived through an ice age hunting woolly mammoth in the icy wastelands that once covered most of Europe. But then the Indians from whom Roh was descended almost certainly had been in Europe during the ice ages too, Griff realised. Perhaps it was that women had spent more time crouching around fires in caves and rock-shelters with babies while the blokes were out running through the snow hunting mammoth and cave bear.

They finished sponging and dressed quickly in the clothes they had taken off last evening. They would be cutting down on clothes-washing in the days to come he guessed. More important things to do and anyway, in this cold they wouldn't be sweating too much and there certainly wouldn't be the usual dust cloud blowing in from outside. Griff had been trying to work out a priority list of things to do as they lay in bed and it was starting to fall into place. Get reinforcements over the downstairs windows starting in the guest bedroom and then get the grain and firewood in there. They had plenty of sheets of galvanised iron and he figured they would do to cover the windows, held in place with the three-centimetre thick planks from the base of the guest bed. Luckily there were always plenty of the really thick nails Griff used around the farm which were strong enough to pin the planks and the metal on to the bricks that lined the inside of the rooms. The outer layer of the house was basalt, probably harder than steel to drill, but the local bricks were not much tougher than dog biscuits. The bags of grain would be stacked hard against the planking and the steel sheet and would provide all the strength that the brickwork lacked. They also needed to get firewood on to the terraces and then complete the sloping haystacks over the wood with plastic sheeting over the top of that. They had to start the process of curing the sheep skin, get Sonba working on the generator, allocate household chores, move the car to the cattle shed, get more wood into the carport and cover it with fodder, reinforce all the windows and doors, slaughter one of the male buffaloes, dress it, and hang it up on the big rain tree, harvest the last of the guavas, build trays to grow the sprouts to keep the scurvy at bay. The things that had to be done seemed endless. Roh and Griff worked through them. She would brief the women and help with the reinforcing while the men brought in the grain, the firewood and the hay and stacked it. Roh said she thought it would be better to use the carport beside the house for the draft oxen. If they stacked green timber logs around the open sides of the carport and then lined that with hay and plastic sheeting, she said the bullocks would be okay. They had their rugs to keep them warm and they would be sheltered from the wind. That would mean they would need to have only the milking buffalo and her calf in the guest bathroom, leaving the whole of the guest bedroom free to store firewood and grain. It was a good idea and they would do it.

Suman and the women had already made tea and were working on breakfast when Roh and Griff got downstairs. The gadees and their wives and children drank only tiny, demitasse-size cups of tea loaded with sugar. Griff and Roh made their own tea. They had large mugs spiced with grated ginger and a little milk but without sugar. They usually had two mugs at breakfast along with muesli, home-made yoghurt from buffalo milk and chopped fruit. There was still some left so they had that. After a few days they would all be on curried mutton, chapattis, wheat sprouts and stewed guava or steak and eggs and bean sprouts for three meals a day.

Wood buyers were coming in by 7 am and it was noticeable that there were fewer than the previous day. It seemed people were succumbing quickly to the terrible cold. Some would have died trying to flee to other places where they thought things might be better, warmer, with more food. That was sad, but Griff and Roh knew there was little they could do about that. They were stretched saving their own crew. They worked taking a break every forty-five minutes or so for a warm-up and a cup of soup. Suman was a marvel. It was hard to know how old she was. Like many of the older village people she was illiterate, had few teeth, no idea of her year of birth. She was probably in her mid-fifties, looked seventy five, widowed, children grown up, but was made of iron. Not much brain but a solid worker when instructed and loyal and uncomplaining. Roh and she had shouting matches from time to time when Suman did something she wasn't supposed to do, or vice versa, but neither bore grudges and they always made it up. Suman had worked for Roh's parents when they had lived on the farm decades ago. Suman and Griff got on well. Griff kept out of the fights and thought her food was almost always excellent, although she had a tendency to slip salt and sugar into the food if not constantly reminded that she shouldn't do it. Griff made a point of rinsing his used lunch dishes and clearing the table and she appreciated that. He had made the big table in the kitchen to provide an extra work and storage space for her. She was from the lowest class, Dalits, previously known as untouchables and Roh was from the highest of the high caste so there was always an underlying frisson of tension between those two. Griff, as a white foreigner or gora, was also high caste but, paradoxically, outside the caste system and he made a point of not assuming any airs or graces when dealing with Dalits or any other low class or low caste Indians. That was something high caste Indians found hard to disguise. Roh was able to because she was as aware as Griff of all the nuances but even so, just occasionally she would allow a little coldness to creep into the voice or to show the iron fist in the velvet glove. No-one wholly escaped the culture they were born into.

After two days of solid work that left them exhausted at night and barely capable of conversation, they had the house in pretty good shape and a routine was falling into place. People knew the tasks and did them without complaint. Emptying the waste buckets, bringing in clean buckets of snow, mucking out and swabbing down the floors where the animals were and bringing in fresh straw; cooking and washing and chopping firewood. Roh and Griff shared the dirty chores with everyone, but Suman and the other women, Roh excepted, always did the cooking. Roh and Griff enjoyed cooking, but there were too many other tasks and heavy work that they needed to be occupied with. It was no time for radical social and cultural change. Bai and Saheb carrying buckets of turd, sweeping up sheep and cattle shit and swabbing floors was revolutionary enough, although all their staff knew that they would do and in fact did these things in the normal course of their activities before the cataclysm. The fact that they would get their hands and clothes soiled helping with the dirty work gave them respect and loyalty that other employers never got. Their people knew that they would never ask them to do something they were not prepared to tackle themselves and they worked the harder for it.

Griff realised that they really needed to have snowshoes. The snow was starting to pile up metres deep everywhere and walking through it one sank down. Lifting the legs required a much bigger effort than usual. There was bamboo in the garden that Griff could cut to make frames for snowshoes and they had rawhide and rubber tubing. After dinner he set to work with bamboo that he cut during the afternoon. He had never seen a snowshoe in the flesh, so to speak, but had seen them in films and photos. He steamed the bamboo lengths into the required shape and wired them firm. He then bound two lighter bamboo pieces front to back to provide a base for the rubber tyre boots and wired them firm with a cross piece. He was able then to use rawhide strips to criss-cross the shoe to hold everything in place and to give the shoe what it needed to sit high on the snow rather than sink into it. When he finished the first pair, he went out to the veranda, put them on and gave them a workout in the snow. They kept him high on the snow and he was able to move relatively quickly and easily. There was no question of being able to run but he could manage a sort of steady slow jog, something like cross country skiing but slower. He made another pair for Roh and left it at that. He would make shoes for the men tomorrow before they set out.

They fell into bed that night tired but happy and cuddled as always. Perhaps it was the happiness and sense of accomplishment that did it for no sooner had they warmed up than they gave way to the tug of lust. Convincing proof that a standing dick has no brains and a wet pussy no wisdom. The added fatigue ensured at least that they were asleep in minutes. As he dropped off Griff guessed Roh must be ovulating and pumping out pheromones. Richard Dawkins was right; humans were ruled by their genes and their compulsions.

Their lovemaking went in cycles. There were times when they went at it like ferrets and then the libido ebbed for a week or so.

They woke around 6 am feeling fresh. It was the fourth day and Griff reckoned they must be getting fitter with the extra physical work. He told Roh he thought it was time to do a survey of the village to see if there was much activity there and to scavenge for extra food, petrol and other useful things. She thought it a good idea too, but she was worried about the effect of the snow on the bullocks' legs and feet. Griff said he thought he could make car tube leggings for the bullocks that would keep them dry and reasonably warm. They agreed they could bind the lower legs with bagging and then pull the rubber leggings up over them and secure them with a rope over the withers. They would need 12 tubes for that and they no longer had anything like that left. They could make leggings for one bullock and take their one sled out to collect tyres and tubes.

By mid-morning, with the help of many hands they had finished the snowshoes and had fixed leggings on to the biggest bullock and given him a trial walk around the wasti. He seemed comfortable, so they set out for the village which was half a kilometre away. They had one bullock pulling a sled and two bullocks trailing on hitch ropes. This was the first time they had been out the gate since the polar freeze began. It was a different world, so far as they could see in the darkness and whipping snow, although that wasn't far. It was interesting though that their eyes seemed to have adapted in some way to the darkness and it wasn't pitch black. The countryside was the cleanest they had ever seen it. All the rubbish that the locals constantly strewed about the place, food wrappings, rags, cigarette packets, dead dogs and calves, liquor bottles and human shit, were all buried deep and even the straggly Prosopis thorn trees, mesquite, looked more attractive with snow drifts around them and pockets of snow caught in the foliage. There were very few lavatories, private or public, in the village and the locals crapped alongside the roads or in the paddocks. Pigs dined off the fresh shit and dogs off the dried shit and what was left blew about in the dust and helped to spread hookworm. It was not wise to go about in bare feet but many of the locals did. There was no public rubbish collection system and the piles that accumulated in the

42

village areas were burnt from time to time. But there was still a good amount lying around elsewhere. Hardly a square metre of ground along the roads didn't have litter of some sort on it. Roh and Griff wouldn't let any of their farm staff throw litter of any sort but wood buyers and other visitors threw it around like confetti at a wedding. The main objects of their rage about litter were the indestructible gutka packets, small plastic envelopes that held a cancer-causing mixture of chewing tobacco and spices. This stuff was one of the few population control elements at work in India, causing slow death by mouth and throat cancer. It was also a great contributor to one of the vile rural habits of spitting. Their staff wouldn't spit or throw down a gutkha packet when they were around but they occasionally did when they thought they weren't about. Roh and Griff concluded that the locals didn't see litter in the same way that they did. The villagers' aesthetic sensibilities, such as they were, were attuned to different things. Roh told Griff once about the people who owned a successful plant nursery a few kilometres along the road towards the town. They had huge middens of rubbish, mainly plastic chemical packets, plastic seedling trays and glass and plastic bottles, on the verge outside the nursery. Roh had asked them why they didn't burn them or dispose of them somehow.

"Why should we do that," they asked indignantly. "Our customers can see, when they drive up, all the chemicals we have to spend money on to grow the products they want to buy."

No matter how much Roh and Griff told their own gadees not to throw litter and to pick up the stuff that blew in or was dropped by visitors, they could walk past litter without even seeing it. For them it was just a normal part of the environment. Most of the houses in the villages and towns as well were lacking in any effort to make them attractive, apart from a few kitsch ornaments and religious posters, and the yards were mostly treeless, bare dirt. Rubbish was thrown out the door and swept to the side, but the odd thing was that when they came across something beautiful they could appreciate it. Before Griff had built a new front gate which could be bolted from the inside, he'd walked out of the house one day to find a man lying in the shade in the middle of the front lawn with his bicycle by his side.

43

"What are you doing?" he asked him.

"Just resting. It's a nice place," he said, as though any fool could see that.

"Well, do it somewhere else, this is private property," Griff told him. The man got up, took his bike, and left and the idea that he might plant a tree and a patch of lawn at his place wouldn't cross his mind, Griff thought. To him, Griff was just that pest of a foreigner who arrogantly stopped Indians from rightfully enjoying their own land.

The wind howled incessantly and the cold seeped through all the weak spots in their heavy clothing. It was a battle to move against it when they walked. But the snow glasses worked well and helped protect the upper face. The lower face was covered by scarves or cloths. Sonba rode in the sled with tools to remove wheels and tyres and also to cut two more car-roof sleds. Roh, Subhash, Ramesh, Wasanta and Griff walked. Griff carried the gun. He had made rubber sleeves for them from motorcycle tubes. These could be pulled down over their woollen gloves or mittens to keep the hands protected from snow and wind. They had to roll them back when delicate work was done but it was surprising how many things they could do with them in place. Wielding spanners and other tools and loading and firing the gun were not amongst them. As they got to the main crossroad in the village they found half a dozen cars. There were no people around and not a sound apart from the wind. The owners must have been able to get away on trucks and had abandoned their cars. Sonba and Subhash set about removing tyres while Roh and Griff picked the two best cars to remove the roofs from. These were the old Ambassadors which had quite a pronounced curve and sides. Modern cars had fairly flat roofs. Using the axe and hacksaw they soon had the roofs off and ropes attached to the front pillars to pull them along. Griff had made halters from chain threaded through pushbike tubes to fit around the necks of the bullocks to which the ropes could be tied for pulling. These seemed to work well. The usual collar for a bullock was an inefficient wooden beam that sat on the neck of the animal between the head and hump that was found on most indigenous Indian bullocks.

Sonba, Subhash and Wasanta had filled two plastic bins with petrol, and, with the tyres and tubes, that filled one sled. Griff suggested they take the chance to have a look at some of the stores and they went to a nearby chemist's shop. The front was shuttered but the owners lived in the adjoining house. They knocked on the door and called out. No answer. They tried the door and it opened.

They went in with torches. The house was as cold as a fridge freezer. No-one on the ground floor so they went upstairs to a small sitting room. In the middle were two people swathed in blankets on either side of a half-barrel fire which had long burnt to ashes. Broken furniture, which they guessed was to be used in the fire, lay beside them. The house had been stripped of burnable items. They called to them but they didn't stir and when they went across to them they could see the old couple were dead. Cold and stiff. Roh checked them. She knew these people and was surprised that their grown children and grandchildren were not around. They must have fled, leaving the parents behind. Roh thought the old people might have taken poison. If not, they would have died of the cold or starvation. They left them as they were and went down to check the pharmacy. Rural pharmacies often had a pretty eclectic array of goods ranging from medicines to biscuits, chocolates, batteries, drinks. Most of that sweet stuff was gone but Roh looked around at the medicines and drugs and took items to add to her stores at home. From there they moved on to a drygoods store nearby. The front of the shop was open and looted clean as was the storeroom at the back. Subhash, however, knew this family and believed that they had a cellar beneath the concrete back storeroom. He had never seen it, only heard about it. They hunted around for some entry way and eventually found a heavy steel trapdoor at the rear hidden beneath old torn bags and papers. It was flush with the floor except for a small space for a hand to lift it. They couldn't lift it even when a crowbar was slipped into the small hand space. It must have been bolted from underneath.

Sonba went to work on it with a wrecking bar, cold chisel and hacksaw and in half an hour he had it open. Stale smoky air came out when he lifted the trapdoor. They shone torches into the cellar. It was extensive and piled high with sacks and tins. In the far end they could see some still figures and called to them. There was no answer and no movement. They left Subhash as guard on top and went down the

45

stairs. They checked the people first. The room was also bitterly cold and the fire which had been in a large drum was cold and dead like the people. There were a couple of boys huddled together on a charpoy under quilts, a middle aged couple under blankets on another charpoy and two old people sitting in plastic chairs by the fire. Roh had a good look at them and said she thought they had died from asphyxiation and probably smoke inhalation caused by burning the fire in a room with no ventilation. It certainly wouldn't have been from hunger that killed them. The room was a treasure trove of wheat, dried corn, onions, potatoes, chick peas, dried green peas, lentils, spices, garlic, rice, flour, and other things. There was a twenty-litre drum of molasses, boxes of candles, boxes of firecrackers and bundles of large torch batteries. There were also several twenty-litre tins of kerosene. These people had obviously moved stores from the upper storeroom to the cellar in anticipation of a prolonged wait for rescue.

The group loaded their two new sleds, stacked some of the kero, molasses, firecrackers and candles, all the batteries and a bag of dried green peas and another of lentils at the foot of the stairs ready for their next visit and then left for the trip back to the farm after closing and hiding the trapdoor under the old bags and litter. They would return to take the lot away in due course. It was lunchtime by the time they got back and Suman had a hot meal ready. After lunch they had a brief rest. They had time for a trip to the dry goods store after their rest and set off with the three sleds. They rode standing in the sleds and carrying their snowshoes which they would need for the trip back. They would load the sleds fully with the goods and walk back beside them. After the first two sorties with stuff from the dry goods store they estimated it would take another two or three trips to get the lot.

After unloading and stacking the goods in the house it was dinner time. Suman had already been into the dried peas, lentils, spices and onions and made a wonderful thick, hot soup that they drank from mugs in the sitting room enjoying the cosiness. They toasted each other in soup. Subhash said he felt certain for the first time since the crisis began that they would be able to survive until rescuers arrived even if it took months. It was a great team, he said, and he had never known such willingness and cooperation and lack of slacking-off or complaining. Roh and Griff agreed. It was a happy crew. Ramesh asked where he thought they would all go and what they would do when they were rescued. Roh and Griff hadn't discussed that yet. Griff took it for granted that they would all go to Australia initially where his family lived and that he would help them settle there. He realised that Roh would want to find her parents and that might take her to the United States for a while or even permanently. It seemed a long way away from their present, practical life. Too far to be anything more than a fantasy.

Griff told them that it would not be possible for anyone to live in India any more, but that many countries would be taking and resettling refugees from India and China and other places. He said he would work to have them all granted settlement in Australia although it was not possible to say exactly how the refugees would be dealt with. There would be big problems for the countries taking refugees because of the huge numbers. He said he thought that there would already be hundreds of thousands of Indians and Chinese arriving in Australia on boats and it might be that the Government would try to settle large numbers in the north, probably in tent cities at first. The people who couldn't speak English would have to do language training before they could move into the community, but there was nothing to seriously worry about. They would have challenges to face but they would be well treated. He said he was hoping that he might be in a position to buy a small farm near Perth where they could live and work together, but that was a long way off and it might not be within his power to achieve that. That seemed to reassure them and most of them settled into quiet contemplation and ultimately acceptance of things that must have seemed almost incomprehensible to farm workers, some of them illiterate, and most of whom had never moved more than a few hundred kilometres from the place in which they were born.

But these people's lives were such that they understood they were merely leaves floating on the surface of currents that moved them without their control or say so. They knew that the random turbulence of life could swamp them and take them under at any time. They didn't have great expectations and, as a result, their levels of contentment, as far as Griff could see, were usually higher than those of people in western societies who were constantly restless and dissatisfied. He had seen that among the poor in Indonesia and other places as well as in India. It was enough for them that Roh and he told them they believed they could get out of this strife and that they would look after them as best they could.

After dinner they looked at the globe of the world again and Roh showed them how the axis of the world had moved putting India into the Arctic area and the USA and Australia into the tropics. This was amazing to Suman who had never had any schooling. The idea that the earth rotated and moved was something she had never thought of. The world and its place in the solar system was not something she had known or thought about. There had been few idle moments in her life to lie back and fly free of the mundane in her mind. The possibility of an almost limitless universe was beyond her grasp. But if Bai and Saheb said it, then it must be so.

The next day they would concentrate on getting the rest of the stores from the dry goods shop and, if there were time left over, explore a little more in the village. They went up to bed, tired but content and snuggled up.

"Do you reckon that Namji and his wife and Wasanta and his wife have been shagging since they have been living with us?" Griff asked Roh.

"I don't know. I suppose so. It would be difficult with the watchman on duty."

"You're kidding, the watchman always sleeps and anyway they are pillow biters. It's un-Indian to make any noise while fucking, isn't it my love?"

"I don't know and I don't care. You're the fucking expert. Not everyone wants to fuck every day like you."

"I don't want to fuck every day."

"Well, we fucked last night and you're ready to go again now, aren't you?"

"How do you know that?"

"Because I can feel your big dick pressing against my backside."

"That's because you are so beautiful and sexy and pumping out irresistible pheromones."

"I don't need to fuck, Griff, but if you want to that's fine. Go the whole hog." She slid her pyjama pants down to her knees. Griff gave his best rendition of a grunting pig as he slowly wormed his way in from behind.

"Are you gruntled, Miss Piggy?" he asked. She gave a couple of sleepy snorts. She was probably asleep by the time he finished.

After a breakfast of beef curry with freshly made chapattis and stewed guavas with yoghurt and tea of course, they harnessed the bullocks to the sleds and set off for the drygoods store. There was still no sign of anyone along the way to the village or at the store and they went and began loading. By lunchtime they had cleaned out the store. At lunch they decided to do another sortie in the afternoon to get batteries for the storage bank for the motorbike generator. They went back to where the six cars were in the centre of the village. While Sonba got the batteries and a few motor parts that he thought might come in handy, Griff checked out the nearby bicycle shop and a hardware store. The bike shop and adjoining house were abandoned but he found five steel-barrelled bike pumps and one large steel-barrelled motor car tyre pump of the sort that you put between your legs and hold in place with foot pieces. He had plans for them and took them with him. The hardware store seemed virtually untouched by looters and there were plenty of large plastic screw-top containers and metal bins of about twenty-litre capacity. Griff needed the plastic containers for their petrol and diesel supplies and the metal bins for the SOS system. After Sonba had loaded the batteries, they moved across to the hardware store to get the bins and a lot of other bits and pieces, such as nuts and bolts, nails, screws, tins of grease, hinges, fencing wire, ropes of various gauges and leather straps, belts and buckles for livestock.

During lunch they also decided that they needed to get the motorbike generator set up and working as soon as possible. Things had been very quiet so far but Griff had a persistent feeling that the situation could easily change and that it could happen suddenly. He hated the thought of being caught unprepared and he was getting tired of constant gloom and the reek of kero storm lanterns, in addition to the inescapable cold. There was hardly a time except when they were in bed or standing by the fire when they weren't aware of the cold and there were many moments when it was painfully sharp and Griff was reminded of how quickly death could come in a time like this. To get the generator working they needed more batteries and more petrol. The 350 cc motorbike engine was essentially 1950s technology and its fuel consumption was quite heavy. Sonba said he had been hoping to find a petrol driven gen-set in the village because that would have obviated the need to press ahead with the motorbike system, but he hadn't sighted one.

Their afternoon sortie was for the first time along the main road towards the town twenty kilometres away. In the first half kilometre they found only one vehicle, a big Indian-made luxury four wheel drive with a family in it. It was the big-shot who'd had the argument over wood to burn his mother and his family. They were all dead. They got the battery but the petrol tank was empty. There was a box of food with some real coffee grounds, fruit, biscuits and expensive whisky. They took that and the fine warm coats that the family were wearing, as well as their blankets. In the front passenger space they found a satchel stacked with wads of high denomination banknotes and gold jewellery. India was a cash economy still and people, particularly business people, had huge stashes of black money on which they had never paid tax, hidden in their houses. It was natural then that a fleeing family would take money and gold with them. Roh told the others that they would share out the money and satchel contents with them when they got home. The roof of this vehicle would make a fine big sled so they went to work with the axe and hacksaws to remove it and replace one of the smaller sleds. They left the dead family sitting in their roofless vehicle. The snow would soon cover them. Another half a kilometre along the road they came upon a cluster of five vehicles. It seemed a truck had rammed the back of a car immobilising both vehicles. Other cars, trying to get around them, had bogged in the deep snow in the ditches beside the road. There were dead women and children in some of them. It looked like the men who had been driving had left to try to get help and not been able to return.

50

The families had frozen to death or asphyxiated. The car windows were almost all closed. Sonba began taking the batteries out while the rest of them went through the vehicles for food and valuables and then started digging the snow away to get the wheels off. Two more satchels with wads of banknotes and jewellery turned up, but no food that was worth bothering with. They took the tyres and tubes off the wheel rims to cut down weight and space. With all of them working hard to keep warm, they finished there in an hour.

Another half kilometre along was a roadside eating and drinking place. A rough concrete box with an attached bamboo pergola that served greasy, semi-toxic snacks, chapattis, chicken curry and not very cold beer. Roh and Griff wouldn't have eaten there for fear of possible death but the locals who had cast iron stomachs and the cane cutting families in the sugarcane season ate there. Outside the greasy spoon was another cluster of cars and trucks but no lights or glow from a fire. In the squalid kitchen there was a dead fire in the middle of the room and about a dozen people, all men, equally expired. The only good thing about the place was that the beer would be well chilled now. They got petrol; four twenty-litre containers, and another of diesel. There was a carton with twelve bottles of Danish beer made under licence in India. They took that and left. A dozen bottles of beer shared among them at dinner time wouldn't lead to any trouble and would help to generate a festive air at a mid-winter party to celebrate the successful setting up of their ice palace and fortress. Roh and Griff wouldn't allow any spirits in the place and Griff would make sure that Sonba and Namji, known to have a taste for liquor, would have no more than their small ration, probably two glasses.

They set out for the farm and by the time they had finished unloading and sorting it was dinner time. Roh and Griff had sponge baths, dressed in their night gear and sauntered downstairs to dine. Their night wear was functional rather than beautiful. Roh had red tracksuit pants with a high necked skivvy and a pullover and thick woollen socks. Griff had thick black track suit pants with a black t-shirt, woollen pullover and an old leather jacket along with socks and a beanie. In bed he stripped down to the t-shirt. Their bedroom was cooler than the sitting room. The sitting room was neither hot nor cold so one needed to be clothed to be comfortable. In bed Griff's body generated so much heat he couldn't wear pants or socks, although Roh did. She felt the cold in her feet and legs.

Over dinner they talked about the work for the next day and decided that since they had ample tyres, batteries, petrol and diesel, they would work on chores in and around the house. Sonba would work on the motorbike generator with the help of Roh and the others and Griff would tackle a couple of projects he had been turning over in his mind. He explained how they would create a large SOS signal out of car tyres to go on the big open garden area on the opposite side of the house to the wasti. They would put another such sign on the top terrace roof. These would have to be swept clean of snow every day. In addition he told them about the kero tin flares that they would prepare in advance and take out to indicate the landing area when they heard a helicopter nearby. Griff said the Australian soldiers had used these fires in the North African desert to keep warm during the cold nights. They were easily made by cutting the top out of a tin, filling it close to the top with sand or soil, soaking the soil with petrol and then lighting it. They would prepare the kero tins with soil tomorrow and stack them on the front veranda. When they heard a chopper approaching, they would pour in the petrol, carry them out and place them and then light them. They should also do a couple of flares for the top roof terrace beside the SOS sign.

Chapter 3: The siege

Next morning as they were having breakfast the dogs began barking and went to the door. There was heavy pounding on the door and a voice shouting: "Open up, Government inspection." They all knew the voice. It was Jagdish Godse, a Government official who was a native of the village. He was egregiously corrupt and had made millions, hundreds of crores of rupees, perhaps as much as the equal of ten million dollars from selling favours. He had control of many State Government affairs for this district, which covered hundreds of square miles with probably ten million people. Maharashtra was a big, rich state with a population of more than 100 million. He had ploughed much of that black money into the purchase of properties in the names of his relatives and friends. Benami properties, they were called. His main farm covered close to a thousand acres. There were State government regulations that limited most farms to forty acres. Broad acre farming was definitely the way things had to move in India to enable it to provide the food its growing population would need, but it had to achieve it without appalling corruption. Godse was smooth and plausible but Roh and Griff knew what a crook he was.

"Who is it?" Roh called.

"You know who it is. Godse. Open the door. I have to make an inspection."

"An inspection of what?" Roh asked.

"What people you have there and what supplies."

"We will tell you that and you can write it down. You know that we tell the truth."

"I have to see for myself, otherwise it is not an official inspection."

While Roh was having this conversation, Griff climbed up and shone a torch through the small gap at the top of the window that faced on to the veranda. There were three men and a teenage boy who looked like Godse's son. He told Roh.

"That is too bad because we are not going to open up. We have ten adults and one girl and we have adequate supplies of food and fuel to keep us going for a while. When will rescuers be coming?"

"We do not know when army people will come to help us. But now we must do a survey of food stocks for the Government's information. If you don't open the door we will have to break it down and we are armed. If you resist you will be shot."

"Do you think we should let them in?" Roh asked Griff.

"Not on your life. This is a ruse to get into the house and take over. If we let them in we'll be in serious strife," Griff said.

She nodded agreement. Griff climbed up to the window gap again and fired the shotgun into the air. There was a stunned silence following the massive blast of the 12-gauge and he called out: "We have guns too and if you try to break this door down or get in some other way we will kill you, so you had better get moving back to your place."

There were hurried footfalls on the veranda paving. After ten minutes or so, Godse called out again.

"Tai, Saheb, listen to me. We are desperate. We are running out of food and fuel and we cannot keep my house warm. That is why I said we needed to make an official inspection. We will starve or die of cold if you don't help us. You don't have to let me and my brothers in but please take my son. I can't bear to think of him suffering and dying as we will have to. Please take him in. He is a good boy and will cause no trouble."

"Wait," Roh called to him. "What do you think Griff?"

"I'm deeply suspicious. I don't believe for one minute that he would be short of anything. He has access to Government storehouses with hundreds of tonnes of food and fuel. He would be better set up than we are. But in the last analysis, it is your house, your people and your country. My advice would be don't do it, but it is your decision. If you do decide to take the boy let me handle it because they are probably trying to work a fast one on us."

"Like what?"

"Rushing the door when we open it."

54

"He seems a nice boy and I can't imagine that he would harm us if we let him stay and Godse may be in some sort of difficulties."

"Up to you," Griff said.

"Alright, say we agree to take him only. You organise it."

Griff went over to the front window and called out that they would take the boy. They should all stand out on the patio where they could be seen. The boy should come and stand next to the front door but the other three should stay at the back of the patio while the boy came in. Subhash and Wasanta opened the heavy inner door and then unbolted the outer door while Namji stood by with the gun at the ready and Griff kept the torch on them. He noted then that Godse, while giving his son a hug, was talking to him as though he were giving instructions and the boy was nodding. The three then moved back and the boy came to the door. Subhash grabbed the boy, pulled him in quickly and re-bolted the doors. Griff told Godse that no harm would come to his son if the boy behaved himself and that they should now leave and not return.

Griff told Namji to search the boy for weapons and Roh gave the boy, who was about sixteen, a briefing on the rules of the house. She got his name. Deepak. She said he should sleep in the kitchen area with Subhash and Ramesh. He was quiet and seemed cooperative although not really friendly. That was perhaps understandable if he were parting from his father and might not see him again. However, Griff wasn't willing to trust him for one moment. The boy had trouble meeting his eyes. He was sure that his father was up to some sort of ruse, but it was not possible, without being nasty to the boy, to ascertain what it might be. They would just have to wait and see and hope to be able to outsmart him. They gave him breakfast. Griff told Subhash not to let him out of his sight. He asked the boy where they had come from and how they had come to their farm. He said they came in a big van from his father's farm further along the road. The van was loaded with food and fuel and they were going to try to get over to the main highway running to the south. They thought the highway might be kept clear of snow with heavy machinery. Griff thought that was improbable but didn't say so. He asked him how it was living in his father's farmhouse. It was very cold. They couldn't

55

get warm. They had lit fires in barrels but it didn't seem to warm the place which had a very open design. Griff asked him where his father was going now. He said he didn't know. He felt sure the boy wasn't being honest with him. It was the face, eyes and the body language. But there was nothing Griff could do short of hurting him and he wasn't going to do that.

They all pressed ahead with the chores. There was a place on the sheltered side of the house where the snow was not so deep and Griff was able to get enough soil to fill five drums almost to the top. The soil was already beginning to freeze hard and it wasn't easy digging. They left the drums on the veranda ready for eventual use and put out the SOS sign with the tyres. It took twenty tyres to make the sign. They would need to get more tyres for the sign to go on the terrace roof and Griff wanted to get more tyres anyway to make the first sign more clear. He reminded them that the tyres would need to be swept clean of snow every day and if they heard a chopper they should drop everything and rush out to clean them so that they would stand out clearly and set up the flares. The other thing they would need to do was to pack the snow down firmly where the chopper would land so that it wouldn't sink in and come to grief. He would make a couple of rams to use to pack the snow down hard.

That afternoon Griff got fertiliser from the godown on the wasti and mixed up a trial batch of fertiliser, white flour from the dry goods store and diesel to make a sort of pastry. He didn't know what the proportions should be and he thought he may have put too much diesel in the mix. It was a trifle wet when he put it in the plastic bottle and then inserted a firecracker to act as detonator. He had inserted the detonator into the explosive mixture and the moisture may have leached into the firecracker and caused it to fail to ignite. The next batch he mixed was a lot drier, like shortbread pastry. He put the firecracker in, lit the fuse and threw it out on to the snow. It went off with a satisfyingly big explosion. Roh came running to see what was going on. He told her. He said he would be making grenades in jam jars and tins with tacks and nuts and screws.

"But what is the threat that you are so frightened of that we need this sort of deterrent?"

56

"Anyone who comes and tries to break in. I know you think it is unlikely and let us hope it is, but if something does happen, I want to be prepared."

"You've got a gun."

"Yes, but it is not enough if there are multiple attackers."

"Oh well, you'll get a kick out of that won't you. Blowing people up with jam jar bombs."

"I hate violence. I hate committing violence on other people but most of all I hate other people trying to do it to me. I'm a pussy cat until people start trying to do me over. Then I get angry."

Roh threw up her hands in resignation and went off. Griff pressed ahead with the new mixture and made about two dozen bombs out of jam jars, jam tins and small plastic bottles. They put small nuts and screws in the containers. Griff showed the men how to puncture the lids to insert the detonator firecracker and explained that they shouldn't punch the holes now, as the mixture might dry out. They would keep the bombs and the firecrackers together and put the detonators in at the time they needed them, if that ever came. They wrapped the tins in plastic bags to keep the mixture moist and Griff took the boxes of bombs and the firecrackers up to their bedroom.

In bed that night they talked. Griff said he was worried that something might happen with the boy's father and uncles. He didn't trust the boy. He felt he was not being straight.

"He can't look me in the eye and his body language isn't good when I speak to him."

"I think you are imagining it, Griff. He seems a nice gentle lad to me, although I admit he doesn't seem all that relaxed. Don't worry. Nothing can happen. Godse has gone."

Two nights later, about 3 am, Griff was woken with a whack in the face. Godse was standing over him with a torch in one hand and an automatic pistol in the other hand. The two brothers were standing behind him with handguns. One was covering Roh and the other was on Griff.

"You will have to get up, pardeshi. You are going for a walk in the snow, foreigner." He dragged the bedclothes off them. Griff was wearing only a t-shirt.

"What do you mean he is going for a walk in the snow?" Roh shouted.

"Just that. He is a foreigner. He can walk back to his own country. We don't need foreigners here using our women and our resources."

"You would do this to a man who has been kind enough to take in your son and look after him?"

"My son is an Indian. He has a right to be here. Foreigners have no rights. We tell foreigners what they can and cannot do in our country."

"You can't make him go outside without getting dressed. He will die."

"He will have to go out as he is. That will make him run. He will get back to his country more quickly." Godse's brothers laughed.

Roh screamed and ran at Godse, but the man who was covering her grabbed her arm and twisted it behind her back. She groaned and sobbed quietly.

"At least let me give her a goodbye hug," Griff said.

"Yes, go ahead, but don't try anything silly or you will both get shot."

Griff put his arms around her and hugged her tight.

"Be strong, help the others, I'll be back, do whatever he says to stay alive," Griff whispered into her ear.

"Alright, that's enough. Downstairs now," Godse said, poking Griff with his gun.

They went down and the son who was holding the shotgun unbolted the door. Griff quickly grabbed a pair of his old brogues from the shoe rack beside the front door as the men shoved him out into the freezing cold and then bolted the door behind him. He knew that he would have to act very quickly to stay alive. He could be dead from the cold in fifteen minutes.

On the front veranda was the pile of heavy jackets that they had taken from the luxury four-wheel drive occupants. He grabbed them on the run along with a couple of car tubes and sprinted across the wasti barefoot to the cattle shed where he had stored the car. The keys were hanging on a pole near the car and he opened it and got in. It was diesel and while Griff was no mechanic, he guessed that the heating of the diesel plugs would mean that the car was more likely to start than a petrol motor in this freezing weather. It took a few cranks before it fired but then it seemed to be fine. It was only a week since it had been driven and it had about two-thirds of a tankful of fuel. Griff put the heater on full and opened the windows on the sheltered side enough to keep a little fresh air flowing in. He pulled on the biggest jacket that they had taken off the dead family and zipped it up. The wife's jacket he wrapped around his loins. A frost-bitten dick was the last thing he wanted. Luckily, the brogues which he'd bought in Edinburgh some years earlier, had a pair of socks in them and he pulled them on. He was ready now to go across to his workshop to do the necessary. There was a spare workshop door key on the car key ring. On the way he checked Wasanta and Seema's room. There was an old army blanket that he took and a kero lantern with a tiny bit of fuel in it. There was a battered stainless steel cooking pot and a kettle and a shegdi. He went to his workshop, got matches and lit the kero lantern. There was a well-worn pair of cotton chino work pants and a denim shirt hanging up in the workshop and a pair of stiff leather riggers gloves, rigid with the cold. He quickly put them on. He took a box of teakwood offcuts for the shegdi and some paper and the bottle of coconut oil that he used to lubricate the stone he sharpened his chisels and plane blades on. From his tool cabinet, now much depleted, he was able to get a battered Swiss Army knife, a pair of scissors, a bag needle and some strong twine and then returned to Wasanta's room. There he got the fire going in the shegdi, filled the kettle with snow and put it on. There was a packet with a little tea in it and some sugar in their food cupboard. While the water was heating he cut a poncho from the blanket to put on over his shirt and under his jacket. It hung down to his knees which was good because it kept his loins warm. From the second jacket he removed the sleeves and pulled them over his lower legs. He had to go back to the car then to get the child's jacket. He cut the sleeves out of it and used them to pull over his shoes. From the car tubes he cut leggings to reach from his ankles to the knees and galoshes to cover his shoes. He made the galoshes with flaps so that he could tie them around the ankles to keep his footwear dry and to give him flexibility in the ankles for climbing and running. Around the galoshes he tied some leather thongs to give him grip in the snow. The rubber was slippery. He used the rest of the child's jacket to make a hat that covered his ears and lower face. From the body part of the woman's jacket he made a muff and suspended it just above waist height with a cord around his neck. The leather riggers gloves weren't enough to keep the cold out and when he wasn't using his hands he would put them in the muff to keep warm. He returned to the workshop, got a used paint tin, and cut a thirty-centimetre spine from the crippled umbrella he used occasionally in the monsoon. Using the sharpening stone he ground a good point on the steel spine and rooted around in an oddments tin until he found a small piece of aluminium tubing. He sealed off one end and bent it over, wrapped some rag around the spine and jammed it well into the aluminium to form a handle which he then bound with rag. The handle was about ten centimetres long and the spine twenty. That was more than enough for his needs.

Back to Wasanta's room with the paint tin half full of snow. He put it on the fire to warm while he made some tea. No fresh milk, sadly, but there was some powdered milk and sugar. Usually he didn't use the stuff, considering it to be poison, but he would need every bit of energy he could muster now. Revived by the tea and his warm outfit Griff went to the godown where the fowls were. There were two eggs and he grabbed them and an old hen before she was even awake and wrung her neck. With the Swiss Army knife he quickly skinned the hen and gutted it, keeping the crop, heart and kidney, and put them in the battered steel pot. There was a packet of masala with a remnant in it and one small desiccated onion which he added to the pot. From his workshop he got a couple of handfuls of the broken wheat used to feed the fowls and added them to the pot. He made a visit to the now empty grain godown and scraped together some chick peas and corn that had spilt from bags, blew the dust off them, washed them with snow, and added them to the fowl in the cooking pot. As soon as the water in the old paint tin was hot he put the plastic bottle with the coconut oil in it to thaw. It was like a lump of stone. When the oil was ready he took some and massaged it into the riggers gloves to make them supple and water proof. With some more of the oil he soaked a length of twine and made a small oil lamp in an empty jam tin. Griff knew the kerosene lantern wouldn't burn for much longer. He lit the oil lamp and turned off the lantern which he needed to conserve in case he had to use it outside. The oil lamp threw a much dimmer light and that suited him fine. He fixed a bag over the window so that if Godse's men came poking around the wasti it was less likely they would see any light from the room. There was space enough under the door for fresh air to get in.

He took stock of his situation while he waited for his chicken stew to cook. It was now just 5 am and he guessed that Godse and his lot would be sound asleep and would remain so until 6 or 7 am. It was unlikely even then that they would come out into the wasti. Griff felt pleased. Things were going well so far. He had warm clothing, some food and drink and a couple of weapons as well as a snug place to sleep. He felt really bad about Roh. Her situation was much more parlous than his. Godse and the other two, whom he did not know, were capable of despicable things and in this lawless situation would feel that there was nothing and no-one to stop them from doing whatever they wished. He knew how ruthless some men could be when they felt they were in an unassailable position of power. Still, he had great faith in Roh's ability to think on her feet and she was tough. She would have to cope for four days to lull Godse into a feeling of security before Griff made his move to try to save them. But if they harmed Roh in any way, he would never forgive them. He would deal with them ruthlessly. She was the dearest thing in his life and the thought of her suffering physical pain or distress hit him like a knife wound. The thought of it choked him and made his hands shake with fear, frustration and anger.

He boiled the hen until the meat fell from the bone and put it aside to cool before eating. Meanwhile, he went back to the workshop and cut some two metre lengths of thin cotton rope, rolled them and put them into his jacket pockets.

After shoving Griff out the door, Godse told one of the men to take the shotgun from his son and take the watch until morning. He told the son to get some sleep and Roh to get upstairs to bed.

"I'll sleep down here, if you don't mind, I prefer the company of these people, to you and your brothers."

61

"That is not possible. You will probably be stirring up trouble with them. I have plans for you. Now, get upstairs."

"No thanks, I'll stay here."

Godse stepped forward quickly and hit her on the side of the head with the gun. Roh gasped with pain and shock, staggered and fell to her knees.

"Now get up and go upstairs." Godse kept his gun pointing at her and followed her up the stairs.

Godse and one of his brothers followed. They pushed Roh into the middle of the bed and then took off their shoes and got in, one each side of her.

"Well, Madam Rohini. You dress like a western woman and behave like one. I don't suppose you know much about our Indian culture."

"I imagine I know at least as much as you do. My family have written scholarly works about Indian society."

"Ah yes, the scholarly family. You will know all about The Mahabharat then."

"I would be an unusual Indian if I didn't."

"Then you will know about our great heroine, the model for all Indian women, Draupadi."

"What point are you trying to make, Godse?"

"You will know that she was married to five brothers. One of them was a fool who lost her in a gambling bet along with most of his other possessions. Your feeble foreign husband or lover or whatever he is, has lost you in the gamble of life. You now belong to us. These other two men are my brothers and you will be our Draupadi. What do you say to that?"

"Draupadi took the brothers willingly as her husbands who were themselves noble. You are not noble, but I am not in any position to enforce my independence. You have the power and the weapons to make me do what you wish, but if you force me to have sex with you and your brothers that will be rape."

"As you say, you are in no position to oppose anything and you would not be wise to adopt a threatening tone. If you try anything stupid, I will give you another hit. Now you can shut up and go to sleep."

He told his brother to stay awake and keep watch until 6 am and then wake him to take over.

Roh was exhausted by the night's activities but it took her a while to fall asleep. She felt scared and uncertain but at the same time a confidence and strength from what Griff had said before he left and from believing that he was clever and innovative enough to survive somehow. She tried to imagine how he might survive but couldn't see it. Eventually, she fell into troubled sleep.

She woke shortly after 6 am, hearing Godse telling his brother to go downstairs and see that tea was made and brought up.

"Alright, Draupadi, now it is time for you to do your wifely duty, so you had better get your pants off."

"I have to urinate first."

"Go then. We have ample time."

Roh went to the bathroom and when she had finished there, ran quickly downstairs calling to Namji and the other farm hands to help. Godse was going to rape her, she said. Godse's brother, the one who had accompanied him during the night, rushed to her and twisted her arm behind her until she cried out in pain. He pushed her ahead of him up the stairs to the bedroom. He shoved her inside and then pulled the door closed.

"I told you if you tried anything stupid you would suffer. Now get your clothes off and get into the bed and do your wifely duty, Draupadi."

Roh was crying with anger and frustration. But she remembered what Griff had told her. Do what had to be done to survive. She went to the cupboard where she kept personal items, first aid stuff and medicines. She knew Griff had put some condoms there. She moistened herself with lubricating jelly, returned to the bed and gave Godse a condom.

"If you don't put that on you will have to fight me. I won't give in easily. If you put it on I won't oppose you."

63

There was no doubt that Godse was more powerful physically than Rohini but she was strong and fit and would be able to do quite a bit of damage to Godse before he overpowered her. He could see that.

"I don't agree with these unnatural western practices, but I will make that concession for you."

"Fine. Go to it then."

"You seem to be in a terrible rush. Is it excitement that prompts you?" he said, laughing. "I will have to go and urinate first."

He returned and climbed on top of her. It was all done silently for about two minutes until he grunted and fell off.

Roh got up and went to the bathroom to wash and then returned and dressed. Godse appeared to be asleep so she went downstairs. The rest of her group were sitting around looking miserable and some were crying. She went to them and told them not to worry. Things would work out and they would be safe.

"But what about Saheb?" Sonba asked, sobbing. "Is he dead? How could anyone survive out there with no clothes? He must be dead by now."

"Don't worry about Saheb," she said quietly. "He is a clever man and I am sure he will find some way to survive." She said it as confidently as she could, but in her mind there was a persistent doubt that the odds were against him. She couldn't see how he could survive without a fire, warm clothes and food.

Breakfast was usually a lively event with conversation and laughter and discussion of the day's work program, but this day it was silent. Godse had his breakfast taken up to the bedroom. Roh told the other two brothers that there were essential jobs that had to be done, such as the cleaning of the livestock rooms, the emptying of the slop buckets, collecting clean snow for drinking water, cleaning and cooking, chopping wood and bringing it in. This required staff members to go in and out. After one of them discussed that with Godse, the brothers said that only one person was to be outside at a time. Namji should do all the outside work and the other staff would hand things to him at the door and take back what he passed in. After breakfast they stood guard, one on the inside of the front door and one

64

on the outside, with pistols in their hands while Namji did the chores. By lunch time all the chores had been done and the staff sat around.

After lunch Namji said he was going to go outside with some food for the Saheb if he were still alive or to put his body in a safe place in one of the godowns if he found him dead. He went to the door and began to open it. One of the brothers whacked him on the side of the head with his pistol and he fell to his knees. Sonba jumped up and pushed the brother away and began to open the door for Namji who stood and moved toward to the door. One of the brothers shouted at him to stop or he would shoot. Godse called out from the bedroom asking what was happening. The brother told him. Godse said no-one was to go out. Namji kept going and the other brother shot him in the back of the head. Namji fell dead and the brothers shoved him out of the door and bolted it. Sonba fell to his knees sobbing like a child. Namji's wife Laxmi and daughter screamed and began beating their foreheads with their hands. Laxmi lifted her arm so that her wrist with her glass bangles, one of the symbols of her married status, were smashed against her forehead causing it to bleed. Bangle shards flew about the room. The other women rushed to comfort her and began wailing also. The men were shocked into immobility. Rohini shouted that they were murdering bastards, who had turned a peaceful, happy house into a hell.

The rest of the afternoon passed quietly. No new interesting projects were begun and what little conversation took place was in whispers. After dinner some played cards and Rohini read a section from the history of India to the non-card players and then made some diary notes. At 10 pm, Godse told her to get upstairs to bed. He said one of his brothers would have the pleasure of her body that night so she had better prepare herself. If she didn't, he would allow his brother to beat her. She did so, as she had with Godse senior. It was over in barely two minutes and she washed and then fell, eventually, into a fitful sleep.

Outside, Griff was in Wasanta and Seema's room stewing some guavas after having eaten his dinner of beef and cracked wheat stew. He had made his stew with some meat he chopped from the carcass hanging in the rain tree. He had spent most of the day packing straw bundles around the car so that it looked like a hay stack, leaving only a narrow tunnel entrance on the inside of the cattle shed. He also lengthened the exhaust pipe with a three metre piece of water pipe so that the exhaust gasses were vented through the chaff-cutting machine room well away from the car. He would run the car engine with the heater on to get it cosy before bedding down for the night. He had removed part of the back seat so that he could sleep lying down. He had made bedding with car mats, straw and empty wheat bags. After eating his dessert he went to work to grind a fine point and sharp edges to a twenty-centimetre piece of mild steel to form a dagger. He had shaped it roughly with a hacksaw and bound the handle with thick twine. In two hours of work with a file and the sharpening stone he had made a fine dagger and a leather sheath so that he could tuck it into his right rubber legging. That gave him two good weapons. He put the remainder of the stew and guavas in the food cupboard, doused the fire and the oil lamp and went in a roundabout way to the car so that there wouldn't be any footprints leading to it. It took a while for the car to warm him and his bedding, and he lay in bed considering his situation. It seemed pretty good. He was warmly clad, he had weapons, food and a cosy place to sleep. He just needed to lie low for another three days before tackling the house. He would reconnoitre morning and afternoon to check on the house and make sure of where he would climb to the top terrace. Once in the house, if he were able to get in, he would have to play it by ear because he wouldn't know where Godse and his two accomplices were. He turned off the car engine and climbed back into his bed fully clothed in his wild outfit and soon fell asleep. Inside his snug hideaway, insulated from the polar storm, he could barely hear the wind raging outside. The weight of snow had stifled the rattling of the corrugated iron sheeting of the cattle shed roof.

No need to rush out of bed in the morning. He lay there thinking of Roh and dreading the things that Godse and the others might be doing to her. He let the hatred of them stew in his gut so that when the time came he would act against them without compunction. They had tried to kill him and he could not forgive that and if they did anything to Roh he would be utterly ruthless in dealing with them. He would be cool, quick thinking and methodical.

That morning, after a breakfast of warmed up stew and guavas, he did a careful tour of the house. He could hear women working in the kitchen. He was stunned to find Namji dead on the front veranda frozen stiff. A good part of his head was blown away. It grieved him that he would have to leave the body as he had found it, otherwise Godse and his mates would realise that he was alive and staying somewhere safe near the house. He went back from the veranda the way he had come brushing his footprints away with a bag. Griff estimated the snow was now more than four metres deep around the house. He realised he would have to spend the day making himself some snowshoes. He cut bamboos from a patch between the back of the house and the guava orchard to make the frames for the shoes and took another tube from the pile near the house to make the binding thongs. He heated water in the kettle after breakfast in Wasanta's room and used the steam from the spout to bend the green bamboo to the shape he wanted and then bound it into place. They were an improvement on the first snowshoes he had made. They were light and kept him high up in the snow so that movement was less taxing and enabled him to move and turn faster.

As he worked he realised it was most unlikely that Godse or the other two would come out looking for him because they would not like having to dress in the snow gear that Griff had made for his people. He doubted also that they would have the gumption to make similar outfits for themselves. Most middle class Indians were tool illiterate. They couldn't use saws or hammers, planes, chisels or even pliers with any facility and regarded doing anything with tools as beneath their social status. It was one of the greatest impediments to the development of good skills in a great many fields from engineering to veterinary work. They didn't like to get their hands dirty and so no-one got trained in the proper and precise way to do things. They did all their learning from books. Roh found that the so-called Masters of Vet Science whom she employed as assistants had rarely handled animals during the entire time of their training and were hard put to know the difference between a goat's bum and its fanny. It was extraordinary, because she had done her degree in Australia where there was an emphasis on practical training and you failed if you weren't prepared to get your hands and your clothes dirty. Griff knew that a lot of the middle class locals who knew that he worked with tools to do things to the house and around the farm regarded him as low class. To them he was just a mistri: a tradesman. But the principal of one of the private schools in the town who was bright enough to see how these caste attitudes were holding back her country, had asked Griff to teach woodwork to her students. They had come along well. The best student was a girl. That surprised and puzzled Griff for a while until he realised that the answer was obvious. A lot of middle class women in Indian society worked with their hands in the home and the office while the men did almost nothing with their hands apart from scratching their balls and writing. The group of ten or so students had made a fine chair for the principal's office and some benches for the students as well as a rope malkhamb frame and jungle gym in the school yard. The malkhamb frame stood six metres high like a squared letter N. It had two uprights with a cross bar at the top from which hung a thick cotton rope on which students performed climbing and hanging gymnastics of a sort that western society students would have great difficulty doing. Western society boys and girls of Griff's era could usually handle tools fairly easily. Different cultures, different needs. He ate more beef stew with stewed guavas for lunch and dinner and spent the night as before.

His greatest hardship now that he was well set up was finding a place out of the wind to crap and wash his bum. He warmed some water and used an old blouse of Seema's as a towel. He had given away the idea of washing. It was just too cold to even contemplate it. Griff mused that the two great inventions of the Indians were washing the bum after crapping and the zero in mathematics, although the ancient Babylonians were rather insistent that the latter was their idea. He didn't know who was right, but he was certain that smearing poo around the backside with paper was a filthy western habit. There was a wonderful story he had heard a few times about an Indian classical woman singer who was being interviewed about her performance at the Albert Hall in London. She remarked that when she looked over the audience of thousands, she inexplicably thought of all those dirty bottoms and almost swooned with horror. Griff agreed. But Indians, particularly high class Indians, had an utter fear and loathing of shit, so much so that ironically, in many cases, their lavatories were revolting. They had clean bums and dirty lavs and the westerners had dirty bums and clean lavs. Except the French who also had clean bums and dirty lavs.

He had a quiet night like the night before and woke refreshed. He crushed some wheat with a hammer and made porridge and stewed guava for breakfast and thought about the day's activities. It was time perhaps to make a sortie to the village with a container to get more diesel for his car and possibly some additions to the diet. He was getting greens from the guava skins but a few dried green peas and lentils and an onion or two would be nice. His car wouldn't run out of diesel before he made his raid on the house but if it failed he would need to retreat to his car. He would wait until his people finished their outside chores before heading off to the village.

Griff guessed that sometime during the morning one of his men from the house would come across to the room where the fowls were to check and, if need be, refill the automatic grain feeder and to give them fresh water or rather snow while collecting the eggs. About 11 am Wasanta appeared to do that and to have a look around. Griff whistled him over to the cattle shed. A huge grin spread over the usually phlegmatic Wasanta's face.

"Saheb, Saheb, Raam has saved you. Are you alright?"

"Ho. Raam and I are very close these days."

"Achaa, achaa. Me kai karoo – good, good, what can I do?"

"One small thing. Tell Bai to get Suman to open the bolts on the top terrace door at 3 o'clock tomorrow night. Not tonight, but the next night, samajle ka?"

"Ho, samajle, Saheb."

"Okay, you repeat it to me."

"Baina sanga, Sahebanni sangitlay ki udya ratri teen wajta Sumanla tiche dar ughadayla sanga."

"Barobar. Chhaan. Phacta Baina sanga. Dusrya konala nahi."

"Good. Tell no one but Bai," Griff responded, and asked then what had happened with Namji.

"Namji was coming out to look for you, Saheb, and give you some food or take your body to the veranda but the brothers wouldn't let him and shot him."

Griff didn't know until then that the two men with Godse were his brothers. He asked if Wasanta was sure all three men were involved in the shooting.

"Yes. The two men apart from Godse are his brothers. Everyone was there when it happened and saw it. Two brothers were downstairs and Godse was upstairs. All three had discussed it and Godse told the two downstairs that no-one was to go out. One brother then told the other brother to shoot Namji when he was going out the door."

That settled an important scruple in Griff's mind about what to do when he got into the house.

After more beef stew for lunch, Griff strapped on his snowshoes and headed for the village at a brisk pace. He had a small torch that he found in the car glove box, but he would use that only when he got to the village and needed to look around in the abandoned stores. He went first to the hardware store and took a large plastic screw-top container for the diesel and another smaller one for kerosene for his now dry storm lantern. He filled his two containers and put them aside and then went looking through other shops and houses for food. He found a couple of onions and potatoes, a jar with lentils and some ginger root. In one house he found a plastic tub and a torch with plenty of power left in the battery. He took them. He had rope in his pocket. He loaded the diesel and kero in the tub, tied a rope to the handle on one end and then around his waist and headed back to the farm. The tub slipped easily over the snow and he made good time. Back at Wasanta's room he filled his kero lantern, put the diesel into his car, added chopped potatoes, onions and lentils to his stew pot and made a cup of tea with some shavings of ginger. He craved a good cup of coffee but that would have to wait until he secured the house and dealt with Godse and his brothers.

Chapter 4: Breaking the siege

At 2.30 am Griff climbed out of his bed in the car, strapped on snowshoes, checked his weapons and good torch and made his way to the house. He stashed his snowshoes in the snow next to the wall, and got under the plastic sheeting that covered the two big haystacks on the northern side of the house. These ran at an angle of about forty-five degrees up to the roof terrace. It was impossible to climb up on the plastic because of the angle and the snow piled on it. But under the sheeting he could climb easily on the hay bundles. Before 3 am he was waiting by the door and heard Suman sliding the bolts. They hardly made a whisper and Griff guessed that Roh had surreptitiously oiled them during the day. The door opened and he slipped quickly in.

"Everything quiet?" he asked Suman. It was, she said.

"Where is Godse?"

"In Bai's bed."

"And the brothers?"

"One in Bai's room and one on guard at the front door as watchman."

"Good," he said and told her to stay in bed. Everything would be alright.

He took his leggings and shoes and socks off, left them in Suman's room and tiptoed downstairs. At the door to Roh's and his room he stopped and listened. No sound but two snoring men. He guessed Roh was awake but she didn't move. He went downstairs. In the glow coming through the Pyrex glass in the door of the stove he could see Rani's and Digger's ears flick up and they looked at him and stood up. He crouched down and went quietly to them, told them to stay and gave them a pat each. The brother on guard duty was sleeping on his chair. Griff went to him with his umbrella spine in his hand. His head was leaning back against a cupboard behind him. He put his hand on the top of his head to hold it firm and at the same time shoved the needle sharp spine up through the lower jaw, through the soft palate and into the brain. He withdrew it immediately and shoved it between his ribs and into his heart. He twitched several times while Griff held him firm and then died without a sound. Griff hid the shotgun in the buffalo room, put the guard's automatic in his belt and then went quietly back up the stairs to the bedroom. No change there. The same rhythm of snoring. He moved across to the bed to see which brother was on the right side. It was not Godse. He was on the other side of Roh. Griff leant in close to see the position of the brother and then despatched him with one quick shove of the spine up through the jaw and mouth. He gave a moan and a few twitches while Griff held him steady. While he was moving around the bed to tackle Godse, he suddenly sat up and said "kai?" Griff whacked him firmly on the side of his head with the automatic and shone the torch in his eyes.

"Get your hands outside the bedcovers and show me where your gun is. Don't touch it," he said.

He pointed to inside the bed. Griff pulled back the bed covers and could see it sticking out from under his pillow. He was wearing all his clothes except his shoes. His brother was the same. Griff told Roh to take the gun and find the other brother's gun. It was also under his pillow. He told Godse then to roll on to his stomach and put his hands together behind him. He pulled one of the ropes from his jacket pocket. It already had a loop at one end. He fixed the loop with a quick knot that was tight on his neck but not so tight he couldn't breathe and then tied his hands firmly and looped the spare end of the rope around his head again and pulled it tight. There was no way Godse would be getting out of that without a helper with a sharp knife. He got him on his feet and downstairs to the sitting room where he tied him in a chair and put a quilt over him. He couldn't risk the son getting up to some stunt, so he woke him and tied him and then left him in his bed.

Everyone was stirring now. He told them everything was alright now and to go back to sleep. He would tell them everything in the morning.

Roh and Griff rolled the dead brother out of the bed. There were only a few drops of blood. Griff took off his snow gear and climbed in.

They snuggled up. Roh was crying with relief and joy and saying she was so sorry she had been duped by Godse and his son. No apologies needed or wanted, Griff said and stopped her talk with a kiss.

"Go to sleep," he said. "We'll talk in the morning." It was only 3.30 am and they fell asleep feeling warm and secure again.

Suman woke them at 6.30 with mugs of tea and Griff's favourite dish that he had created and called an Indian crepe. It was fusion cuisine: a hot freshly-made thin chapatti smeared with jam and yoghurt and rolled like a crepe. He greedily ate three leaving only two for Roh. They got up and went to the bathroom for a pee and wash. Griff dragged the dead brother out to the landing returned and closed their door.

"You don't have to tell me anything, Roh, or apologise for anything. You did what I would have done, stayed alive till your luck improved. If you want to talk about it you can, but you don't have to."

"I need to talk about it, Griff, to get it off my mind."

She told Griff how the brothers had forced her in turn to have sex and she had told them that it was rape. She made them use condoms and they did, although she had to threaten one brother with scratching his face to a bloody mess when he started arguing about the condom. She told him also about the killing of Namji.

"They fucked like fowls. At least it was over in less than two minutes every time. Women are just a hole to shoot their semen into. A convenience, like a lavatory. In fact I'd say they spent less time on it than they do on their other natural functions." She cried a bit with the anger.

Griff kissed her and massaged and stroked her until she fell asleep again. Griff soon joined her and they woke at 7.30 to the smell of breakfast wafting up the stairs and the happy conversation of their crew at the breakfast table. They dressed and went downstairs.

Godse's son was still tied up in his bedding. He seemed agitated and asked why he was tied up. Because he couldn't be trusted, Griff said. They'd trusted him once and he had betrayed them. If he gave his word not to go near his father Griff would undo his bindings. He said he would abide by that and wanted to know what would happen to his father. Griff undid the bindings and told him he would find out soon enough but, meanwhile he should behave himself or he would be tied up again. If he went near his father, or spoke to him, he would be tied up and taken upstairs. Meanwhile he should have some breakfast. Griff gave a cup of tepid milky, sugary tea to Godse, holding the mug so he could sip it.

As he finished, Godse said: "Let us talk things over, Saheb. We are both strong, clever men and we shouldn't fall out at a time like this. You are such a smart fellow. I can see all the things you have done here to help this group survive." He gave a disgustingly insincere grin followed by a hollow laugh.

"I thought we had already fallen out, Godse. You sent me out to die in the snow."

"Oh no, Saheb. I was just testing you." Another hollow laugh."I knew you would be back. That is why I looked after everything here for you. Your wife, your staff, your dogs."

"You forgot Namji. You looked after him too, didn't you?"

"He was a stupid fellow who wouldn't take good advice. What have you done with my brothers? And what are you going to do with me?"

"They are both dead. I killed them. They were murderers. They killed Namji. But let us not talk now. I want to have some breakfast and then we will have a trial. Since there is no law now for us to hand you over to, you will have to be tried before our group for your bad deeds."

"No, Saheb. Let us not do that. I am a very rich man. I have millions of American dollars in my house, which you can have. If you take me there I will show you where to get them. You will be a multi-millionaire in your own country when you get back there."

"Thank you for your kind offer but I regret I am not interested. Our staff may be. You can tell them where the dollars are stashed and they can go and get them after the trial."

"Bai, Madam, did you hear that. I have millions of US dollars hidden in my farmhouse. You can have them. They are all yours. Just let me go and I will leave you and not bother you again."

Roh ignored him.

"Do you have any sense of morality at all Godse?" Griff said.

"Don't you realise that this is the end of the world. This is the Iron Age, Kali-yug, the last phase of life on this planet when everything is degenerating and there is no morality. In such a time one has to do whatever is needed to survive. I know the Indian scriptures. That is what they say," Godse said.

"Well, according to my reading of Indian mythology, the Iron Age is supposed to last 400,000 years and so far we have had only 5,000 or so. This is not the end of the world, Godse. It is only the end of India. The rest of the world is proceeding pretty much as normal except for the vast masses fleeing from India and China and other places to warmer parts of the world."

"What warmer parts?"

"The United States and Australia, Africa and parts of Europe."

"How do you know that?"

"Because I worked it out."

Godse threw his head back and roared with laughter. "You worked it out. Out here in the middle of India?"

"Yes, I worked it out."

"How could you do that?"

"To you I may be a stupid foreigner who works with his hands, but I may also be a bit smarter and more knowledgeable than you imagine."

"But what is the proof of what you are saying?"

"We heard it confirmed on the television news," Roh interjected.

"So what do you say is happening?"

"The earth has changed its axis so that it runs through Tibet and India has become part of the Arctic region. Soon it will be buried under ice and snow. Snow is already five metres deep outside."

Godse looked for a moment as though struck by a lightning bolt.

"This is the punishment of god upon Bharat Mata for dealing with unclean foreigners and degenerate western ways." Godse's head dropped to his chest.

"Your degenerate ways seem home-grown to me, Godse, but you will have your chance this morning to let us hear your strange, self-serving ideas."

Griff left him and went to the breakfast table. After breakfast Griff fed Godse and then gathered the whole group together. He asked Roh to tell them that he believed they should have a trial straight away to hear and note what Godse and his brothers had done and to decide what to do with Godse. Did they agree with that? Yes, they agreed. When she finished he asked Sonba and Wasanta to take the two dead brothers outside and bury them in the snow on the wasti.

When the table was cleared and other basic chores out of the way, including a toilet break for Godse, they gathered again in the sitting room. Griff sat at the dining table with a writing pad and pen and told them what had happened during the night. He said he believed it was important to have a trial at which all of them decided what to do about Godse. There was now no legal authority that they could turn to and they would have to uphold the laws as best they could for their small community. He said it seemed to him that the charges against Godse were breaking into their building without legal reason and holding the people captive; complicity in the murder of Namji; the rape of Rohini Bai, by all three brothers, and the attempted murder of himself by driving him out into the blizzard with nothing but a t-shirt and a pair of shoes. He asked if they all agreed with that. They did, they said. Were there any other things Godse should be charged with, he asked. They said no.

"So those are the charges against you, Jagdish Godse. How do you plead?"

"Not guilty. This not a court, you are not a judge and this is illegal," he shouted.

"This is the only court you are going to have for the time being, Godse, so you had better make the most of it."

"I am not going to take part. This is a joke."

"Yes, and a novel situation for you, Godse, because this is one court and one judge and jury that you cannot bribe to get the decision you would like. So let us get on with it. Namji is dead so that he cannot give evidence about how you, Godse, got entry to the house, but I understand that Wasanta saw what happened, so we had better hear his story. You will have to interpret, Roh, and you will both have to swear to tell the truth. Say after me: I swear to tell the truth." They swore.

Wasanta, after an initial briefing by Roh, said: "I had been asleep but about 4 am I heard a noise and woke and I saw Godse's son walking towards Namji. Namji was sitting in his chair by the door but he was dozing with his head back. Before I had time to do anything the boy had grabbed Namji's gun, poked him with it and told him to unbolt the door. Then Godse and the other two came in. We all sat up but Godse pointed a gun at us and told us to be quiet. Then he went upstairs and brought you down."

Griff wrote down the statement as it was made.

"I think we should hear evidence now from Godse's son." Roh interpreted again.

"Deepak Godse, do you swear to tell the truth?"

"Do I have to give evidence?"

"Yes, I'm afraid so."

"What will happen if I don't?"

"You will be tied up like your father and tried as an accomplice to your father's misdeeds."

"What do you want to know?"

"Please swear to tell the truth and then tell why you took part in opening the front door to let your father and uncles in."

"My father told me to do it."

"Do what?"

"To wait until 4 am on the third night after I was taken into this house and then to sneak up on the night watchman, take his gun and make him open the door."

"Did you want to do that?"

"No, I was frightened, but my father said I had to do it and I was scared also that if I didn't do it, he would break the door down and shoot people. He has told me many times that a son has to do what his father tells him. Good Indian families are like that, he said. Not like western families we see on TV where the children don't take notice of their parents and do what they like, drink alcohol and have dirty habits."

"What dirty habits are they?" Griff asked.

"Going out with girls and having sex."

"Did your father say anything more to you about how to let him and his brothers in?"

"Yes, he said that when I had the gun, if the watchman wouldn't open the door, I was to shoot him."

"Why did your father and uncles come to this house?"

"Our farmhouse was too cold. We couldn't keep warm. We had fires but they were not enough. We couldn't sleep at night. My father knew you had a fire and he thought your house was warm and that you had lots of food. We had lots of food too but we couldn't keep warm."

"But you had another house in the village nearby that you could have gone to. Isn't that so?" Griff asked.

"Yes, but as we were driving past here to that house, my father said we would stop and see what people and food you had."

"So your father didn't come here on Government business like he said?"

"No, he only said that because he thought you wouldn't let us in."

"How did you come here?"

"In a van. It is parked outside on the road."

"Is there anything in the van?"

"Yes, there is a lot of food and kerosene, diesel and petrol."

"Do you know where your father and uncles went after they left you here?"

"Yes, they went to our other house in the village and stayed there."

"Were they able to keep warm there?"

"Yes, it is a better house with lots of warm bed quilts and a fireplace and rooms that can keep the wind out."

"So they could have stayed there indefinitely?"

"Yes, I think so."

"Good. Thank you. You may have to answer more questions later about other matters."

"Well, perhaps we should look at the question of being held captive," Griff said.

"Can Subhash say something about that?"

Rohini interpreted again and Subhash was sworn.

78

"After Godse and his brothers came into the house were you free to come and go, Subhash?"

"No. After they had made you go out into the snow they said that you would not be coming back and that they were now in charge of the house. They were holding their guns in their hands and they said that if we tried to attack them or disobey them they would shoot us dead. Godse fired a bullet into the wall to show us that the guns worked. He said that we should go on doing our daily chores but only one person could go outside at a time and that was Namji. We were always to tell them when we had to do outside work and they would stand guard at the door while things were passed in and out."

"So one of the brothers was always on guard at the door with a gun night and day?"

"Yes."

"And no-one could go out without their permission?"

"Yes, that's right."

"And no-one except the brothers was allowed to have a weapon or to do guard duty at the door."

"That's right."

"If you all agree with Subhash, raise your hand."

All hands were raised.

"Does anyone want to add anything to that or disagree with any part of it?"

"What about the killing of Namji?" Sonba asked.

"Yes, we are going to deal with that next, Sonba. Any other points anyone wants to make? If not, we will move to the charge of killing Namji."

No one spoke and Griff then asked Sonba to be sworn and to say what he knew about Namji's death.

"Namji was very upset at breakfast about you being forced out into the snow, Saheb, and he thought you would probably be dead. But if you weren't, he wanted to take some food and clothing out to you. He got your clothing from Bai and put it in a bag and then he got a bag of food from Suman and went to the door. The brother on guard asked him what he was doing and he said he wanted to take this food and clothing out to you and he showed the contents of the bags to the brother."

"The brother said he was not to go out. Godse had said the Saheb was not to come back in and nothing was to be taken out to him. Namji said it was not right to do this to the Saheb who had done so much to set the house up to enable all of them, including Godse and his brothers and son, to survive this great disaster. He then reached for the doorbolts and the other brother who was at the breakfast table called out to shoot him. Godse then called from upstairs to ask what was happening and the brother at the breakfast table told him that Namji was trying to go out to take clothing and food to the foreigner. Godse said no-one was to go out. Sonba had opened the bolts on the inner door and was opening the bolts on the outer door when the brother at the breakfast table cried out to stop Namji and the other brother did that just as Namji was pushing open the outer door. The one who shot him took the bags of clothing and food and the two brothers pushed Namji's body out the door on to the veranda and then closed the door." Sonba broke down sobbing.

"We are so glad you have come back, Saheb. We would all have died if you had not come back."

"No, Sonba, you would have survived. You have seen how to set the place up and keep it running and you have all worked well together. Bai would have looked after you as well as I could."

Griff asked if anyone wished to add anything to what Sonba had said. They shook their heads.

"Does anyone want to contradict anything Sonba said?"

"Does that include me?" Godse asked.

"Not yet. You will have the chance to answer in detail to all the points you wish to dispute when the other people have spoken. But, I thought you had said you were not taking part?"

"Ah yes, I have changed my mind. I have an answer to all these accusations."

"Good. We look forward to hearing them in due course."

"Now we must deal with a very serious and also very delicate matter, the rape of Bai by Godse and his brothers. It is up to Bai to say as much or as little about this as she wishes." He asked her to swear to tell the truth about this matter and then make her statement.

"Straight after they had forced you out into the snow, Godse took me at gunpoint up to my bedroom. I said I wouldn't sleep upstairs but would stay down here with the others. Godse got angry and hit me on the head with his gun. One of the brother's twisted my arm and made me go up the stairs to the bedroom. Godse said that I was to play the part of Draupadi, the wife of the Pandawa brothers. My husband, Saheb, had lost me in a gamble, the gamble for survival he said, and he and his brothers had won the gamble. He said I would be wife and sexual partner to him and his brothers. He said they had the guns and the power to exercise their will and that I would be wise to accept that. Because of that and because Saheb had told me, just before he was pushed out into the snow, that he would survive and come back and that I should do what they demanded to enable me to survive and to help you others, I did not physically fight them. I did not want to make them angry in case they used their guns on us.

"I told them all in turn that I did not want to have sex with them and that if they insisted it would be rape. I said that if they wore condoms I would not fight them but if they refused to do that they would have to rape me by force and I would do whatever I could to hurt them. They all used condoms. Godse insisted on sex the first morning, one of his brothers, that night and the third brother the next night. The third brother wanted to argue about using a condom. I told him I would hurt him if he didn't. That is all," she said.

"Are there any questions or uncertainties about Bai's evidence?" Griff asked.

Godse's son then said he didn't believe she was raped. She agreed to have sex. She wasn't fighting or screaming and she also had sex with him.

"Is that so, Roh?" Griff asked.

"Yes," she said wearily. "I didn't mention that because he is just a boy and his father brought him and insisted at gunpoint that I let him have sex with me. I could see that he was frightened and being bullied by his father and I didn't want to aggravate the situation. I helped him get it over with as quickly as possible. I made him wear a condom and

I put it on for him and it was apparent then that he was able to do what his father ordered."

Griff turned his attention back to Godse's son.

"Do you still wish to maintain that she wasn't raped but consented willingly to have sex?"

The boy shrugged his shoulders. It took all Griff's self-control not to get up and slap the sullen boy across the face. Instead he stared at the boy with a burning intensity. The boy flushed and turned away.

"Alright, let us look at the next matter, that Godse and his brothers tried to kill me, by forcing me out into the snow with nothing but a t-shirt and a pair of shoes." He asked Roh to give her story.

"Godse and his brothers woke us up in bed, with guns. They made us get up. Saheb was wearing only a t-shirt. Godse said that Saheb was going to take a walk in the snow. I shouted at him and said that it would be a sentence of death to put him out wearing only a t-shirt and that he should be allowed to dress. Godse said that Saheb was a foreigner and had no rights in India and he was going to have to go back to his own country. If he were cold that would make him run faster and get there more quickly. He then made us walk down to the front door where the other brother was standing guard with a gun and pushed him out through the door. Saheb was able to grab a pair of shoes as he went out. They then closed the door."

"Does everyone else agree with that, so far as they saw it after the group came downstairs from the bedroom?" Griff asked. "If so, raise your hands." All raised their hands.

"Okay, let's break now for some lunch and also to provide time for Godse to gather his wits about anything he wishes to say on his own behalf and that of his brothers and his son."

They ate lunch mostly in silence. Subhash gave Godse his food after he had eaten his own lunch. They rested for an hour and then resumed the hearing.

"You know the four things we have charged you with, Godse. The first is that you broke into our house using force while carrying weapons and held all those within against their will without any authority on your part. What do you say to that?"

"I am a senior official of the State Government. I do not need any authority apart from that to go into any place I wish."

"I don't believe that is so. I think you will find the law will say that you need written authority such as a warrant to enter a property uninvited."

"I gave you a reason. I said that I needed to inspect what you had in your house and the people there and to see what you were doing."

"Yes, but that was not the true reason was it? Your son has already told us that he did not believe you had any Government instructions or business and that you wished to occupy our house because it was warmer than your farmhouse and because you believed we had ample supplies."

"He is just a boy. He knows very little."

"It seems he was old enough to do your bidding to disarm our guard and take control of the house and to let you in although he did not wish to do that?"

"A son should do what his father tells him."

"So it was just a normal Government inspection?"

"Yes."

"And what were you going to do after you had made your inspection?"

"It might have been necessary, if the place was adequately supplied, to make it a safe haven for other people who were not so well served."

"A safe haven, eh. So people would have been free to come and go as they pleased?"

"Yes."

"But you put an armed guard on the door and turned the place into a prison."

"Yes, that was because you had guns."

"We had one gun which you took from us. We had no other guns."

"You fired the gun at us."

"Yes, I fired the gun near you, not at you, because you had threatened us with guns. If I had wished to kill you I could have. I fired the gun so that you would know we had a gun and because you had given us no good reason to believe that you were here on Government business and that you were lying about your true intent."

"I am a Government official. I have authority."

"Did the people who were in the house after you occupied it, threaten you in any way?"

"They might have, if they had had the opportunity."

"Alright, let us pass on to the next charge, that you were responsible, along with your brothers, for killing Namji. What do you say about that?"

"He disobeyed an order that no-one was to leave the house without my permission."

"What authority did you have to give an order that no-one should leave the house?"

"As the only Government official here I was in charge of the house."

"That is disputable, but what harm would have been caused by allowing Namji to go outside?"

"He wanted to take food and clothing out to you. It was a waste of time. You would have gone away or you would have been dead."

"But I hadn't gone away and I wasn't dead."

"No, but I didn't know that."

"You told me a little while ago that you were only playing a joke and that you knew I would survive and be back, didn't you?"

"You were a foreigner. We didn't need or want you here and we couldn't waste food on you."

"There are months' worth of food supplies here, aren't there? And plenty of clothing?"

Godse shrugged but did not answer.

"So that was enough reason to kill Namji, was it?"

No answer.

"So let us pass on to the next charge then, that you and your brothers raped Rohini Bai. What do you say about that?"

"She did not object. She is a degenerate person who lives with you without being married and does not believe in god. She sleeps with a foreigner. She would have sex with anyone."

84

"She said quite clearly when she made her statement about the matter that she did not want to have sex with you and that if you forced her to, it would be rape, didn't she?"

"She may have said that but she did not fight. No real Indian woman would allow a man other than her husband to have sex with her. She would rather kill herself."

"I am well aware of quite a number of Indian wives who have been ravished by men other than their husbands. They haven't killed themselves. The law courts are full of them. Bai mentioned that you said she was like Draupadi, the wife of the Pandawa brothers in the Mahabharat. That you had won her from me in the gamble of life. Do you still maintain that?"

"What does it matter? You have now won her back."

"Yes, that is so. Tell us, you were married weren't you?"

"Yes."

"Did you let your brothers sleep with your wife?"

"That is a different matter."

"Yes, it seems so. Where is your wife?"

"She is dead."

"What happened to her?"

"She died in an accident."

"What sort of accident?"

"A fire."

"What sort of fire?"

"When she was cooking in the kitchen, the kerosene stove exploded."

"Ah yes, the stove explosion. It's very strange that so many of your Indian women have died in stove explosions."

"I don't know what you mean."

"What I mean is that thousands of wives a year die in India from exploding stoves fires. It seems hard to believe that there could be so many faulty stoves."

"What does it matter to you?"

"I can't imagine a worse death than being burnt to death by the person who is supposed to love you and protect you. Why not just divorce your wife?"

"We are not supposed to have divorce. That is an evil western habit. That is the will of god."

"So a painful death by fire is preferred by god to divorce, is it?"

"It must be. Widows are supposed to die on their husbands' funeral pyres."

"Tell me, did Draupadi resist and kill herself when her husband gambled her away to another man?"

"She did what a good wife should do, she obeyed her husband."

"There is not much logic or humanity in your arguments, Godse."

"I say what I know. I am a religious man who has studied the sacred texts of our people."

"And do your religious texts say that it is alright to go about raping women?"

"Not decent Indian women, but she is no longer a decent Indian woman. She has lived with a foreigner outside marriage and she has lived outside India and picked up degenerate western ways of life. Look at her, she doesn't dress like an Indian wife and she has haughty manners as though she is as important as a man. Anyway, what does it matter now? This is time of Kali-yug. Everything is corrupted. The Agni-Purana says that around this time there will be increasing ignorance, that men will marry daughters of castes that are not theirs and that is a great sin. We know that this must be the time that the Agni-Purana speaks of, because it says it is the time when foreign barbarians will conquer India and rule here."

"I thought colonialism was long gone. Anything else?"

"Yes, we know that this must be the time of the end of the world because our sacred texts say that Vishnu will come on his white horse, Kalkin, to wipe everything out so that the world can begin again in a pure way. This white snow is the symbol of Vishnu's white horse and his sword that will wipe everything out."

"Tell me another thing. You said earlier on, that you had made millions of dollars that you keep in your house and that we could have them if we turned you free, didn't you?"

"What does that matter?"

"How could a person who is a Government official accumulate such vast sums of money without indulging in countless corrupt practices?"

"In this time of Kali-Yug when the world is coming to an end and everything is corrupted, that is the only way one can operate."

"I see. Well, let us pass on to your explanation of why you forced me out into the blizzard with a t-shirt and a pair of shoes."

"This is the end of the world anyway. We are all going to die soon. I don't believe what you say about other countries being alright. This is the end of the world. You can do whatever you want to me but you will all be dead soon too."

"Not while I have any say in it. So is there anything you want to say about what you and your brothers did?"

"No, nothing, except that I am an important Government official and you have no right to do anything to me."

"We'll see about that. Alright, we have all heard what Godse has had to say. My view now is that we need to think about what we will do with Godse. He has shown himself to be treacherous and it will be difficult for us all to keep him here as a prisoner. He has a truck and supplies outside and an adequate house not far away in which he can live. I believe that if you find him guilty of having done any one of the things that have been alleged against him, he should be exiled from this house. His son may stay if he wishes, but only if he promises to behave himself and not to act against our interests or to collude in some way to enable his father to take over the house again. We will need to vote on this matter. Anyone who wishes to say anything about this should say it now."

Subhash said he believed that if the group voted that Godse had done these things he should be killed, but if the rest of the group wanted him to be exiled he would agree to that.

"Let us vote on it straight away Saheb. We know what Godse did. He is a bad man and a killer."

"Anyone else wish to speak?" Griff asked.

There were murmurings of no.

87

"Alright, if you believe Godse is guilty of any of the charges made against him raise your hand." All hands shot up, except Godse's and his son's.

"If you believe that Godse should be expelled, raise your hand." Again the hands were raised.

"Now there is the matter of Godse's son; whether we should let him stay or make him go with his father. Perhaps we should ask him first. Do you want to stay or go with your father?"

"I will go with my father."

"Are you sure?"

"Yes, I am sure."

"If you go I don't think we will allow you to come back in, unless we know for certain that your father is dead. You have betrayed us once, and it seems to me that you are very strongly under your father's sway, so have a little think about that. Are you still sure you wish to leave?"

"Yes, I will have to go with him."

"Fine, you had better gather what things you own. Suman will give you enough food for twelve hours and you will go in an hour. I will escort you out to your van. If you give Sonba the keys now, he will get the van going for you."

Griff took the keys from Godse's pocket and gave them to Sonba who put on his outside gear and went out. Suman prepared the food. Griff put on his outside gear, got a torch and took the shotgun from Subhash. He took the bullets out of Godse's pistol and held on to it. Godse wouldn't get it until he was in the van. Griff would keep the bullets for the brother's pistols which he'd hidden in Roh's bedroom. He was quite sure that Godse would have plenty more bullets in his house.

"Now, Godse, you and your son had better listen carefully to this. If you come back here to cause trouble I will kill you outright. If you come back because you are in desperate need and we can see some assurance of that we will try to help you. Your stupid, selfish behaviour so far has resulted in three deaths for which you have shown no contrition, so far as I can see, and you have also endangered your son. Cause more trouble and I will hunt you down. Now let's get going. I will give you your gun without the bullets when you are in the van. Perhaps with all your millions of dollars you will be able to buy some more bullets."

Subhash unbolted the doors and Griff cut Godse free. They gave him his coat, gloves and hat and the bag of food. He went out followed by his son. They were clad warmly enough to get them to the van which was only fifty metres away. Griff followed with the torch and the shotgun on them. Sonba had the van going and the cabin warmed. Godse and the boy got in. Griff handed over the pistol and waved them on. They drove off slowly. Godse knew the road well enough and his village house was only half a kilometre away. Griff and the others went back to the house and re-bolted the doors.

Everyone was standing around looking pleased. It was late afternoon and Griff thought there was no better time to open their Danish beer to celebrate getting rid of Godse and getting life back to normal. They could now get on with their lives and survival program. Griff had stashed the beer in the hay on the bedroom terrace where it was safe from sight and the itch of temptation. It was also nicely chilled. Griff carried the box downstairs. They poured a glass for each and toasted "to survival". Everyone wanted to know what Griff had done when Godse had pushed him out into the blizzard. He told them. They laughed and clapped hands. He said then that he thought they should have a holiday soon. Perhaps tomorrow they should have a house cleaning and clothes washing session and the next day a good bath and change of clothing. The day after that a holiday with games. He'd noticed after coming back in from the fresh air of the wasti wilderness that the house was getting a bit fuggy. Probably a combination of sweaty bodies, dirty clothes and limited house cleaning during the Godse occupation.

The day after that they would get the motorbike generator working. But Roh said she thought it would be better to get the generator rigged up first and then they would have a really good reason for celebrating. They agreed that was better. In fact Subhash thought it would be best to get the generator going the next day. Good light would help them with the cleaning and washing.

Chapter 5: Midwinter frolics

Sonba was an early riser and started work on the generator as soon as Roh and Griff came downstairs. They set the bike up in the first floor bathroom. Above the bathroom was a low-ceiling storage space, entered by ladder from the stair landing outside Roh's bedroom which was ideal for the battery bank. They had scavenged plenty of batteries and put them aside earlier and by midday had them all in place and wired up and Sonba was ready to start the bike. After lunch Sonba kicked the motorbike engine over. It had electronic ignition and went first kick. The noise and resonance coming from the bathroom were horrendous. Fortunately, no one would have to be in the bathroom when the bike was running and it would have to run for only thirty minutes or so each morning and night. It was as though the strong light after so many weeks of constant gloom had taken them back to a world they had forgotten. The glare of sixty-watt globes showed them what a wild-looking bunch they were in their homemade and mismatched clothing, in the organised rat tunnel chaos of the sitting room, and they burst into gusts of laughter that triggered more of the same. They tottered around pointing at each other and yelling like school kids.

They decided they would continue to use lanterns for the other rooms so that the power could be conserved for a rooftop light and the front veranda and patio lights. That afternoon Griff made the lantern cabinet for the roof light and they rigged it up. The shape of the lantern allowed the house to be lit up with a beam that shone down as well as out. If there were any rescue planes or choppers around they would be able to see the light from kilometres away. The veranda and patio lights would enhance that too. Next day they washed clothes and cleaned the house. The following day was their holiday. They got the essential chores out of the way early and then began the games. They had games of skill which required lobbing a paper ball into a rubbish bin at seven metres, balancing races with books on their head, and egg and spoon races using boiled eggs which eventually became part of their lunch. They raced up and down the clearway from the front door to the kitchen and finished with endurance races up the stairs to the loft. When everyone was knocked out they played card games, betting thousands of rupees from the money they had found in the stranded vehicles. Just for the day. All money went back into the kitty to be divided up properly at a later date. It was a great day and the men and Roh finished it off with another couple of glasses of beer before dinner. The other women chose to have tea.

Life went back to the normal routine the next morning. By lunchtime things were in chaos. Ramesh who had gone to feed and water and check the poultry didn't come back. Subhash went out to check on him, carrying one of Godse's brother's pistols. Minutes later he came rushing back to the house shouting for Saheb and Bai.

"Saheb, Bai, come quick. Ramesh has been killed. Bring your gun, there is a man out here somewhere."

It took Griff a few minutes to get his snow gear on and he ran out with the shotgun leaving the other pistol with Wasanta. Griff told him to keep the door bolted until Subhash or he called on him to open it. Subhash said he had walked across the wasti calling to Ramesh and shining his torch around. He could see a shape on the ground near the fowl room. He kept swinging the torch about and was sure that he had just caught a glimpse of movement going out of sight behind the dairy shed. He shouted but the figure took no notice. He thought it was a person dressed in white. He then moved to the shape on the ground near the fowl room. It was Ramesh. He was dead and his throat was cut. He must have been dead for ten minutes or so because the bleeding had stopped and the blood was frozen. Subhash showed Griff where he saw the figure in white. There were still footprints of snowshoes visible in the snow. The two of them carried Ramesh back to the veranda. Griff told Roh what had happened and that he needed to go quickly and alone to follow the snowshoe tracks. They would bury Ramesh after he returned. He put fresh batteries in his torch and set off to track the snowshoes. He had a pretty fair idea where they would lead and that was to Godse's village house. He kept the torch off and switched it on only quickly now and then to check the trail, shielding it with his hat in the hope that the murderer would not see him following. As expected, when he got to the sealed road, the tracks turned towards Godse's place. It wasn't definitive yet, but it was looking more likely. The good thing about having to wear snowshoes was that it made an ambush fairly unlikely. It was hard to rush someone while wearing snowshoes and they also made quite a bit of noise. As he got level with Godse's gate he could see the tracks turning in. There was a dim lantern light in the house, but no noise. He turned and headed back to the farm. He would come back and watch from hiding. He calculated that the killer would return to the farm tomorrow to try to get another one of the group. Godse and his hitman would be working on a plan to reduce the group's strength by knocking off their men one at a time while they did their essential outside chores. They could then move in and take over the house and supplies.

That afternoon, they buried Ramesh in deep snow in the wasti and Griff decided he should start a diary straight away to record what they had done from the beginning of the disaster, because it looked as though things were becoming complicated and nasty. It didn't take long to bring it up to date. He had the notes he had made of the kangaroo court they had held for Godse. He added the information about his caution to Godse at the time they expelled him and his son, the murder of Ramesh and following the tracks of the likely killer to Godse's house.

Next morning, after breakfast, Griff dressed in his outside gear with a white pillow case wrapped around his hat and head and a bed sheet over his clothing. They normally all rose about 6 am, washed and then the men did some pre-breakfast chores like milking and feeding the buffalo and her calf, and the oxen - checking and feeding them and the sheep, while Suman, Seema and her daughter Laxmi and Jyoti prepared breakfast. They did the cooking on a shegdi and a kero primus stove in the kitchen and then kept it warm on the stove in the sitting room. They had breakfast about 7.30 and began outside chores about 9 am. Griff was sure that Godse was involved in the killing of Ramesh. He knew the group's routine. Griff told everyone at breakfast what he was going to do and that they were not to go outside until he returned. At 8.30 he took a pistol and a hefty teak club and some thin cotton rope for binding and went out to lie in wait. He didn't want to kill the assailant. He wanted to get hold of him and find out where he was from, who was directing him and why. The wind was blowing strongly from the south-east and Griff needed the element of surprise. He also needed to be in a spot where he wouldn't miss the bloke coming into the wasti. Griff guessed the fellow would have to come up the road. Travelling cross-country would be too difficult. That meant he would then turn into the farm at the main wasti gate. Griff waited on the north-west side of the road opposite the farm gate and hoped the bastard would come soon as it was bitterly cold and he couldn't be moving about. He had to crouch still beside a clump of acacia scrub and every minute in that cold meant it would be harder to spring into action. The intruder on the other hand would be limbered by snow-shoeing from Godse's house. Griff needed to be on him before he knew it and to disable him quickly. Luckily, he didn't have long to wait. Ten minutes after he took up position a shape loomed from the direction of the village and mushed past him towards the gate. He was travelling well and looked young and fit. He was wearing proper white camouflage snow gear, which didn't please Griff at all because it probably meant the bloke was a northern army border guard used to living and fighting in the snow. His movement kicked up a flurry of snow that washed over Griff. The wind was still strong, so, with the noise his own shoes were making and the wind, Griff doubted the bloke would hear him coming, particularly as his head and ears were really well covered. Maharashtrians were known for hating to have a cold head. They could go out into bitter cold in light clothing so long as they had a scarf wrapped around their head and ears and under the jaw. It was clear from the way he was moving that he wasn't expecting any opposition. Griff went after him fast and, just after getting through the gate, swung the club at the side of his head. Unfortunately, the front of his right snowshoe came down on the tail of the other fellow's snowshoe and caused him to pitch forward slightly so that the blow which would have knocked him out struck him only a glancing blow. Stunned and surprised, he turned to look at

Griff and at the same time fell because Griff's snowshoe was pinning his and put him off balance. He was on his back but his gloved right hand held a dangerous-looking army knife with a serrated blade. Griff clubbed the hand hard, knocking the knife into the snow. He rolled away, but getting to one's feet in snowshoes is not the easiest or fastest business and Griff sprang towards him and gave him a solid whack across the back of the head that slowed him down but didn't drop him. He had a thick woollen balaclava under his white snow hat. Griff gave him another whack, a harder one this time and that dropped him flat. He got a piece of rope out and bound the man's wrists behind his back with a loop around his throat. He was starting to come around and Griff got him to his knees and then moved back a couple of paces and told him to get up. Griff showed him the pistol and told him to move across to the house. When he got to the front veranda, Griff called to Roh to open the front door and stand clear as he was bringing the assailant in. They got him in and tied him to a chair. Griff untied his left hand so that he could have a warm cup of soup and Roh had a look at his head to see if there was any broken skin and bleeding. There wasn't but a hard-boiled egg was already rising from the second blow he had taken. Roh told him that she and Griff needed to question him. He was a young good-looking bloke with proper army mountain gear. Roh said she thought he might be a relative of Godse who served with the Indian Army on the mountain posts along the India-Pakistani border.

After Roh and Griff had had a warm drink, they sat down to question him. Roh asked him who he was. He said his name was Shakunt, he was Godse's nephew and he had served with the Himalayan division in the Pakistani border area. He had been on leave when the crisis broke. He was staying at that time with his mother in his parents' house in a village a few kilometres away. They ran out of fuel and food and his mother died of the cold. He then decided to go in search of his father who worked with his older brother, Godse. When he arrived at Godse's house in the village he found his uncle and cousin there. They told him that Rohini Sane's foreign lover had killed his father and other uncle when they went to Sane's house to see if they could offer any help. Godse had told him that it was his duty to

94

punish Sane and the foreigner for that and also that they should take over the Sane farmhouse which was full of looted food stocks and fuel. Godse had told him the house routine and how many men and women there were in the place.

Rohini told him that what his uncle had said was a lie and gave him the real story of what had happened. Subhash confirmed that Rohini's story was the truth. Shakunt said he was shocked to hear what he had been told. He was deeply hurt by the realisation that he had been fooled by Godse and that he had been induced to attack Roh's house and to kill Ramesh. He seemed a decent young fellow and genuinely remorseful about the attack on Ramesh. He said he had always had suspicions about the dishonesty of Godse but he was so overwhelmed by the death of his father and uncle that he had easily fallen prey to Godse's manipulation. He didn't know what to do. He couldn't make it back to his army unit in this weather and he didn't want to go back to Godse's house. Griff conferred quietly with Roh and then said that if Shakunt promised to abide by the house rules and help with the work, he could stay with them. Griff said he believed they would be able to hold out until rescue came, probably when the daylight began to return in a month or two.

Shakunt wanted to know how they knew that daylight would return. Griff and Roh explained to him the shift in the polar axis and how that meant that they would get a long period of daylight when the summer came to the new Arctic region. That surprised him. He hadn't realised what had caused the onset of the polar conditions but thought it had to be some great natural disaster or a nuclear war.

He told them that the only weapon he had was the knife Griff had taken from him. He said his hand that had held the knife when Griff knocked it free, was painful. Rohini had a look at it. It looked like a cracked bone in his third finger, she said, and strapped it with a small splint and plaster.

Shakunt proved to be a useful addition to the household. He was a strong and willing worker. Griff had told Subhash to stick close to him and to report back. The reports were always good. He had shown no squeamishness in helping with the dirty work of cleaning out the sheep shit and putting down fresh straw in the bullock enclosure and the buffalo room and in carrying out the buckets of toilet waste and burying them deep in the snow.

About that time they discovered a bonus in their food situation. Suman told Roh that the sprouts were ruined because 'dog shit plants' were growing amongst them. Roh called Griff and they had a look and burst out laughing with delight. They found that button mushrooms were coming up among the bean sprouts. The locals didn't eat mushrooms because of an old wives' tale that they grew out of dog turds. That belief probably dated back to the time of the British raj, when dogs were fed on meat instead of vegetable scraps and chapattis, and a dried-out dog turd looked rather similar to a newly-sprouted mushroom. Roh and Griff had tried to convince Suman in the past that mushrooms were tasty, nutritious food. From time to time they found mushrooms growing in their garden. She didn't argue, but you knew she hadn't changed her opinion. The mushrooms had almost certainly grown from spores in the sheep manure that Griff had used as an underlayer in the sprout trays. The warmth in the sitting room kitchen area and the added light from the motorbike generator must have triggered them. Roh explained to the team over lunch that day that the mushrooms were good food and a welcome addition to their limited diet. They agreed to give them a try and Roh told Suman the various ways they could be used. They ate a lot of beef and lamb stews and soups so the mushrooms went well in them. Roh had also found that two of the few onions they had left were sprouting and got Griff to fill some old buckets with compost and soil and planted them. If she could get them to seed they would be able to get a regular production line going in tear-jerkers.

The kitchen was now looking like a cross between a greenhouse vegetable garden and a junk yard, with trays of sprouts and mushrooms, buckets of onions, boxes of tools, offcuts of materials needed for various jobs, rolled-up bedding, clothing and plastic containers of fuel, as well as a kero stove and two shegdis for daily cooking. Now that they had electricity, the fridge was back in use, not as a cupboard, but to serve the purpose for which it was made. They could have kept perishable food outside the kitchen door but that had two disadvantages: the stuff would be frozen solid and in need of defrosting and since the door had to be kept locked most of the time, it was a nuisance to be ducking in and out through the bolted doors. The kitchen was too warm to leave food on the benches.

Griff and Roh hated clutter. As the store of grain sacks lowered in the guest bedroom, they decided Subhash and Shakunt could move their sleeping quarters and gear into the guest room and sleep on top of the sacks. They spent a week reorganising and tidying. They replenished wood and hay stocks on the patios and cleaned out the slow combustion wood stove in the sitting room properly. Up until then Griff had only done partial cleaning, by scraping out ash in the mornings before loading in more wood. This time he got a half drum beside the fire, lifted out the burning logs and charcoal with tongs and a small shovel and cleaned out all the ash down to the sand base. He was then able to put the burning logs and embers back into the fire and load it with fresh logs. The room temperature dropped alarmingly during the operation which lasted about half an hour and reminded them of how dependent they were on keeping the fire burning day and night. Once the cleaning was completed and the fire reset in the stove, the temperature rose again fairly quickly. Griff dumped the ash in the heap where the animal droppings and the straw from the floors of the animal stalls were put. The composting process generated enough heat to melt the snow on top of it while it produced the soil they needed to replace that in the sprout trays.

Three weeks had passed since they had ousted Godse and his son, and two weeks since they had taken in Shakunt. Griff decided to risk his judgement that Shakunt was genuine and a part of their team now and asked him if he thought that Godse would make another move against them. Shakunt said he had been wondering about that himself. He said also that he had been thinking about various episodes over the years he had known Godse and now realised that he was a sly and calculating person with a vengeful attitude towards anyone who crossed him. As he had risen in the government and become richer and more powerful, he had become even more vindictive.

"Now that I have seen that you are good people and how you work together and were kind enough to take me in and overlook the killing of Ramesh, I am angry with Godse. I will never trust him again and I want to kill him. He is a snake and the best thing to do with a poisonous snake is to kill it. I am willing to go back to his place and kill him, Saheb," he said.

"Well, I am not sure that I want to kill him straight off. I did tell him when we put him out of the house that I would hunt him down and kill him if he tried to harm us, but I have discovered I am reluctant to kill except in a mortal confrontation. But I would like to know if there is anyone else in his house with him apart from his son, and if there are any signs of funny business afoot," Griff said. "Perhaps you and I could go across to the house together to have a look."

Late that night, Griff and Shakunt snowshoed across to Godse's house and had a good look all around it. There seemed to be no guard and no lights. Shakunt had a key to the kitchen door and opened it. They removed snowshoes and Griff took off his tyre-boots and they went in. The rubber tube-boots were quiet on the slate slabs of the kitchen floor but as soon as they entered the inner rooms, the rubber squeaked alarmingly on the marble floor. Griff tapped Shakunt on the shoulder and whispered that it was impossible for him to go on unless he stripped to bare feet or wrapped something around the rubber footwear. If he stripped to bare feet they would have real trouble trying to escape quickly and that was dangerous since Godse had the unpleasant combination of a gun and few scruples. Shakunt said he knew the house well and would press on to check out the rooms while Griff waited at the kitchen door. Since Griff didn't know the house and was in danger of blundering into things, he agreed to wait. He told Shakunt not to harm anyone unless attacked and unable to escape.

Griff went outside to put on his tyre-boots and snowshoes. A good ten minutes passed in dead quiet and then suddenly there was shouting and a rapid exchange of angry conversation. Griff stuck his head through the kitchen door in time to see Shakunt racing through the kitchen. There was a bang from a handgun. The bullet whined off the wall above Shakunt's head. Shakunt flung himself through the door. He gave the door key to Griff to lock it while he put on his snowshoes and they then mushed around the corner of the house as fast as they could. Griff knew that Godse wouldn't come out into the snow after them and it was too dark for him to be able to shoot at them from inside the house. Once in the roadway they eased up and mushed back to the farm at a steady pace. The wind and noise from the snowshoes and their clothing was too loud for conversation without shouting so Griff waited till they got back into the house to ask what had happened.

Shakunt had looked through all of the upstairs rooms leaving Godse's room till last, he said. When he opened the door the hinges squeaked and Godse sat up and shouted at him. He shouted back saying Godse was a treacherous snake and that he was going to kill him, then slammed the door behind him and bolted down to the kitchen. It seems Godse leaped out of bed with a gun, raced after him, and fired from the foot of the stairs.

"I heard the bullet whistle over my head, Saheb. It wasn't a nice tune," Shakunt said and then burst into nervous laughter.

"We will have to be careful now, Shakunt, because he may come here and try to cause mischief again."

Two nights later Subhash woke Griff and Roh, hammering on their bedroom door and shouting 'fire'. They dragged on coats and rushed downstairs. The fire was in the haystack and wood stack on the kitchen terrace and it was well alight. Luckily the snow was now so deep that it was more than halfway up the height of the stack and that was where it had been lit. That meant it was burning up, not down to where the wood was. The snow that had accumulated on the plastic tarpaulin was good and bad. The melting snow was falling on to the burning hay and causing it to generate choking black smoke that mixed with the foul chemical smell of the burning heavy tarp. But it was also helping to reduce the flame. Griff could see the only way to fight the fire was from outside and then all they could do was to scoop buckets of snow up and throw that on the flames. At least there was no lack of snow. Griff sent Roh, Seema and Suman up to the roof to throw buckets of snow down from the terrace on to the fire while he, Subhash and Shakunt went outside and threw buckets on the lower parts of the fire, leaving Wasanta to guard the front door. They had hardly scooped up a bucket when above the crackling and roar of the fire they heard gunshots from the plantation trees behind them and bullets smacked into the stone wall near them. Griff gave Shakunt his pistol. Shakunt dropped to the ground and fired a couple of shots in the direction of the shooter. He then jumped to his feet and ran towards the trees. As soon as he reached a tree with enough girth to give him shelter, he switched on his torch and moved it in a wide arc. At the far reach of the beam, he could see a figure retreating fast towards the road and sent a couple of shots after him. He then returned to the fire to help Griff. The work of the women from above was telling and the fire had died down to a couple spots in the stack and they were soon put out. Luckily no timber seemed to have caught, but they had lost at least half of the hay. Roh shouted down to Griff that all the hay that was even slightly singed would have to be thrown away as the animals wouldn't eat it. Shakunt and Griff worked on to pull out and throw into the snow all the damaged hay and even the stuff that smelt of smoke. There was more hay in stacks on the wasti and Kamala farm so Griff wasn't worried about running short, particularly since the number of sheep was reducing.

Back inside they all gathered around the stove and warmed their hands around mugs of tea. Roh praised them all for their good work in getting the fire out, before heading back to bed. In bed, Griff told Roh that he was going to have to settle the problem of Godse. He had been prepared to leave him be even after the killing of Ramesh, but it was clear that Godse wanted to continue to make trouble and that was a threat to all of them. He said he would try to save Godse's son but he was determined to finish Godse off. He spent a while thinking about how he would do it before falling asleep.

Next day, he outlined a plan to Roh and the others. He still had the bombs they had made a month or more back. They would wait several days to let Godse stop worrying about a revenge attack and then go over there. Meanwhile, they would have to put a guard on the roof terrace to keep a look out for a possible return by Godse. Then they would take the bombs over to Godse's place and call on him to come out unarmed, otherwise they would bomb him out. Griff knew that Godse wouldn't come out unarmed and he didn't want to kill him in cold blood if he did, but he hoped to save the son somehow.

There was no sign of Godse for a week and they checked the bombs, blew one up in the wasti to be sure that they were still viable and made other preparations. Griff took the shotgun and gave Wasanta his pistol to guard the house door. Griff, Shakunt and Subhash would make the trip to Godse's with two bullocks and their biggest sled. They took extra clothing for Godse and his son in case it was needed and extra batteries for their torches.

They left late afternoon and were at Godse's in thirty minutes. Griff fired a shotgun cartridge through the upper part of a top window in the second floor and shouted to Godse to come out without his gun and his hands on his head. After a couple of minutes, Godse shouted out an obscenity and fired his pistol at them. Griff replied that if he didn't come out peacefully, they would bomb him out and that he was putting his son's life in danger. Griff lit one small bomb and flung it on to a terrace on the upper floor. It went off with an impressive bang. Minutes passed quietly and then a voice called to them from around a corner of the house. It was Godse's son. He had his hands up and in the torchlight they could see that he carried no weapon. They called him over and Shakunt frisked him thoroughly. Griff told him to go to the sled outside the compound wall, put on warm gear and stay there. Before he left Griff asked him if he thought his father would come out peacefully. The boy said he wouldn't. His father had sent him out after telling him he was going to stay and fight.

Griff shouted out again to Godse, telling him to leave his gun and come out with hands up, otherwise they would bomb him. The only answer was a shotgun blast fired at them through the plate glass window. Griff sent Shakunt to the back door with six bombs and Subhash to one side with another six and stayed in front. He lit one large bomb sheltering the light from Godse's sight and then threw it at the main window on the upper floor. It went off with a tremendous roar. Seconds later, another two thrown by Shakunt and Subhash shook the place. Griff lit another and flung it through the window in the ground floor. More followed from Shakunt and Subhash. Griff called to the others to wait while he shouted out to Godse. There was no answer from Godse but a minute or so later there was a single shot. They waited another half hour calling out to Godse but getting no answer and Griff decided they should go into the house. Shakunt led the way. The inside of the house was littered with blackened rubbish and broken glass. They flicked torches on and off as they moved up the stairs to dazzle and confuse Godse about their position. There was no sign of Godse until Shakunt opened his bedroom door. This room was relatively undamaged which was more than could be said for Godse who was sitting in a chair with his clothing in tatters and half his head missing. A shotgun lay beneath his right hand which hung over the side of the chair. Godse had been ripped in a hundred places by shrapnel from exploding bombs but it was clear he had taken his own life with a shot to the head. On the bed were two suitcases with a note sitting on top of one of them. Griff read it out.

"You have won this battle, foreigner, but perhaps you too will be swept away by Vishnu when he comes. If you survive hiding in your cave and Vishnu spares you and my son, I wish you to give my son one of these cases and to keep one for yourself to share with your partner. Godse."

Griff put the note in his pocket and opened one of the cases. It was filled with US dollars, packed in bundles of $100 notes. He guessed there must be more than $1 million in each case. He handed one to Shakunt and took the other while Subhash collected Godse's guns and they went downstairs. Griff was bothered by what was for him an unusual sensation. A conflict of emotions. He wanted to feel a sense of elation that they had finally solved the Godse threat but that was being overridden by depression about having caused another death in their struggle to survive. This was accentuated by his realisation that even Godse was not bereft of humanity. He needn't have said that Griff and Roh could share the money with his son. Griff didn't care about the money for himself, but he realised that if they survived and all got safely to Australia with the money, it could help the group as a whole to make an easier recovery with a new life there. That was better than leaving it to be buried under a mile of ice where it could do no good at all even to the environment. Griff was quiet and thoughtful on the way back to the farm. They now had the care of Godse's son whom he wouldn't have trusted as far as he could throw him uphill into a strong wind. Griff sensed it wasn't just teenage shyness. The reticence had remained throughout the period Deepak had lived with them in the house even though they had all been helpful and friendly towards him. He was shifty and couldn't look Griff in the eye. He suspected the only reason Deepak had chosen to come with them was because he knew it was his one chance of survival. Out at the sled, Griff gave one of the suitcases to Deepak and told him that his father had asked him to give it to Deepak. Griff said it contained money and that he would store it safely for him if he wished. Deepak just nodded.

Griff noticed as they mushed back to the farm that the weather had moderated. The wind had ceased to howl around their ears and was now merely whistling and the snow had stopped falling.

When they got to the house, Roh was beaming at the front door with the news that she was getting some television reception. They had been trying the TV, morning, noon and night, since the generator began working, but there had always been too much interference. Even now it was patchy. Griff went up to the roof terrace and wiped the snow from the satellite disk. That improved the reception a little. They had the set on the BBC news program.

"The Director of the United Nations Natural Disaster Rescue and Recovery Program said today that refugee camps being set up in the USA, Canada, Australia, New Zealand and Europe would be restricted to 100,000 people per camp," the announcer said.

He went on to say that so far, the US had twenty camps completed, Canada twelve, Europe twenty-five, Australia ten and New Zealand two, and more camps were under construction in each country. The Director said that the decision to restrict camp size was to reduce the possibility of criminal gang activity and to make it easier to maintain law and order and arrange supplies.

The BBC pictures showed shots of camps in Europe, Australia and the US, built with shipping containers, canvas tents and corrugated iron. Shopping centres, hospitals and community centres had been built from huge iron farm sheds. The picture of the camps in Australia's Northern Territory and near the Ord River Scheme, in the north-west, showed people moving around the streets on push bikes. No cars or motor bikes were shown. But there were commercial

103

vehicles; vans, buses and trucks. Each residence had a space for a vegetable garden and a couple of shade trees. Some of the vegetable gardens were well-established and producing crops. They could see tomatoes, peas, beans, lettuce and cabbage.

The Director went on to say that the weather in the new polar regions was expected to begin to abate for longer periods as the Arctic summer approached and that would enable more rescue missions overflying India and China and other places badly affected by storms and flooding.

They left the TV on while they had dinner. It showed the aftermath of terrible storm damage and flooding in northern Europe and Russia. It was of biblical proportions. Boatloads of half-starved people were still floating out. The downside to this was a massive reduction in world food stocks but the upside was that much of the crap of the materialist culture in the developed societies, if not washed away or blown away, was giving way to a focus on providing basics. Everywhere people were growing their own vegetables and keeping fowls. Even in the big cities of the US, Europe and Australia, people were growing vegetables on apartment verandas and roofs. The crucial factor in siting camps in Australia was availability of fresh drinking water and water for growing crops. The Ord River Dam was huge, thirteen times the size of Sydney Harbour, and already the centre of a vast tropical fruit, rice and vegetable growing area. Apart from the camps, many families in provincial towns in Australia and in the US and Europe had taken in refugees. Some were relatives and friends from devastated locations but most were strangers. It was estimated that at least as many people had been taken into private homes as there were in the camps, possibly even double the number. Millions of people were expected to flee from coastal cities around the world as ocean levels were already rising from the melting of the old ice caps and the uptake of water into the new ice caps was a slower process. In addition, there were millions more refugees from India and China in African countries in makeshift locations and wandering desperately. Many of these were doomed to die of thirst, starvation and disease. Throughout the developed world, the spirit of the London blitz in World War II seemed to have come alive again and people were actually happier. The desire to help make things better, as communities did during the Sydney and London Olympics, had happened. The preoccupation with self and self-pity, self-mutilation, suicide, and starving and overeating "diseases" had dropped away remarkably. Nothing like the threat of death to get people interested in staying alive, Griff mused. Obesity was declining rapidly. A drastic shortage of many food stocks was helping with that. Governments were grappling with the problem of how best to conduct food rationing. Now that the social workers had some real problems to hug, they had no need to torture themselves and the community about such things as stranger-danger, toddler tension and adult men and women recalling the sexual experiences of their childhood as a torment that could be assuaged only by large amounts of money. Refugees were no longer throwing themselves off buildings. In the camps they seemed grateful to have survived, to be safe and to have three meals a day. They were helping each other rather than fighting over trivialities such as race, tribe and religion. People in the camps were biking each morning to collection points on the edges of the towns from where they were taken by truck to new farming locations where they helped establish and run huge market gardens, plant new orchards and plantations and build and run poultry and rabbit farms.

It was estimated that between twenty and thirty million people had been able to escape from the disaster areas, but that was a pathetically small figure considering the stupendous loss of life that must have occurred. The populations of India and China combined had been close to 2.5 billion and there had been many more lost from the Middle East. The Arab-Israeli problem no longer appeared to exist; they had more serious problems to contend with from biting temperatures to flooding and storm damage. Few people were still thought to be alive in the hinterland of India, Tibet, Mongolia, China and nearby devastated countries, but fly-over rescue missions continued.

Roh and Griff stayed up watching the TV for hours after the others had crept off to bed. When they at last went to their bed they worried about whether the rescue missions would eventually get to them before giving up the search.

"Do you really think they will find us, Griff?"

"Yes, I'm sure. They will be searching for many months yet. And if they don't come soon, we'll be tunnelling up to the surface of the snow." He gave a grim laugh.

"It's reaching the top of the second floor windows and we are going to have to be careful about ventilation."

Next morning Griff made an inspection of the snow levels and their rescue alert systems. They had been clearing the snow daily from the front patio and the area where they took out the draft bullocks and sleds and had a gentle gradient from the ground level up to the new "ground level" on top of the snow. They had to do that to be able to keep their SOS sign clear and the snow in the chopper landing pad hard-packed. Griff tested one of the kero fires they had prepared two months previously. It didn't go well at all. He realised that quite a lot of the petrol must have evaporated so he topped up each of the tins again and then tested one. It went very well. He worked with Subhash, Shakunt and Sonba to clear the snow away from the ventilation spaces at the tops of the ground floor windows and to bring in more hay and cut wood for the stove. Griff had tried to get Deepak involved in the outside work but found he was worse than useless as he constantly got in the way and showed little real interest in manual work. Griff told him to help Suman with the household chores and he seemed amenable to that.

After lunch, four of them harnessed the big sled and headed for the village to get the skyrockets and to try to top up their petrol supplies. They scouted on the other side of the village where they hadn't been before and found no signs of life. Everything was buried deep beneath the snow with only the top of some of the taller buildings showing through the snow. They thought they knew where the shop with the firecrackers was but they couldn't find it in the deep snow. Nearly all these shops were basically concrete boxes so the roofs hadn't collapsed and filled them with snow as many of the small private houses had. It was hopeless trying to find cars deep under the snow that might have petrol, but Shakunt pointed out that there were two cars in the garage at Godse's house as well as the large van and he thought they had fuel in them. They had to clear the snow away to get into the garage but once in, they found to their surprise that there was a hundred-litre drum of petrol and two Tata four-wheel drives, one petrol and one diesel. They had full tanks. The truck was parked in the driveway and buried under the snow. They dug out the snow around the rear doors and found they were bolted. Cutting them open, they found a great haul of foodstuff and drums of diesel for its diesel engine. Griff thought it best to leave the fuel in the vehicles and take it from the hundred-litre drum. They siphoned fuel out into their plastic containers. Griff wanted the SUVs intact and ready to go just in case they might need them at some time.

After lunch Griff and Roh went up to their room for their usual brief rest and pulled quilts over themselves.

"I've been thinking about what to do if the rescue flights don't find us soon. This is a fairly isolated village and the rescuers might easily think that no one could possibly survive here. In the dark our lights stand out clearly for a great distance, probably twenty kilometres in clear weather. They won't be so noticeable when the daylight starts to come. It might be best if we make plans to leave for Pune soon," Griff said.

"Tell me more."

"Our supplies can last until well after the daylight comes. The problem then is that with the light and warmth the snow will begin to melt. It would be impossible to go anywhere while the melt is in progress. There will be flooding and mud and the roads will disappear, creeks will run like rivers and rivers will run with such force that they will take the bridges with them. If we are going to make it to Pune we will need to leave in two weeks."

"Do you think there will still be people in Pune?"

"There's sure to be some authorities still operating there. There was an air force base there, remember. They may even be running rescue surveillance flights from there. But if there is no-one there we will press on to Mumbai."

"God, that is a long way to walk."

"Yeah, but it's mainly downhill."

Roh chuckled at that. "Seriously, Griff."

"Well, Shivaji and his soldiers used to do it, and we can too. Of course, they didn't have to do it in the snow. We would need to get to the main highway before the creeks came up. With only a light melt, we would never get through the creeks. But the highway bridges are well above the rivers. We would need to leave before the melt began, particularly if we have to press on to Mumbai."

"When do you think the melt might happen?"

"That's a bit hard to say. It's the end of March now and I'd guess that the melt will start around mid to late May, so we would need to leave here by mid April."

"That means we've only got another two weeks here."

"Yes, and we'll need all that time to make the preparations to leave," Griff said.

"Have you thought about how many days it would take to get to Pune?"

"At twenty kilometres a day, six days walking, but I'd allow eight or nine."

"That means, say, ten days food for us and the bullocks, and camping gear."

"Right, my love. It will be hard, but I've got an idea to make it considerably more comfortable and hopefully quicker."

"Oh yes, what's that?" Roh asked, somewhat ironically.

"We'll take the two four-wheel-drives in Godse's garage. The two bullocks and the buffalo with two laden sleds can travel in front, flattening and packing down the snow. The two SUVs can then follow and each of them can pull a sled. We can take it in turns to be out on the lead sleds while the rest of the group luxuriates in the warmth of the SUVs. It will be a slow boat to China, you could say, but it will be bearable."

"Griff, you are a clever boy. That means we could sleep in the SUVs too, doesn't it?"

"It does. But meanwhile, I will make another trip to the shop where we found the firecrackers.

"What do you want now?"

"More skyrockets, if possible. From now on we should always have someone on watch on the roof terrace, and if we see or hear a plane or chopper, we can fire skyrockets to help make sure they see us."

"Another good idea, Griff. Clever boy."

"Yes, I'm not just an ugly face. We will have to make and fit snow chains on the SUVs. The sleds will help to pack and flatten the snow but the SUVs will be carrying five passengers each and they will need chains to help them make way on the snow. "

"Have we got enough chain?"

"Yeah, there are miles of it in the hardware shop in the village, in addition to what we have in our godown."

"Do you know how to make them?"

"I've never actually made any, but I used them to go cross-country skiing when I lived and studied in Canberra for a couple of years. They're not complicated."

"Is there anything you can't do, Griff?"

"There are things, now that you mention it, but I am not going to tell you what they are."

"Why is that, Superman?"

"In this new era in which men are being feminised, a man has to maintain a sense of mystery."

"Okay, if that is the case you had better lie back tonight and take it like a woman. I think I've got over the Godse outrages."

"That's good to hear, but do you really love me, or do you only want my body?"

"You'll find out tonight. Now, have a rest. You'll need your strength."

That afternoon Griff, Shakunt and Sonba took a sled to the village, dug down to the hardware store and pulled out enough chain to moor the Queen Mary in a storm, along with other bits and pieces that Griff thought might be useful, including padlocks to secure the snow chains and more heavy plastic tarpaulins. He was able also to get two large stainless steel bins with clip-lock tops and three similar plastic bins with screw tops. They would need containers like that to carry cooked food for the trip to Pune. The only thing they would cook on the trip would be tea and coffee, but they would also need to warm soup and stew. They would do that on two kerosene-fired stoves.

It took them a while to locate the shop that had firecrackers. With the snow so deep, most of the single-storey houses and shops were no longer visible and in the gloom it was hard to estimate distance exactly. Eventually they located the place and got down to the cellar. It was as they had left it and the bodies were frozen solid in the positions in which they had died. Griff took a large carton of skyrockets and they left.

As they mushed back to the farmhouse Griff was aware that the weather was definitely milder and he thought warmer. Probably because the wind was not blowing so strongly, there was less of a wind chill factor and he was conscious of the need for urgency if they were going to tackle the Pune journey. That night, after dinner, he sat with Roh and the others and they told them about the plan to travel to Pune and how they would do it. Sonba, the mechanical whizz, liked the idea of the sleds to flatten and pack the snow down. Griff told him they would have to make snow chains for Godse's vehicles. Sonba asked if it would be possible to take Godse's van too. Griff had not overlooked that, but on reflection thought it might be too heavy to negotiate the snow unless empty. But even empty it could be useful as sleeping quarters during the trip. If they could rig a small snow plough in front of the van and put snow chains on its wheels it might be a goer. They would make chains for it and a v-shaped snow plough. It could also pull a heavy sled to pack the snow down and the two SUVs could follow, each pulling a sled with food, fuel, bedding and clothing. If the van and snow plough worked, they could dispense with the draught cattle and ought to be able to make a good enough speed to reach Pune in two days. Normally, the trip took three hours from the farm to Pune but Griff thought they would be lucky to average ten kilometres an hour while travelling and they would have to stop for meals and toilet breaks and a night's sleep. Definitely two days, but take provisions for two weeks.

They talked more about modifying the van and how and where to do it. There was a small metal-fabricating workshop not far from Godse's house. Sonba was quite familiar with it and its equipment. It had electric welding gear and an electric-powered hacksaw and an electric bolt-hole drilling machine. They would need all that to make the snowplough. But the only place they had an electricity supply was at the farmhouse. They would have to get the gear and the truck to the farm to work on it. They would start next day. They would take the big sled to the fabricating shop and load up the gear. It would be very heavy and that suited their purpose. From there they would make a path from Godse's van to the farm. Since they had no snow chains yet it would be a slow and perilous journey. And before it could begin they would have to dig the van out and warm the engine gently to thaw it and the lubricating oils before trying to start it. As bad luck would have it, when they got the sled to Godse's house they realised that the van wheels were wider than the sled, but it wasn't all bad news as the van had double wheels at the rear. Sonba thought they could get by without having to put chains on the rear wheels if they deflated them a little. They went off to bed, full of anticipation about the next day's challenges. Griff had forgotten about Roh's desire for carnal pleasures. Roh hadn't. Her supple fingers soon renewed Griff's memory and he rose to the occasion. He did as earlier instructed. He lay back and let her have her way with him. By the time she had finished he was sufficiently aroused to crawl over broken glass, if need be, to attain his own satisfaction. Without the need for that he reached his goal more quickly. No wonder the western churches regarded sex in their strangulated way as one of the sacraments, Griff mused.

"Was that heavenly for you, my love?" he asked.

"Utterly divine," she said, snuggling into his back.

"I sometimes feel, after sex, that there might be a god after all and that he loves us," Griff said. "Benjamin Franklin must have been a fat old man and past it when he said that about beer. He didn't mention sex."

"He might have felt that about sex as well, but the times didn't allow one to say it," Roh added.

"True, my love. But he used to take part in the frolics at the Hellfire Club during his visits to merry old England."

"Perhaps things were different in Puritan America," Roh said drowsily.

Chapter 6: Getting ready to mush

After breakfast they loaded a sled with tools and Griff, Sonba, Wasanta and Shakunt set out for the fabricating shop. Griff left Subhash as the guard. Roh said she would do a survey of their food stocks and what they would need for the trek to Pune. She would get Deepak to help her and do some of the household chores, she said.

At the fabricating shop they dug down to the shed. Part of the roof had collapsed with the weight of the snow but they got the electric welding gear out with ropes and then the electric hacksaw, along with some lengths of mild steel and ten-centimetre square tube. Griff hadn't done a design for the snowplough and the more he thought about it the more problems he could see with it. He began to realise that it would dig into the snow unless it were welded rigid and then that would create its own set of problems. He called Sonba aside and told him that he thought the snowplough idea was no good. Sonba wanted to argue.

"I've got a better idea, Sonba, that will be easier to make and more effective. We'll make a roller with a length of concrete sewerage pipe. It will roll over the snow and pack it down and it will be easier to steer the van. It won't need to be rigidly fixed. It will just ride up and down. We will be able to move faster. The only difficulty will be in turning corners but there are only eight between here and the highway and then it's straight running pretty well all the way to Pune."

Griff smoothed the snow with his boot and hand and drew a picture of how the roller would work.

They would cut away part of the bodywork at the front of the van, weld a ten-centimetre-square steel tube to the chassis across the front, slightly wider than the width of the wheels. From that, two steel beams would project forward to hold the roller which would be filled with concrete to give it weight. An axle would run through the middle of the roller and sit in bearing sockets. The roller support or steering arms would have to be able to tilt so that the roller could ride up and down freely. If the steering arms for the roller were not too long it should be able to turn fairly easily. Sonba thought it a good idea.

"The problem, Sonba, is that we will need a concrete pipe about two point four metres long and sixty centimetres in diameter. Do you know where we can get one?"

"Ho, Saheb. There is a creek on the other side of the village where the government had started to build a bridge. They dumped pipes to channel water under the bridge but didn't finish the work. We can go there and get a pipe now."

They went. Sonba was right. He knew where the pipes had been left awaiting use. They probed until they located the pipes and then dug down. When they got one out with ropes it was three metres long. There was a flange on one end that would have to be removed. Sonba said it could be cut off with the electric grinder. By the time they got the equipment and the pipe back to the farm for a late lunch they were completely shagged. Late afternoon they made a trip back to the van for Sonba to cut away the front body to expose the chassis and make measurements. While he did that, Griff and the others checked the supplies in the rear of the van. There was a rich haul: food, including tea and spices and a bag of potatoes, as well as a drum of diesel. They left the diesel in the van and took some of the food for the house.

Each night they watched the TV for any information about rescue flights in India, hoping for something that would indicate the Indian Air Force was still operating out of Pune. Griff calculated that if there were no flights operating from somewhere in southern India, they would have to come from Singapore, the Middle East or Russia or from American, French or British aircraft carriers in the Indian Ocean. If they were operating from aircraft carriers or from Pune, their chances of being discovered and rescued were good. Of course, there were satellites too, but they would be able to operate successfully only when there wasn't heavy snow and cloud. That applied to all forms of surveillance in fact. It would improve greatly when the summer came, but the melt would come with the summer and it would be hell then. The floodwater and mud could leave them stranded inside the house for months. They would have to go, and the sooner the better, while the snow was firm and could be packed hard.

Roh and Griff talked late into the night about the food and gear for the Pune journey, which Roh would organise. He told her about the plan for the roller to go in front of the van, obviating the need, he hoped, for the oxen. If they could do the trip without the oxen they would be able to move much faster. They drifted off to sleep hoping that the journey could be made without the bullocks.

What seemed like only minutes after they fell asleep, they woke to shouting and screaming coming from downstairs. They dragged on coats and rushed down. Deepak was standing in a corner of the kitchen with a large carving knife in his hand and making threatening jabs at Subhash and Sonba to keep them away. Namji's widow Laxmi was screaming and her daughter, Jyoti, whose hands were dripping blood, was moaning with pain and shock. Subhash and Sonba were shouting at Deepak and he was shouting back.

Griff added his voice, loudly: "Gup, gup," shouting at them all to shut up. They did.

"Put the knife down, Deepak. I'll see that Subhash and Sonba don't touch you. Put it down. If you don't I'll give you a whack on the head with a pick handle." Deepak slid the knife onto the bench beside him.

"Right, what's the story, Subhash?"

"Deepak was pestering Jyoti for sex and she was telling him no. He threatened her with a knife and she screamed and woke Sonba and me. We got up and went to Deepak who was pointing the knife at Sunita. He said he would stab her if we attacked him. Jyoti tried to grab the knife and her hands got cut. Deepak jumped up then and got into the corner and that is when you came down."

"Is that how you saw it, Sonba?"

"Yes, that is how it was, Saheb."

"Is that so, Deepak?" Deepak who was looking down didn't respond at first, just shrugged his shoulders. Then he blurted out: "He stole her from me," pointing at Subhash.

"Nobody steals people unless they are in the slave trade or kidnappers. Even then they can't steal emotions. If she doesn't want your company, keep away from her, Deepak. Okay, it's all over. Let's all of us get back to normal. Go back to bed and stay there."

Roh was already treating Jyoti's cuts with antiseptic and binding them with bandages. Griff waited with them until it was finished. Roh asked her if she was happy to go back to bed now. If she wasn't she could bring her bedding and sleep on the floor of their room. She said she was fine. Griff noticed that her bed was next to that of Subhash and also that Sonba had gone to bed next to Laxmi.

"There's more to this than we've heard so far. See if you can get the full story tomorrow, Roh," Griff said as they got back into bed.

"I've suspected for a few days that there were tensions and new relationships developing but I didn't think it would be as explosive as this. I'll try to find out tomorrow," Roh said. "But you well know that, at best, we may only get half the truth. Remember the fish mystery?"

"How could I forget," Griff said, laughing.

The fish drama had happened a couple of years back. They were cleaning out and deepening one of the great farm wells, twenty metres wide and ten metres deep, in the summer. Roh and Griff knew there were some large fish in the small amount of water left in the bottom and had told the head gadee or mukadam (mookadum) that they wanted the fish. The mukadam and four other gadees were working on that job. Griff and Roh had checked them while doing the rounds of the farm and saw four large fish in a bucket. At the end of the day Roh asked the mukadam where the fish were. He said he didn't know. If there had been fish, he hadn't seen them and he didn't know what had happened to them. All the other gadees denied any knowledge of fish. Roh had told him that that was how it was there. There were some things you never got to the bottom of.

"Bottomless wells of deception, you might say," she said, and they had laughed at that

Next morning they got the daily tasks out of the way quickly and then started on the preparations for Pune. Roh and Deepak and Wasanta were taking it in turns to keep a watch on the top roof terrace for planes and choppers, with matches ready to light skyrockets. They were sheltered from the wind by what had been the house water tank. It was a one-and-a-half-metre high PVC tank from which Sonba had removed the top and cut a narrow doorway. There was a stool inside it so that they could sit with the head clear to watch and listen for planes and choppers. It wasn't the most exciting job, but it was good for day-dreaming. Roh spent some time in the watch-tank with Deepak and asked him about his feelings for Jyoti and what had happened. She felt a little sorry for him, but not a lot in the light of her previous experiences with him. He was, after all, alone in the world now, apart from his cousin Shakunt and they were not close. His mother and father were dead and he faced a very uncertain future at a tender age, having lived a sheltered and comfortable life.

Shortly after, with Deepak still up on the terrace, she was able to speak to Jyoti and Seema. Meanwhile, Griff, Sonba, Shakunt and Subhash worked on making the roller for the van and the snow chains. Griff decided that they should make snow chains for the rear wheels of the van and for all four wheels of the two SUVs. The work went well but noisily - they had to have the motorbike generator going all the time to keep the battery bank charged. The electric hacksaw got through the steel cutting steadily and by the end of the day they had cut all the steel lengths needed for the roller and completed and fitted the snow chains. Griff had used two different sized chains for the snow chains. Using large bolt cutters, they had cut heavy chain for the cross pieces and used a slightly thinner chain to thread through the links of the cross pieces on each side of the wheels. The circle chains on the sides of the wheels were locked with strong brass padlocks. The next day's work would be tricky because they would have to fit the roller axle dead centre and fill the pipe with cement. The axle would run all the way through the roller and be held in place with radial steel centring arms at each end. They would then block one end, stand it on that end and then pour the cement in and leave it to set. Fitting the bearings on each end of the axle wouldn't be hard, nor would the welding of the arms to hold the roller.

That night in bed, Griff asked Roh what she had found out about the strife between Deepak, Jyoti and Subhash.

"It seems that when Deepak was here the first time he showed an interest in Jyoti and she responded. However, after he and his father left, a relationship developed between her and Subhash."

"How old is Subhash?"

"He is twenty-seven."

"And she is?"

"Sixteen."

"And do you think they are having sex?"

"Possibly. She probably didn't have sex with Deepak when he was here earlier."

"So you think he knew that and was cranky that Subhash was having some and he was on the outer?"

"Most likely. You never get the full story, and as you know, these rural girls are usually married off about sixteen to a cousin who might be as old as thirty. Subhash would be a good catch for Jyoti. He is a higher caste and he has some education. Laxmi may even have given the nod to Jyoti and Subhash with a view to them getting married if we got out of this situation. "

"Would they use contraceptives?"

"Probably condoms. I asked if they had contraceptives. She said they had condoms. It seems Subhash got a carton of them from the chemist shop that we had visited on our first trip to the village."

"That's good at least. And what about Laxmi and Sonba?"

"Yes, it seems like they have formed a relationship. I got the impression that Sonba is not going back to his family. He feels he has been dumped by them."

"Ah, well, it's interesting to see how quickly new relationships form in a situation like this where people are thrown together and have to depend on each other more than usual. You know, I read that during the Nazi holocaust in Europe in WW II, the gypsies, being railed to the concentration camps for extermination, shagged like rabbits even in public view."

"I suppose if one is facing death, all the inhibitions that flow from social strictures seem irrelevant."

"Yes, well, we are not facing death yet. I still prefer privacy."

"Me too. Do you think we are private enough now?"

"Only if you promise not to scream and moan."

Next day, Griff and the men pressed on with getting the roller completed. Griff realised that they would have to get the van across to

117

the farm to do the welding of the crossbar onto the chassis to hold the roller arms. That wasn't going to be easy. They would have to create a snow ramp from where the van was parked at ground level up to the surface of the snow. It would need to be gradual and a lot of snow would have to be hauled away. They had a bullock-drawn scraper that was used on the farm for grading fields so that the irrigation water would flow properly and evenly. Sonba agreed that it should do the job, particularly if four men helped to pull the scraper, which was about the width of sedan car wheels. The work took a day and a half. They then had to light a fire under the van to warm the engine before they could start it. Heating the engines was a bit of a tricky job. They had to jack up each vehicle and raise it thirty centimetres or so above the ground with bricks under the wheels and put a sheet of metal immediately under and touching the engine block. Then they could light a small fire under that. They couldn't risk the bare flame touching the engine for fear of starting a fire in the accumulated grease, oil and dust. The metal sheet also caused some of the heat to go around the edge of the metal and, after hitting the bonnet, channel back down onto the motor. They fitted the chains to the rear double wheels and Sonba drove it up the snow ramp and onto the surface where it slowly followed the sled back to the farmhouse. They thought it best to leave the two SUVs in the garage at Godse's after checking that they had fuel. They would fit the snow chains later when they needed to leave for Pune. Griff planned to return the next day with Sonba to warm the engines and start the motors. However, Sonba took the batteries out, carried them to the farm on the sled, to be recharged and then returned them to the SUVs. Heated by the fire, as they had done with the truck, the engines kicked and ran without trouble.

Roh said she was making good progress with the preparation of stews and soups. She had decided that the time had come to kill the buffalo heifer and use it for the stew and to cut steaks. The women had led it out to the rain tree, Roh had shot it with one of the pistols and they had then hauled it up into the tree for skinning and dressing.

Griff hadn't realised that the heifer had gone, but as he contemplated Roh's good work, he rather fancied a prime veal steak. They rarely ate steak as people in the west did. Meat was always cut

118

small or minced and incorporated in curries. The locals didn't waste an ounce of a slaughtered animal. Everything, from the intestines to the testicles, was chopped and added to the curry. And it was full of bones and bone chips. Indians, of course, ate with their hands and for them there was no greater delight than hauling a bone out from their plate and sucking the marrow out of it. The slaughtering was an uncertain craft and Roh and Griff often joked that it was done with a blunt saw and the back of an axe. The meat was never hung overnight to let it set and then sliced into known cuts. But Roh knew how to hang and then dismember a carcass properly. There was nothing worse or more dangerous, Griff reckoned, than cutting the mouth on or swallowing jagged bone chips, except perhaps fishbones. He had once had a trout bone stuck in his throat.

Griff had intended, before the great crisis struck, to build a smoke house so that they could smoke haunches of young male buffaloes that they slaughtered on the farm. Roh bred her own buffaloes and seemed to be cursed with the talent of getting more males than females. The males were virtually valueless and were sold off to Muslim traders. There had been a particularly despised and useless but corrupt Chief Minister some decades back by the name of Pandule and male buffalo calves were called pandoolays by the local farmers on the basis that they were good for nothing. They had to be fed if one kept them, they didn't give milk and few Hindus would eat the meat. They could only be used as sires or sold to Muslims for the meat market. To Roh and Griff, the idea of buying meat from the local slaughterhouse was too much to even contemplate. They had seen the haggard, skin and bones beasts awaiting slaughter and it was a miracle to Griff and Roh that any meat could be gleaned from such a carcass. From time to time they bought some meat there for the dogs when they didn't have a sheep they wanted to slaughter for the household. Because of the conflicting and hypocritical religious-based attitudes of farmers towards their livestock, a great deal of usable meat was wasted. Although there was a lot of talk about the sacred nature of cattle and other animals and the sacrilege of beef eating, when cows became too old to bear a calf and yield milk, they were tied up to starve to death or let loose to roam and feed off other farmers' fields. Similarly with

119

male bullocks. Griff and Roh found it appalling but knew it was a waste of breath to try to talk them out of it. Roh was willing to despatch old and lame animals humanely. The farmers merely nodded their heads or agreed and then went away and did nothing. Animals hit by vehicles, including donkeys, camels, horses and cows were left to die in agony. It could take a week sometimes. No one would give them a bullet, but Roh would slip out at night sometimes and give them a fatal injection. The whole business of animal suffering was a puzzle to Griff. Unwanted puppies and kittens were dumped along the roadsides, but then the same was done in Australia by the squeamish who didn't have the guts or the gumption to put down unwanted pups and kittens as soon as they were born and that had led to the near annihilation of Australia's small native fauna by feral cats and wild dogs. The foolishness of the human race never failed to amaze Griff and he often ranted about it until Roh had to tell him to shut up.

By lunch the next day, they had filled the roller with cement and done most of the welding. When the cement was set they could attach the arms to it and the cross bar on the front of the van's chassis. Griff was anxious to get it done and test it. If it didn't work, they were back to the old plan of going at bullock pace behind a sled. If they were forced to do that, they would be getting perilously close to the melt and that would be a disaster. They needed to get moving and it was making Griff edgy. He didn't like that. He liked to be ahead of things. He could never leave anything to the last minute. When he went up to do his stint on the roof terrace that night, watching for rescue flights, he found Deepak, from whom he was taking over, asleep on the floor of the loft and let his temper get the better of him. He shouted at Deepak and called him a lazy bludger who wasn't pulling his weight and was putting all their lives in danger.

"You are well fed, safe and comfortable and you can't even do your small share of work to help us all survive. What is wrong with you?"

"It's not comfortable out here alone in the cold."

"It's the same for all of us. We have to do it to give ourselves a chance to survive this mess. If you are not prepared to do your share, you had better leave the house now."

"You can't do that."

"Don't dare me, mate. Make sure you do your tasks properly. Now get going. If you are tired you had best go straight to bed." The kid slouched off.

The next day, they fitted the roller and tested it. It seemed that they wouldn't be able to travel at more than ten to fifteen kilometres an hour, but that was good. Griff got Sonba to modify the heating system in the van so that it would heat the load area as well as the cabin. Most of them would eat and sleep in the van. Roh and Griff would sleep in one of the SUVs. Griff knew that one of the things that was unsettling him was what to do about the dogs and the cattle. He had no compunction about putting a sick or injured animal out of its pain with a bullet to the brain, but the idea of doing that to healthy animals who had served them so well and which they loved, tormented him. Roh and Griff loved the dogs and he couldn't face the idea of killing them. He could manage the cattle. They certainly couldn't leave them to starve or die. They would have to be killed. The dogs would stay with them. Perhaps in Pune, they could be adopted by people at the air base, or if that were deserted they would then cope with the next set of problems. He knew they wouldn't be allowed into Australia because of the rabies threat, even though Roh vaccinated them every year against the disease.

Griff got Sonba to make a set of steps for the back of the van so it was easy getting in and out.

Each person was limited to one case and one overnight bag, if they needed it. Roh and Griff had one suitcase full of money and one of clothing. Deepak had a case of money and a carry bag of clothing. Each of the rest of them had one bag each. Roh and Griff counted out the rupees shared among eight, excluding themselves and Deepak. That worked out at close to 320,000 rupees for each of the eight. They were all delighted with that result. Then Roh helped them divide the gold and gold jewellery amongst them in such a way that they could claim most of it as personal property. It was common for working families to hold quite a lot of their personal wealth in gold jewellery.

On the afternoon before departure, they checked through the lists of things they needed, took the cattle out into the wasti, put a bag over their heads and then a bullet between the eyes. The pre-cooked food had been made into daily portions and frozen solid. Apart from the buffalo beef and lamb stews, stews and curries and soups with vegetables, they had chicken made with their last two fowls. It was packed into bins and the bins were wrapped in large folded heavy plastic tarpaulins on the veranda ready to go on the sled to be pulled by the van. They also had the last four lamb carcasses wrapped in clean sheets and frozen solid. Each of the SUVs would pull a sled with the food, tools, fuel, cooking gear and equipment that Griff and Sonba thought might be needed in case of breakdowns. They still had some carpets that hadn't been used to protect the cattle, and put those on the floor of the van. They had large plastic containers with snow for drinking and washing, which would go in the back of the van along with their bedding, towels and personal bags. The heating in the back of the van would keep the water warm enough to be used for washing.

They were ready to go. The wind was relatively mild. There was a gentle wind and the sky was clear. They could see a few stars. That was cheering, but it was still bitterly cold. They had cleaned and tidied the house and left it in good order in case they had to retreat to it. There were still thirty bags of grain unused, as well as firewood and hay. They took two bags of grain with them as well as a bag of flour and left the rest. Early on the morning of departure they loaded the vehicles and sleds. It was a strange-looking convoy, the van with roller in front and a sled behind, followed by Roh's SUV with a sled and then Griff's SUV with a sled. Sonba would be in front driving the van with Laxmi and Shakunt. Roh would drive the first SUV with Subhash, Jyoti and Suman, and Griff would drive the second SUV with Wasanta, Seema and Deepak. Digger would be in the SUV with Roh and Rani with Griff. Unlike Australian dogs, who were trained to it from an early age, they didn't like going in vehicles. Digger and Rani had always been outdoor dogs, but they seemed to have become used to being indoors once they'd had a taste of the cold outside. They would have to get used to being in the SUVs. They didn't care much for snow. When they had first experienced it, they tasted it, had a couple of rolls in it, shook themselves dry and headed for the front door. They had short hair. They were hot weather dogs. But unlike humans, they didn't complain. When they got a thorn in a foot they tried to get it out with their teeth and if that failed, they limped along or stood with the paw raised, so that Roh or Griff could remove it.

They left the fire to burn itself out and closed the front door but didn't padlock it in case some desperate person, who had survived, turned up and needed shelter. Roh was teary as they walked to the vehicles. They started them and rolled slowly up the ramp leading from the hard-packed icy snow near the veranda and out the farm gate. The snow from the house to the main road had been used recently by their sleds and it was well packed and fairly easy going. It had been used by sleds for weeks and there had been many snow falls since then. The test would come when they turned on to the main road, half a kilometre away. They made about fifteen to twenty kilometres an hour to the main road but then the speed dropped back to ten to twelve. Griff was happy with that. That would mean two days to Pune if they could keep at that speed. They had a five-minute stop each hour to let people stretch the legs and have a pee. Griff had rigged a small plastic tarp on two poles that could be pushed down into the snow so that anyone who wanted privacy could have it.

The drivers, Sonba, Roh and Griff had driven these roads so many times they knew every twist and turn by heart and anyway, in places, the tops of the roadside trees still showed and they had no difficulty navigating, not that it mattered much. They possibly could have gone cross-country but Griff didn't want to take the risk of going over a house roof or some other structure that might collapse and plunge a vehicle into a deep hole that it would be almost impossible to extract it from.

They stopped for lunch after five hours. They were sombre as they prepared lunch of heated stew and tea. Griff then made damper with flour, water, baking soda and a few sultanas in the camp oven and that helped to lift their mood. They still had a few tins of jam and that went well with the damper. Lunch took about an hour and then they pressed on. Griff held a slim hope that they might find signs at the main highway junction of traffic or of graders and bulldozers having worked to keep the freeway open, but that was in vain. But when they reached it they found the snow was as deep on the freeway as it was elsewhere. The speed with which the deadly cold had hit, along with the chaos of would-be refugees, had been too much for authorities. They simply didn't have the experience of that sort of cold weather or the clothing, heating and equipment to cope with it. The death toll must have been beyond belief. Griff and Roh talked about it quietly and guessed that beneath the snow where they stood would be an almost unbroken line of vehicles with bodies in them. They would have run out of fuel or crashed out of control on the slippery surface and created impassable bottlenecks of vehicles. These would have been worsened by reckless drivers trying to drive around the blockages, instead of stopping and cooperating to push the crashed vehicles out of the way. Griff wanted to get half way to Pune by dinner time and at the speed they were making, they would do that. Roh pointed out that it was the first time in the lives of any of them that they had the road to themselves and the joke was that they couldn't go any faster than ten kilometres an hour. Following the freeway wasn't quite as easy as it had been on the roads leading to it, because none of them was as familiar with the new freeway. But here and there electricity poles and tall buildings helped them orient themselves. They watched carefully for lights in the buildings that poked up through the snow but saw none. They had their vehicle lights on and they would have been visible to anyone looking out of the buildings. The weather had been kind to them all day. At late afternoon when they stopped to make tea, there was still little wind and no snow and visibility was good, all things considered. Roh said she was sure the days were getting lighter. It was almost exactly three months since the cataclysm hit them and that meant it was mid-April and the sun was certainly moving north towards the new Arctic region. It would be getting lighter.

They had been travelling only twenty minutes after their tea break when the roller, without warning, plunged through the snow and Sonba was barely able to stop the van from following it. They got out of the vehicles to see what had happened and, standing on the edge of the hole into which the roller had fallen, they could hear running water. Even though they were sure they were on the freeway, the melt must have already started and was running beneath the snow in places. They unhitched the sleds from the van and the SUVs and put a chain on the back of the van. They reversed slowly with the two SUVs hitched up behind the van and helping to pull it back out of the hole. It was slow and the van wheels were slipping. They took a carpet out of the back of the van and lay it on the snow so that the SUV wheels would have better purchase. Gradually they moved the van back and brought the roller out. The problem then was how to proceed past the hole. There wasn't water visible from the surface which meant there was still snow packed in the hole. They would have to fill the hole with shovelled snow, pack it down with their feet and then lay down the long planks they had carried on top of the van in case of a situation like this. Getting the van across was the main problem. If it was able to get across on the planks, the sleds and the SUVs would make it easily. Packing snow into the hole was a bigger task than Griff had initially assessed it to be. Griff and Roh made them all help with the shovelling and packing. They got pots and bins from the kitchen utensils and used them. Griff was worried about the danger of a further collapse, so he did the tamping down with a rope around his waist tied to the roller. If he fell through the snow into the water they would be able to pull him out quickly. It was the sort of situation that Griff was terrified of: falling into a chasm and disappearing into a black hole from which the only escape was death. He liked the idea of having a fighting chance. It was time to stop and prepare their evening meal by the time they had the hole filled, but Griff and Roh insisted that they get across the danger spot before they stopped. The general lie of the land indicated that they were over a depression in the road and the ground began to rise slowly a short way ahead of them. He guessed that they would be safe from the danger of underground streams if they could move about fifty metres ahead. They laid the planks down and Griff decided he would drive the van. He moved the roller slowly onto the planks and that seemed to be pretty solid, so he inched forward until the whole weight of the van was on the planks, while

Sonba and Roh watched for any signs of collapse. The planks bent but they held at the ends and the van rolled to safety. They dragged the van sled across by hand then re-hitched it and the SUVs then moved over. They moved one hundred metres up the freeway before they stopped to collect the planks and prepare their meal.

Over dinner, Griff and Roh discussed the situation and agreed that they should press on as fast as possible until they were too tired to go further. The non-drivers could doze anyway. After an hour's break, they were on the move again. The ground was rising gently and their speed had dropped back to a steady ten kilometres an hour. That was fine as long as they could maintain it. Griff and Roh had decided they wanted to get to the top of the ghat before stopping for the night. There were two reasons for that; there was a decent-sized drainage ditch on the uphill side of the freeway which fed into drains that ran under the roadway, and from the top of the ghat, it was downhill and then level run all the way into Pune. Hopefully, that would mean there wouldn't be any melt water running under the snow and creating the possibility of a disaster for them. Fortunately, the terrain to the edge of the ghat had a gentle rise for most of the way until the last kilometre or so when it became steep. That last stretch would be a worry. They might not even be able to climb it.

Around midnight they reached the point where the ground began to rise more steeply and their speed fell back dramatically. They were still moving but now at only five kilometres an hour. They churned on. All were asleep but the three drivers. About 1 am, bleary-eyed and exhausted with the stress of worrying about whether they would make it, they were confronted by a near vertical mountain face with a small black half-moon facing them. It was the top of a tunnel just short of the peak. Griff realised they had forgotten to take into account the tunnel and the problems it might present. They would have to get out and move a big amount of snow to be able to get the van into the tunnel. It was too much to tackle now. All three drivers could think only of sleep. They roused everyone and got them into the back of the van. Roh and Griff piled in with them. He roped the door so that it left a fifteen-centimetre opening to allow fresh air in and in minutes they had the bedding arranged and were asleep.

Around 6 am there was an ear shattering noise of someone banging on the side of the van and they sprang into life. Griff untied the door and poked his head out. There in front of him was a wild-looking bearded figure dressed in layers of clothing. He was bent over in a sort of supplicant posture and tears were welling from his eyes.

"You come at last to save me," he said. "How are you knowing I am here?"

"Sorry to disappoint you, mate, but we are not the rescue squad. We're in search of salvation too," Griff said. He jumped down and reached to shake the fellow's hand, but the figure lurched forward and embraced him with a desperate hug, sobbing with relief or gratitude. Roh had now joined him and others were getting down from the van.

"We need to have some warm breakfast and this bloke seems as though he could use some too," Griff said to Roh. "Let's see if we can get our breakfast gear down into the tunnel. He's obviously been living in there so it must be easy to get in and out."

Griff disengaged from the bearded one. "Show us into the tunnel. Perhaps we can make some breakfast in there," he said to the fellow and took him by the hand. The man turned and struggled towards the tunnel mouth. It looked to Griff as he shone his torch around that the man had been keeping the tunnel open by pushing the snow away. There was a gentle slope downwards until Griff realised he was standing on top of a car. Shining the torch ahead he could see that the tunnel was jammed bumper to bumper and wall to wall with vehicles. They could walk on the top of them. Shining his torch through the windows Griff could see bodies in nearly all of them. As they got further along the tunnel, which Griff recalled was about five-hundred metres long, he could see that bodies had been pulled out of cars and laid on the bonnets or pushed into the small spaces between vehicles. About half way along there was a cross tunnel that connected the two roadways. On the eastern side of that, heading away from Pune, the tunnel was relatively free of vehicles and it seemed that the bearded man had been cooking there. There were a couple of pots, boxes with foodstuffs and the ashes of a fire. Chemical smells lingered. Griff could tell as they moved along the tunnel that there was air blowing through it. The fellow must have kept the snow free at the other end

127

too. But he must have been burning some pretty toxic stuff dragged out of cars to feed his cooking fires. Griff thought he noticed a faint trace of grilled meat too but didn't dwell on it.

Subhash and Wasanta helped set up the kerosene stove for Suman to warm the breakfast stew and make tea. Roh sat with the bearded stranger and they spoke in Marathi too rapid for Griff to catch anything but the odd word. It turned out the fellow was Ulhas Suryawanshi, an engineering student. When the disaster struck he had been visiting friends at a village near Satara. He was worried about his elderly parents who lived in Pune, and decided to go back there to help them. He had a Maruti Zen, a small light car. He hit traffic jam after traffic jam and managed to get around them all until the tunnel where he got stuck. There were hundreds of vehicles stuck in the tunnel. Some people stayed and they eventually died and he presumed that those who had left to try to walk out of the tunnel to Pune had also died. Some left but returned and then died. There was a small group who managed to stay alive by scrounging food from vehicles in which the owners had died. Nearly every vehicle had keys in the ignition. Each day they would stay in a vehicle and run the heating system until it ran out of fuel. One by one the survivors had either died or left to try to make it to Pune on foot. He had cooking pots he had taken from vehicles. For cooking he had siphoned petrol from vehicles and soaked a blanket with it and lit it. When the blanket was used up he burnt floor mats and clothing from the vehicles.

Over breakfast Griff wrestled with the problem. How in hell were they going to get out of this dilemma? They could go back for ten kilometres or so and try to find the way on to the old highway that wound round the ghat down to Pune. There was no tunnel on that. There was no way forward with their existing vehicles. They couldn't go through the tunnel to the west because it was choked with probably close to a thousand vehicles and they didn't have the time to clear all of them out. Even with a powerful tractor or a JCB it would take weeks. But it seemed to Griff that it might be possible to clear the vehicles out of the western end of the east bound lanes and then travel down that side of the freeway. From the transverse tunnel to the western exit there were probably fifty vehicles but they wouldn't have to clear all of them out. They could move at least one hundred vehicles to one side of the vacant east end of the tunnel, leaving a lane free going west. That would leave ten or so vehicles to push out of the tunnel on the western end so they could make a path to get their vehicles through. The hardest part of that would be moving the cars that were under the snow at the exit point so they could make a gently inclined snow ramp up to the surface.

Griff discussed it with Roh and Sonba. They thought it was their best chance. Roh then explained it to the others. First they would move their vehicles back to a point where they could approach the eastbound end of the tunnel. They would have to clear a snow ramp into the tunnel. Then they needed to find a truck under the snow at the western end that they could start and, using the ropes they had brought with them, begin pulling vehicles from the tunnel and then pushing them out of the way. Griff thought it might take them two to three days to clear a way through. Straight after breakfast they began work. They needed a long steel probe they could push down through the snow to hit a truck. The trucks were twice the height or more of cars so it wouldn't be hard to tell when they had hit a truck. Griff knew that most of the traffic on the eastbound lane was usually trucks carrying supplies inland and, in the circumstances, there wouldn't be all that much eastbound traffic in the snow. He knew that nearly all the trucks were grossly overloaded and once the snow began falling on that uphill climb the trucks would have poor traction. They started probing at the western end of the eastbound lanes. Griff had decided not to take their vehicles into the tunnel until he could be sure that they would be able to get out. If they got stuck there, that would be a real disaster leaving them with little choice but to walk to Pune pulling sleds. He didn't like that idea at all.

About twenty metres back from the tunnel mouth the probe hit what was most likely a truck and they began digging down. It was a non-articulated truck with a massive load of bags of salted, dried fish. Even in the cold the smell was horrendous and got worse as they began to unload the bags and put them to the side. They might need them later. That was a full day's work. They washed themselves with melted snow and talked about the next step. Griff said they needed to cut through the wooden deck of the truck near the differential to get to the main drive shaft. They would attach a rope to the universal joint so that when they ran the truck engine in reverse, it would wind the rope. They also needed to take a wheel off one of the cars, remove the tyre and fix it in the truck deck near where the rope passed through, to act as a spindle to help the rope slide easily without fraying. The rope could then be attached to vehicles in the tunnel to wind them out of the tunnel mouth. The truck would have to be jacked up so that its wheels were off the ground. With the engine running in reverse, it would be a slow but safe pull and the second gear could be used to unwind the rope. Griff thought it would be a good idea to pull the vehicles out and then use another rope attached to a vehicle to drag it to the side and push it by hand over the cliff.

By lunchtime the next day they were ready to start pulling vehicles out. It turned out to be too hard to pull and then push the first car over the side. Sonba suggested they could set them on fire which would help to melt the snow away from the tunnel mouth and greatly reduce the weight of the car. They decided to give it a try. The fire produced great choking clouds of black smoke that drove them away from the towing truck for more than an hour, but did melt the snow down to the road level. They were then able to use a four-wheel-drive vehicle from the tunnel to push the hulk further to the side of the road. It was slow work, but they were able later in the afternoon, to pull out a small truck that had enough power to push vehicles through the remaining wall of snow and over the edge of the cliff which had a steep fall of more than a hundred metres. Another full day's work and they had a path clear through the tunnel for their own vehicles. They then had the problem of building a gentle ramp that could get their three vehicles and sleds out of the tunnel mouth and up to the level of the snow on western side. One thing that helped was that the road to the west fell away steeply and Griff thought it would be relatively easy to build a ramp out of hard-packed snow and other stuff to ride up on. It took them another full day's work to move their van and SUVs into the tunnel and up to the exit point. They used the bags of fish to start the ramp up to the level of the first car, but Griff realised then it was a hopeless task. The angle was too steep and their vehicle would never be able to make it. They would have to do something similar to the way they had pulled the vehicles from the tunnel. They would go a hundred metres down the highway to the west, find another truck and set it up to pull their van up to the level of the hard-packed surface snow. The setback hit him hard. A lot harder than he had been hit since the start of the calamity. He felt like lying down in the snow and having a good bawl. He flopped down and sat with his head between his knees. They had worked so hard over the past ten days and now there was at least another week's work, he guessed, to get the ramp built and their vehicles up to the snow surface. He sat there trying not to feel sorry for himself and fighting back an outburst of tears. Others had thrown themselves down around him. He lifted his head to say something and caught a fat snowball right in the face. Stunned he blinked through the snow to see Rohini packing another snowball. He jumped up, packed one himself and flung it at her. The others were all laughing. Subhash was roaring with his head thrown back. Griff hit him in the face with a snowball and then they were all into it. The air was thick with flying snow. They ran and jumped and flung balls with a near hysterical frenzy that must have grown out of weeks of hardship and the struggle to keep up a good face and do their share of the work in seemingly hopeless circumstances. Griff finally gave up and rugby tackled Roh into the snow. They lay there exhausted, alternately struggling for breath and laughing. They were all down on their backs with arms flung out sucking in their breath when they became aware of a distant "wop wop" sound and then a powerful searchlight came over the top of the nearby hill and towards the tunnel mouth. They leapt up grabbing their torches and switching them on. No point in shouting. The chopper circled and hovered over them. Griff told the group to cluster together and start stamping down the snow to form a hard pad for the chopper to land. He used their hats to mark a cross in the middle of the hard-packed snow for the landing and then they stood back in a big circle with their torches pointing in to the landing spot.

Chapter 7: Rescue

As the chopper floated down, Griff could see that it wasn't going to be able to take them all in one hit. It seemed to have makeshift UN markings. He guessed it would take four or five at a time with limited baggage. It appeared to have a two-member crew of pilot and spotter. Despite their efforts to pack the snow down, the chopper had sunk a foot into the snow even though it had landing skis in place of rails, so they kept away until the blades had stopped turning. The spotter's door opened and a figure of indeterminate sex hopped out, paused and took a photo or two. Griff and Roh walked towards it, flung their arms out and gave it a big hug as the others ran up. It turned out to be a French woman doctor from Medicins Sans Frontieres, Helene Dupre. The pilot was an Indian Army Captain, Viraj Shah. Griff and Roh hugged him too. They linked hands, grabbed Dr Dupre and danced a ring-around-the-rosy while shouting excited nonsense. When they stopped panting with exertion, Griff introduced the group. Shah and Dupre said they were astounded to find them. They had been flying back to Pune after a survivor patrol a few days back and had noticed what they thought was a fire and smoke here. They couldn't stop at that time because they were running short of fuel and had to go straight back to base in Pune. As soon as their work schedules allowed, they made the trip to the site where they thought they had seen the fire. This group were the first survivors to have been found for more than two months. They had given up hope of finding more until they saw the fire and smoke from the group's activities. Dr Dupre took more photos of the group and after that they took her into the tunnel and showed her their three escape vehicles and sleds. She took more photos of those.

Griff asked how many the chopper could take at a time, apart from the crew. It was four with one bag each. Griff said they would need three trips because their group numbered twelve. Rohini said then that they had two dogs as well and the dogs would have to go with them. They couldn't be left behind. Dr Dupre said the dogs could go with them. She thought the base would be pleased to have two such lovely pets. Captain Shah said he would notify the base in Pune of the find and then take the first group back with the dogs. They couldn't bring out a bigger chopper because it was not possible to land the heavier helicopters on the snow. It was a one-hour return journey to Pune base and they wanted to start right away. Griff told Roh he thought she should go in the first flight with the suitcase of money, Laxmi, Sunita and Sonba. That would enable Roh to deal with any authorities. She and Griff went to their SUVs and got the case while Laxmi, Jyoti and Sonba got their bags and the first flight took off, with Digger.

Suman suggested they celebrate their rescue with a cup of tea and they trooped into the tunnel. Suman got the stove going and put the water on and Griff told the others how he thought they should be divided for the flights. Subhash, Suman, Wasanta and Seema would be in the second flight and he, Shakunt, Deepak and Ulhas in the last group with Rani. He suggested they get their bags ready while they waited for the tea to come. Ulhas said that he had to take two suitcases.

"Not possible, mate, you heard what they said. One bag each," Griff told him.

"I have to take my two cases. They have my books and my clothes."

"Well, that means you will have to take half the books and half the clothes," Griff said, and added: "Where are the cases?"

"I will go and get them," he said and disappeared into the gloom of the jam-packed east-west tunnel.

Five minutes later he emerged, straining with the weight of two large, heavy cases.

"Let me feel the weight," Griff said and reached out to take the weight of the heaviest one. He wrenched it up off the ground and as he did so, the handle broke off and the case hit the tarmac and fell open. No books, just gold jewellery which had obviously been taken from the dead in the vehicles. Griff had no moral objections to that, but he wasn't going to let Ulhas take two cases.

"The other one doesn't have any clothes or books either, does it, Ulhas? It is full of banknotes isn't it?"

Ulhas said nothing.

"You can take one case and I suggest you try to keep the weight down."

"You can't make me."

"We'll see about that. I am not going to let you jeopardise our safety because of greed. I am sure there is enough money in the suitcase to keep you going for quite a few years so just shut up and accept the situation. Do you think the rest of us are not in the same position?"

Ulhas scrambled to pack the gold back into the suitcase and then took it back into the east-west tunnel, no doubt to hide it. Griff left his torch off and quietly followed him into the tunnel. A short way in, he stumbled over a naked foot poking out from under a car and pulled it out. He bent and pulled at it. A whole leg cut through the groin came out. There was a large slice taken from the thigh. That explained the smell of cooking meat he had noticed when he first entered the tunnel. He pushed it back under the car and went back to where Suman was pouring the tea. Deepak had his one case of banknotes and nothing else. Griff had one case which held his and Rohini's clothes and four books, *The Meditations* of Marcus Aurelius, Voltaire's *Candide*, *The Rubaiyat of Omar Khayyam*, his diary of the days since the disaster struck and his passport and resident's permit. They sat and drank their tea until they could hear the "wop wop" of the chopper returning and then moved out to the tunnel mouth. When the rotor blades had stopped turning, Subhash and his group ran over and Griff followed.

"Everything okay at the base?" he asked the crew.

"Fine. A big sensation. They were amazed by the photos. They all want to hear about your adventures, how you survived," Helene said.

Griff gave the second flight members a pat on the back each and said he'd see them soon. The chopper engine groaned into life, settled into a rhythm and the machine lifted off, veering sharply away like a falcon on the wind. It was lovely to see. Griff's group strolled back to the tunnel mouth and sat on their makeshift chairs; seats pulled out of vehicles. It was then about 4 pm and Griff expected to be in Pune for dinner at the base. Five o'clock came and then six and seven and Griff realised then that something had happened. It was worrying, but probably nothing serious. An engine adjustment or something like that. He cooked an evening meal for them, warmed-up stew with some damper and more tea. They brought the van up to the tunnel mouth so they could sleep in it with the rear doors open. That way they would hear the chopper if it came during the night. Griff put a soil and petrol fire tin outside the tunnel mouth and lit it. They were up at 6 am and Griff made more damper with jam and tea for breakfast. He heated some water so they had a large dipperfull each for washing and shaving. About 8.30 they could hear the approaching chopper. They got their cases and stood up. As soon as the engine was cut, Ulhas grabbed his case and stumbled as fast as he could to the machine and approached the pilot's door. As Griff and the others walked he could see Ulhas talking rapidly with the pilot who was shaking his head.

"If he is asking you to let him take two cases, I've already told him I won't allow it," Griff said to the crew.

"Yes, you are right. He is asking but I have told him no," Captain Shah said. "He is offering me money but I have told him it is not me, it is the regulations."

"Good," Griff said. "Let's go then."

They climbed in and put their seat belts on and were away. It was an exhilarating flight as they swayed around the hill tops and then plunged down towards the city. In twenty minutes they were touching down at the Pune airfield that Griff knew well. They were led into the staff recreation room and canteen where the rest of the group and what looked like a good number of the base staff were gathered. The room was large, a cross between commercial and industrial and the décor was wildly eclectic. A selection of armchairs and other furnishings clearly taken from abandoned houses along with a ping-pong table and a billiards table at one end and a bar at the other. But the effect was cosy and the faces were friendly and they were given a clap and a cheer as they walked in. Griff went straight to Roh, gave her a hug and then turned to who seemed might be the base commander, from the number of pips and his general aura.

"You can't imagine how grateful we are that you have saved us all. We were on the brink of despair when your chopper turned up," Griff said.

"Are you sure it was despair?" the Commander said. "Dr Sane has told us you were lying exhausted from a snowball fight when our chopper came upon you,"" he added, with a laugh.

"That was our last desperate fling," Griff said.

"Well, you are safe now and from what Dr Sane has told us, it was a remarkable time and you showed unusual leadership and survival skills. We are all delighted to have met you all and I know the media will be wanting to talk to you. We are arranging to fly you in a big military chopper to a navy ship offshore, that will take you to Singapore, and from there you will be flown to Australia. You will probably go to Broome or Darwin for processing. I don't know how much you know about the ramifications of this terrible world disaster but the refugees number in the millions and a couple of those millions are being housed in temporary facilities in northern Australia, among other places.

"This is not a big base and we do not have extensive facilities, but we would like you to have a warm shower and then a quick medical check and brunch and then we will fly you to the ship. I am Commander Jain. I am in charge here and we are honoured to have your company, if only briefly. When you have finished with the doctor, you will need to talk to our Customs officer, Inspector Thakre, about your identity and what goods you are carrying, then you will be free to have something to eat and drink and then to depart. Dr Dupre will show you to our dormitory bathrooms."

Roh translated for the members of the last group whose English was not good and Dr Dupre then showed them the shower rooms. The men came out refreshed from their showers and went to the canteen area where they chatted with Commander Jain and others. The base staff had learnt a lot about the survival struggles from Rohini the previous evening, but were still full of how the group kept warm and their food supplies and lighting from the moment the disaster struck to when they reached the tunnel. Griff told them briefly about how lucky they had been to be living on a farm with plenty of fuelwood, grain and livestock and how they had set the house up. He left out the strife and killings with Godse, but he drew their attention to the presence of Shakunt and asked what they would expect of him, as a serving army man. Commander Jain said Shakunt would have to stay at the base with them unless he chose to take retirement from the army and to emigrate. He would be free to do that, if he wished. Shakunt turned to Griff with a questioning look. Griff said he would be very happy for Shakunt to stay with them. Shakunt said he would go with the group. It wasn't going to be much of a life in the military in India, if there were to be any at all. Commander Jain said the Indian defence forces had virtually been disbanded. The base was actually under the command of the UN Relief Organisation. A quasi Indian Government in Exile had been established in the United States. Some of the members of the Indian Central Government had been able to escape in VIP and other aircraft. They were insistent that they should have a government in exile so that they could maintain sovereignty over India and resettle as soon as conditions allowed. Most Indians agreed. The idea of abandoning the motherland, Bharat Mata, was too much to accept.

The women of the survivor group were greatly refreshed and relaxed after their night at the base. Their hair glistened, their skin was creamy and they wore clean saris and carried their jackets. Rohini had told them that it would probably be a cold trip to the ship and for a day or two on the ship until they got into warmer waters. All the women except Rohini were wearing saris. Rohini was wearing jeans with a long outer shirt and a brown leather jacket and carrying her heavy coat.

"You look wonderful, Roh," Griff said.

She laughed. "They had hair shampoo and hair dryers. It was heaven."

She asked Griff what they should do with their improvised snow gear. They turned to Commander Jain and Griff asked if it would be possible for them to keep their snow gear as a reminder of their ordeal. Would there be sufficient room on the chopper for them to take their snow gear?

"Yes, definitely, there will be great interest in that and you should have it with you. Even your snow shoes. You must take them too. We will provide you with bags to carry your gear. And if any of your group need warm jackets we can provide them for you. The jackets of some of your group look a bit worn and soiled. We want you looking nice when you arrive on the ship and in Singapore," he said.

Griff had noticed that Ulhas stayed behind and began talking to Commander Jain, when he had left for the shower rooms. Ulhas arrived for his shower when the others were finishing. Griff asked the Commander if he could see him privately in his office. The Commander led the way and Rohini and Griff followed. In his office the Commander shut the door and asked Roh and Griff to take a seat.

"I won't bother you for long, Commander, as you probably have many duties to attend to, but I wanted to ask if you were having any problems with Ulhas."

"Ah, yes. He doesn't wish to go with you to the ship and then onwards just now. In fact, he asked me if it would be possible to be taken back to the tunnel as there was something important that he had left there, his study books. I understand he is an engineering student."

"I'm afraid he may have misled you there." Griff related the story about Ulhas' suitcase of gold. He didn't mention his suspicion about cannibalism.

"Yes, I had suspicions about the real purpose of the trip. That settles the matter. I did tell him that it would not be possible to do a trip back specifically for that. He then asked if he could stay here at the base and perhaps, when one of the helicopters went on patrol, he could accompany them and collect his case. I told him that was not possible. He did offer a considerable sum of money, but I had to tell him that made no difference. We do not have the capacity here to keep refugees indefinitely. They have to go to staging points and then on to the camps."

"That is fine. I quite agree and thanks again for your gracious hospitality Commander. We are all deeply grateful." They shook hands.

"It has been my pleasure, Mr Bolton, and I wish to say that you and Dr Sane have shown remarkable leadership and determination as well as innovative skills and I hope that will be recognised. You had better go to see the Doctor now and then have something to eat. And don't forget to take those jackets I offered for your group members who need them."

They walked together to the recreation room and Dr Dupre took them to her clinic.

"This won't take long at all," she said. "I can see that you are all in good condition. You must have kept a good diet. Dr Sane has told me that you have been eating fresh green vegetable in the form of wheat sprouts as well as mushrooms and onions, grains and meat. That is truly remarkable. I will just record your blood pressure and pulse and take a blood sample and have a look at your fingers and toes for any signs of frostbite damage. If you will wait outside and come in one by one we can begin now."

Griff and Roh sat together and talked about Ulhas' attempt to get back to the tunnel to retrieve his case of gold loot. Roh told him that Helene Dupre had told her that Inspector Thakre was, in her view, rather sleazy and might try to demand unofficial fees for clearing them for departure. Dr Dupre had said that there was a legitimate fee of ten per cent of gold that was not personal jewellery and five per cent of banknotes. This was a levy to fund the Indian Government in Exile.

"She's a good stick," Griff said. "That's very useful to know."

"Yes, I thanked her warmly for that."

"Commander Jain seems to be a fine bloke too. He reminded me to collect the jackets for the group members who need them."

"Yes, he is very decent. We should accept his offer of jackets for the other members of our group.The ones they are wearing now are really soiled and worn."

"You're right. They're putrid. Your leather jacket looks great. It hasn't had much wear until now, has it?"

"Well, your jacket looks fine even though it is well worn. Like you, it improves with the years."

"Just wait till I get you alone in a cabin, my love. Yes, it's comfortable. It feels good to be wearing it again."

It was a double-breasted woollen pea jacket of greatcoat thickness, bought in Europe years before on a winter trip with Roh to Prague.

"Remember our trip to Prague? We were looking forward to a white Christmas then. How do you feel about snow now?"

"I think I've probably had enough for the time being. Perhaps in a decade or two we could try it again."

"Yeah, we could have a nostalgic trip with the Eskimos."

"Or get a couple of skidoos and go back to the tunnel to get Ulhas' gold."

"Sounds like a good movie, The Hunt for Ulhas' Gold. However, in ten years that tunnel will probably be under two hundred metres of hard-packed ice and snow. By the way, just between you and me, I discovered a human leg on the last morning, which had a large slice taken from the thigh. Looks to me like someone was having a bit of long pig. I noticed a faint smell of cooking meat when we first entered the tunnel. I think Ulhas may have been the culprit. I haven't said anything to anyone but you about it and I won't unless Ulhas starts getting funny in any way. He doesn't want to come with us. He wants to stay until he can get his hands on the gold, but Commander Jain has told him he has to go."

"Wow, that is interesting. I had noticed that faint tang of cooked meat, now that you mention it."

They sat and held hands while waiting for Dr Dupre to call them. After their check-ups, which were all clear, they returned to the recreation room and asked about the jackets. One of Commander Jain's staff took the group to a store where there was rack upon rack of cold weather gear for rescued refugees. After the first few weeks, the clerk said, the numbers of rescued people had dropped to virtually nil. After one month there had been none, until Griff and Roh's group. Everyone was astounded that they had survived three months and the media were already bombarding them with inquiries. Commander Jain had fobbed the media off, saying the group would not be available for any interviews until they were on board the ship, or possibly even until Singapore. Griff was starting to get nagging fears of a media melee.

"What do you think Roh? Talk to the media on the ship, if they telephone, or put them off until we are in Singapore?"

"Singapore would probably be better. One big press conference to get it out of the way. You should be spokesman."

"Okay, but I want you all with me. I will speak to the ABC, if they call. They are the best and they will handle it well. I detest commercial television and I'm not interested in selling any exclusive rights to anyone. Are you?"

"I'm with you Griff."

With the group kitted out in new jackets, they headed back to the recreation room where a buffet spread had been laid out. Roh and Griff kept away from the spicy stuff. Half a papaya each, a stuffed vegetable paratha and tea was all they wanted. Other members of the group seemed hungrier.

"The next hurdle, Roh, is the Customs bloke, Inspector Thakre. Are you braced to cope with him?

"I am if you are."

"Well, I haven't anything to declare. We have shared the gold out among the others and you have the suitcase with US dollars, I hope."

"Right, no need to worry. I have the case. I gave it to the Commander to keep in his office for the time being. I don't mind paying the five per cent levy for the Government in Exile, do you?"

"Not at all, although I think it is a ridiculous proposition to maintain a government in exile in these circumstances. I hope they will be working or living on their foreign bank accounts rather than expecting Indian refugees to keep them in idle comfort. There won't be any work for them to do, that I can see. Just make-work."

"You might be surprised to see how much they can make out of nothing but, for the time being, perhaps we should give them the benefit of the doubt. It's possible, I suppose, that the polar axis will shift back to its old position or at least to an alignment that enables resettlement in India."

"Yes, agreed, my love. Do you think we should check with Commander Jain on the point that the levy for the GIE is, in fact, five per cent? We want to be on sure ground if Thakre tries to get into us and we have to argue with him."

141

"I've already checked with him. He confirmed it."

"Clever girl. I don't know about you but I'm ready to crawl through a thorny hedge for a decent cup of coffee."

"Perhaps we'll get one on the ship or in Singapore."

"I wouldn't count on it. I fear we may have to wait until we get to the land of the sun-bronzed heroes for a decent flat white."

"You're probably right, Griff. I just wish we were on the way. I am keen to get on with things."

"Me too. Let's find out where Inspector Thakre is and get the troops to him."

They went in search of Commander Jain to ask him when Inspector Thakre could start clearing them and when they were to be flown to the ship. Straight away, was the answer. Jain showed them Inspector Thakre's office. They knocked on his door and he called out for them to enter. They had met him earlier so there was no need to introduce themselves. They said they would like to start their group on clearing for departure if that suited him. Thakre was dressed in splendidly clean whites with white shoes to match. He had a large stomach and a cool distant manner and thinning jet black hair that belied his middle age. Griff noticed that in the places where Thakre's hair was very thin, his scalp had been darkened with dye to lessen the effect of the balding. A danger sign. They would be dealing with an ego of vast proportions unable to see the absurdity of his vanity.

"I must have my lunch before starting on your people. There are extremely many of them and it will be taking a lot of time. There are few of forms to be filled."

"Ah yes, the forms, of course. Some of our group are illiterate, so it may be useful if Dr Sane and I sit in and help with the form filling, if that suits you?" Griff said.

"I will ask them the questions and fill out the forms for them. You will not be needed. Are you a member of the family of Sadanand Sane?" Thakre said, looking at Rohini.

"Yes, he is my father. Do you know where he is? I am desperate to know what has happened to my mother and father."

"I am thinking they left for the United States on the day following the disaster. I was not working here then and Commander Jain was also not here, but I knew your father through my Customs work. I heard he had left for America. I think you have brother there, do you?"

"Yes, I have a brother and a sister there. I am so grateful to you for that information. Would it be possible for me to make a telephone call to my parents, do you think?"

"I am sure if you speak to Commander Jain he will be helping for you to make call to America."

Roh and Griff thanked him and left to see Commander Jain.

"Do you mind if I call my parents first Griff?"

"Of course not. I think I will wait until Singapore, or perhaps on the ship they will let me call my brother. If the media has been as active as Commander Jain has hinted, I am sure my brother will know by now that we are safe."

The Commander was happy to let Rohini call the US on his satellite phone. She thought she would try her brother first. They were not really close. His name was Anil. He was more traditional than Rohini, had tried in the distant past to force her decisions and in recent times seemed to resent her success and independence, although he was a medical doctor with a reasonable practice in Tallahassee.

She got through. Anil answered. "Yes, our parents are here. They are worried about you. Where have you been and why have you not been in touch with them to spare them the pain and suffering of uncertainty?"

"I have been fighting for survival in the snow for three months until now with no means of contacting the outside world. We have just been rescued today," she said.

"I'll get your father," he said.

Sadanand Sane came to the phone. Roh told him how relieved she was that he and her mother had got away safely. She had been desperately worried and had no means of contact with the outside world, apart from occasional news reports on TV, when the weather was not so wild.

"We thought you would have gone to the US. We will go initially to Australia, but I will come to visit you as soon as we get settled there." She explained briefly then how they had survived in the farmhouse.

"Come and settle here in the US with us. Anil has a big house and the family can be together."

"No, Dada, Griff and I are going to Australia and will settle there. Then we will have two bases and you can come to visit us in Western Australia."

"Your mother doesn't want to travel any more. She has had enough of travel. She says her next trip will be to return to India or to the grave."

"Give her my love and my love also to Neelim. I have to go now. I will call again from Singapore to speak to mother." She hung up.

She re-joined Griff and told him about the call. Tears trickled down her cheeks as she spoke of her relief at them being safe and the recollection of the tensions with Anil. It seemed nothing had changed there. He was still abrupt and insensitive and accusatory. She didn't want to live with them or even close to them now. She squeezed Griff's arm tightly and pressed close to him.

"We can make a good life and be fulfilled. They are not very happy. Well, my parents are reconciled to each other now, but the family group is tense. My parents don't get along all that well with Anil's wife and my sister doesn't like Anil's company. And you know that none of them is really at ease with you. The idea of living together with them is ridiculous. It gives me a headache just to think about it."

Griff and Rohini waited in the recreation room while Inspector Thakre took the group members in one by one, except for Wasanta and Seema, who went in together. Subhash, who went through first, told them that Thakre looked at their gold jewellery, weighed it and took a tithe and wanted to take a tenth also of their cash. He said he told Thakre that Commander Jain had told them they were required to pay five per cent. Thakre had nodded and taken five per cent.

Griff and Roh noticed that Ulhas was nowhere to be seen. They went through last. They told Thakre they had no gold to declare and showed him their suitcase of US dollars.

"Do you have any proof that this is your money?" Thakre asked.

"Do you have any particular reason for asking that?" Rohini said.

"One of the members of your group has alleged that you stole this money from him. If that is so, the money will have to be impounded

144

until a special court can be set up by the Government in Exile to hear the matter."

"How long would that take?" Rohini responded.

"I cannot say, but there are already many matters pending. It might be years."

"And that would be goodbye to our money, wouldn't it? We would never see it again."

Inspector Thakre looked at them with a dead fish stare and gave a dry cough.

"Just like that, eh? Somebody can make a baseless allegation and leave another person impoverished without recourse? Supposing I made an allegation that the person who has made this allegation about us is lying and that he stole the money he is carrying, a sum equal to ours, from us?"

"How would you know who made the allegation?"

"Come now Inspector, you don't think we are stupid, do you?"

"If you were to make that allegation, it might be necessary for me to impound both sums of money."

"Yes, well, it won't be necessary for you to impound either sum of money," Griff said. He opened the small leather satchel he had on his lap and pulled out the letter from Deepak Godse's father, which he read out and then held up for Inspector Thakre to see.

"I will have to take charge of that letter," he said, reaching out.

"That will not be possible. This letter is addressed to me and it is my property. You may take a photocopy in our presence and notarise it and we will countersign it as a genuine copy," Griff said.

The Inspector gave them another dead fish stare and, after a pause, looked down and said: "Yes, that can be done."

"I take it from your response that Mr Godse was known to you?" Griff said.

"Yes. The father of the boy. He was well known to us."

"Fine, let us get a copy of the letter notarised and any other paper work and get on our way. We have been living rough for many months now in life threatening situations and we are very keen to get back to civilisation and some warm weather." Griff gave Inspector Thakre a broad smile.

"Yes, of course." The Inspector began shuffling his forms and passed one each to Rohini and Griff to sign.

"Here is your five per cent of our US dollars. I had counted it out for you after Commander Jain told that five per cent was required," Griff said.

"That is good. You are free to leave now," Thakre said.

Griff took the suitcase of money and their other case and they returned to the recreation room where Commander Jain and some of his staff and the group were waiting.

"All clear now?" the Commander asked with a broad smile. He was wearing his full length military greatcoat, gloves and hat and the rest of the group were also dressed in their new jackets, hats and gloves.

"Yes, all clear," Griff said.

"Let's go out to the helicopter then. It's cold out there, so you will need your heavy coats on."

They put them on and Griff and Rohini waited with the Commander while the others filed out, carrying their snow gear in canvass kitbags provided by the rescue station. At the door to the chopper Rohini and Griff thanked the Commander and his staff for all their kindnesses. The Commander wished them a safe journey to the ship and back to Australia.

Griff told the Commander that Ulhas, the engineering student, was missing from the group.

"Yes, he has been detained by Inspector Thakre in connection with matters that require further investigation. I can't say much more than that," he said, but he gave Rohini and Griff a wink. "You can reach your own conclusions about the need for an investigatory trip to the tunnel, but that is not my area of responsibility," he said with a shrug.

They shook hands and Rohini and Griff climbed into the chopper. The door closed, they buckled on seat belts, gave a final wave, and the big machine rose ponderously and moved slowly forward like a well-fed pelican struggling to gain height. It was too noisy to talk normally but Roh spoke into Griff's ear.

"So it looks like Ulhas has talked Thakre into a visit to the tunnel to share the loot, eh."

"Looks that way. Good riddance to Ulhas, I say. He might be lucky to escape with the family jewels after Thakre has finished wringing him out." They had a chuckle at that.

The chopper droned on south and Griff and Roh were surprised at how far they could see as it rose to cruising height. It was no longer black outside. It was definitely lighter and they could see a vague glow of watery light over the rim of the earth to the south. Just north of Thiruvananthapuram they began a slow descent and the pilot announced through a PA system that they would be landing there in about twenty minutes to take on fuel at the rescue station. They were low enough then to see that there was ocean below, although to their left the land was still covered with snow. The pilot said icebergs were not yet any threat, although the Arabian Sea, further north, was still frozen. No doubt in years to come, when the icecap built up, icefloes would become a danger. They landed near a fuelling point. There was a bus standing by and the pilot said they should go in the bus for a tea or coffee and snacks. They had been flying for three hours and it was good to get out and walk. They went to a large canteen and recreation room inside the base that seemed to be a clone of the Pune station with a similar crowd cheering them into the room. They shook hands all round and the Commander made a short welcome speech in which he called them heroes who had shown incredible determination and endurance and it was a great honour to have them at the station if only for a brief visit. Roh and Griff were keen to sample the coffee and snacks but there was no escape from having to make a speech in reply. Roh pushed Griff forward to make the first reply. The Commander translated Griff's English into Malayalam for the few who were not able to follow English. Griff said that they didn't see themselves as heroes but he thanked them for their kind words. He said he thought there was a good lesson for the whole world in the survival of this group. They were from many different social levels, from Dalits to Brahmins and, of course, a foreigner and they had been forced by circumstances to live all in one house in very close proximity. Their survival was due to the fact that they had disregarded all those differences of social levels, education, manners and pre-judged notions and worked together with hardly any disputes. The best hope

147

for the world in this great calamity that had been forced on them by nature, and in future generations in whatever crisis humanity faced, was to work together as they had done.

Rohini also spoke in English. Hindi and Marathi were rarely understood in Kerala. She realised, she said, that the people of Kerala must have lost many millions of their citizens to the disaster but she hoped that millions also had escaped south to safety. Those people who had stayed behind to staff the rescue stations and look for survivors were the heroes in her view and she wished them well and a safe return in time to warmer climates.

The Commander led them to a buffet table where food and drink was laid out.

"I understand there is a great reception waiting for you on the ship," the Commander told them. "So you had better have some coffee to keep awake. It is good coffee, we have our own machine."

They agreed. Coffee it would be. It was good. They all headed off for the lavatories and then it was time to go. After the usual round of thanks they were away and heading south east towards Sri Lanka where their ship was waiting near Colombo. They dozed until woken by the pilot over the PA telling them they would be landing in about fifteen minutes. The chopper settled on the rear deck of the destroyer. Through the windows they could see a crowd of naval officers, sailors and others waiting, some with what looked like TV cameras. When the rotors stopped they slid the doors open, dropped the steps and went out. A distinguished-looking officer in an immaculate winter uniform stepped forward to greet Griff and Rohini.

"Welcome on board HMS Trafalgar. I am Commodore Awati of the multinational fleet on station here and this is Captain Scott, Commander of Trafalgar, who will be taking you to Singapore. It's a pleasure to have you here safe after your ordeal and we all look forward to hearing how you managed to achieve your survival in such a calamitous situation. It is quite remarkable. Let us go into the wardroom where we can talk in comfort and, as you can see, the media is keen to get you into a corner. We have kept them at bay for the moment but you had better brace yourselves for them."

"Ah well, if we were able to survive the rigours of the polar crash, I feel sure we can manage a media blizzard, but let me introduce Dr Rohini Sane, my partner. She will introduce the rest of the group inside, as there are quite a few of them and there is a bit of a bite in the wind," Griff said.

Captain Scott called sailors over to carry the bags of snow gear and they filed in after the two officers.

The wardroom was a tight fit with several officers, the group of survivors, the media pack and a long dining table set out with sandwiches, cakes, various drinks and tea and coffee urns. Rohini asked Subhash to help the other members of the group with getting something to eat and drink.

After the introductions Captain Scott spoke.

"Before we throw you to the wolves, perhaps you would like a drink or coffee? You're probably keen to tackle a cold Fosters, Mr Bolton? And what would Dr Sane like?" the Captain said.

"That's very kind of you," Griff replied. "Rohini and I don't drink much Fosters, actually, but I understand you are making some good wine in England these days. We would both settle for a glass of something light and dry. Our group won't have any wine but they would love a cup of milky, sugary tea."

"Sorry, no English wine, but we do have some Margaret River Verdelho. Perth is our leave station so we re-victual there. Your people can help themselves to the tea and food as soon as they wish."

"That would be excellent," Rohini said. "We haven't had a glass of wine for months. It was a very dry winter holiday."

"Ah, yes.'*Fill me with the old familiar juice, methinks I might recover by and bye',*" Griff added, with a wry smile.

A sailor brought a tray with glasses of wine for Commodore Awati, Captain Scott, Roh and Griff.

"Here's to a safe journey to Australia and some warm weather for you and your group," Commodore Awati toasted. They drank. The wine was good. Griff and Roh exchanged smiles.

"Are you happy to face the media now?" the Captain asked. "I can easily put it off until the morning if you are too tired to face them."

"No, we can see that they are desperate and although it has been a long day, I am happy to give them half an hour now, if Rohini is, and perhaps we can have another session tomorrow morning if they are hungry for more. What do you think Roh?"

"Yes, I'll go along with that."

"Here's to your happy settlement in Australia and a warm welcome there," the Commodore toasted them again.

They responded with thanks to the Commodore, Captain and crew for their hospitality. They sipped their chilled wine and the mood lightened. The Commodore was an imposing figure, of medium height but with a large head graced with a full but well-trimmed beard and a powerful thick-chested body and strong arms. He had a ready smile, a deep voice. A little pompous, perhaps, but friendly with lots of questions. He was a contrast to the Captain who was tall, wiry and laconic.

"Fine, well if you would all sit over there, you can begin." The Commodore pointed to the chairs set up in a semi-circle.

Rohini rounded up the group and they took their seats. The journalists and camera people moved in and the bright lights hit them in the face causing them to blink and shield their eyes initially. The long period of dim light during the survival months seemed to have made them sensitive to strong glare.

"We are ready when you are," Griff said, "and perhaps my partner Dr Rohini Sane should introduce each member of our group. She will also have to translate for them too, as only one or two of them are fluent in English."

Rohini introduced each member to the media and said a few words about how they came to be in the group. Having finished that, she said that Griff would be the main spokesman for the group and it was he who had played the leading role in holding the group together and devising the strategies that enabled them to survive.

"Before you let fly with the questions," Griff said, "I would like to say that if it had not been for Rohini's house and farm and her veterinary and medical skills, we would not have survived. She had a fine bluestone three-storey farmhouse built by her family some years back and ran a productive and prosperous farm. It was a relatively easy business to bring in the grain, fuelwood, livestock and fodder that enabled us to get by," Griff said.

He explained how they had been woken in the middle of the night by the cold and wind and had begun work immediately to make themselves secure. They answered questions for forty-five minutes and the TV people wanted them to show the snow gear that Griff had made. It seemed there were representatives from the BBC, European and American networks as well as Japanese and Australian broadcasters and newspaper correspondents.

"If we promise to put the gear on tomorrow, how about letting us have some sleep now?" Griff said.

There were mutters of agreement and one or two asked if they had any photos. Rohini told them she had plenty, but they were mainly of indoor activities including their mid-winter games day. Tomorrow they could download them from her camera, she added.

Commodore Awati excused himself at that point and said he would return to his carrier nearby, but would return next morning for the continued media session. He was keen to see the snow gear, he said. The Captain asked one of his crew to show the other group members to their berths and took Griff and Roh to theirs. They had a two-berth cabin to themselves. If was tiny but it had a lavatory and a shower. They thanked the Captain who left, then slipped off their boots and flung themselves down on the bunks. The ship was already under-weigh and due to reach Singapore late the next day. It was then after midnight.

"Well, my love, it's been a long and varied trip today from being stranded in a tunnel to being safe on board a ship steaming to Singapore and a hero's and heroine's welcome. Let's not reconsummate our love tonight, I'm already utterly shagged." Griff said.

"Can you manage a kiss?"

"I can, but only just." Griff rolled out of his bunk and lay half beside and half on top of Roh.

"These bunks are a discouragement to anything but sleeping alone or one on top of each other," he said.

"There is a place for each in good time. Let's clean our teeth and collapse." Roh replied. They did, sleeping naked in their separate bunks. Griff woke in the morning to the pressure of Rohini lying on top of him gently kissing his lips.

"You had better go and have a pee so you can perform the needful, sir."

"Oh, lord save me, a sea-sprite or siren has me in her clutches. What will mother say?"

"This is not a naiad, it is a succubus. They are more demanding. Mother is not here."

"Oh well, I suppose you have me at your mercy. I will pop into the lav."

"Bring back a towel to put over the sheets. Who knows what turmoil a sex-stained sheet might cause among a shipload of abstinent sailors," Roh called to him.

"Your servant, ma'am." He returned with the towel, spread it and lay back with arms outstretched. Eventually they dozed in each other's arms. At 7 am, as they were dressing, there was a knock on the cabin door. It was a steward with a pot of tea. He asked that they call on the Captain before breakfast to give him the names and details of each of the members of the group and to bring any passports or travel documents.

"Breakfast at 8 in the wardroom, sir," the steward told them.

At 7.30 they went to the Captain's suite adjoining theirs. When they arrived the Captain explained he was obliged to report the details of the group to the refugee processing office in Singapore for passing on to Australia. He said he had received a list of the names and basic details of the group from the refugee search centre in Pune and he needed to check that and to see passports and IDs. He was accompanied by one of his officers whom the Captain asked to take the details. Griff explained that only Rohini and he had passports and the others had very few identification papers apart from driving licences or ration cards. They were mainly semi-literate or illiterate farm workers. He and Rohini handed their passports for checking against the list and Rohini checked the names of the rest of the group. That done the Captain led them out for breakfast. In the wardroom there were eight or ten freshly pressed officers, including two women, standing about sipping tea and coffee. They joined them.

"Now you are here we can start," the Captain said. "Perhaps you might sit one at each end so that we can better share your company. It's serve-yourself style from the buffet."

Griff and Roh helped themselves to yoghurt and fruit salad and returned to the table to take their places. When they were all seated and the conversation had resumed, one of the officers with the remnants of a north-England accent that he had not be able to eradicate, addressed Rohini and asked: "How is it, Dr Sane, that a cultured and refined lady such as yourself got caught up with a wild uncultured Australian?" Rohini laughed.

"What makes you think that Mr Bolton is uncultured, sir?

"Well, I was joking, of course. I've only met a few Australians but I have heard it said that the only culture in Australia is found in yoghurt." Only he and Griffith laughed. The rest merely smiled.

"Ah, well, Griffith is rather fond of yoghurt which we made daily on the farm, so I guess that has probably done much to lift his culture levels. But have you not been to Australia?"

"No, I joined the ship only recently so I haven't been on a leave visit to Perth yet. I hear it is all beaches, burning sun and flies. Have you been there?"

"Oh, many times. You may find it a little different from your expectations."

"Well, if they have art galleries and museums and restaurants as good as the wine, perhaps it won't be too bad."

"Well, the art galleries and museums are excellent and so far as fine living is concerned, the West Australians are exporting truffles to France and sending wine makers there as well, these days. They have several fine universities too, not to mention extensive parks right in the city area."

"You don't say? But tell me, Dr Sane, about the famous Sai Baba. I have been reading about him and was thinking of making a visit to his ashram to seek some spiritual guidance and solace. Have you made such a pilgrimage yourself?"

153

"No, and I have to tell you that he is the last person in the world from whom I would seek any guidance, spiritual or otherwise. I'm not much inclined towards religious matters or people. I am a medical doctor and a vet so I am rather more concerned with practical matters relating to the functioning of the human body and science. If it is spiritual uplift you seek, perhaps you should talk to Griffith. He is more philosophically inclined."

"So what do you say, Mr Bolton, about Sai Baba?"

"Please call us Rohini and Griffith. That will make us feel much more at home here. So far as Sai Baba is concerned, perhaps the most tactful thing I could say is that his reputation in most things is far from the reality. Anyone who claims to be able to materialise watches and sacred ash from the air, is someone with whom I would not wish to have any dealings, but then it is no different from western religions and their so called miracles, I suppose, is it?" There were a few chuckles around the table.

"So, where do you turn for comfort and knowledge in spiritual matters, Griffith?" another officer asked.

"I don't claim to be any sort of a guru and the words spirit and spiritual puzzle me. Since I have seen no evidence of a spirit or a soul, I don't use the words much. I tend to think in terms of trying to get an understanding of the human condition and the nature of the world and the universe."

"Please go on. So you get no comfort from religion or god?"

"No, only fear and distress when I contemplate what religions have done and are doing to the human race. 'Gott mit uns' is not a mantra for me."

"So, where do you find whatever it is that drives you on? You must have needed something to have survived the great ordeal that you have been through, surely?"

"I am not sure, really. I don't believe there is an intrinsic moral law. I think our morality has all been created as part of the social contract but I am happy to accept that contract for the most part. In my view the best way for the world to prosper is if we all try to get along with each other peacefully and show some consideration for other people's needs. Try to give a bit more than we take and leave the world in a better place than when we came into it."

"So there's no place for religion or *The Bible* in your life?"

"No, I'm afraid not, but there are three other books I read from time to time to refresh my outlook on life."

"Won't you tell us what they are?"

"I am sure you are all familiar with them. Voltaire's *Candide*, *The Meditations* of Marcus Aurelius and *The Rubaiyat.*"

"All slim volumes. What do you find in them that is helpful?" the Captain asked.

"Ah well, *Candide* reminds me of the random brutishness of life and the restlessness of the mind. *The Meditations* shows me the disciplines needed to cope with the world and *The Rubayait* helps me to laugh off the setbacks in life and realise the unimportance of the individual in the vastness of time and the universe."

"Yes, I think it was Khayyam you quoted earlier about the old familiar juice wasn't it? And what about you, Rohini. Indians are often very religious people, aren't they?" the Captain asked.

"Not this one, Sir," she said with a rippling laugh. "I come from a long line of anti-religious people who are more interested in the reality and hardship of the human condition than pie in the sky."

"Well, you two seem very well suited then. And what sustains you in difficult times?"

"That's hard to know. I think it is just a will to survive and to overcome challenges. I get a lot of comfort from my friendships."

Griff and Roh returned to the buffet to get poached eggs on toast and then took their places again.

"No Indian philosophers in your iconography, Griffith?" the Captain asked.

"Oh, yes. I admire Gandhi and most of what he said and there is another Indian whose thoughts also appealed to me though I fear I fail to live up to them," Griff said.

"Oh, what did he say?" the Captain asked.

"He said the fruit laden tree bends low. The truly great are always humble."

"Yes, that's useful to remember," the Captain said.

"Surely you are being too modest Mr Bolton." It was the Yorkshire officer again. He was starting to grate on Griff.

"Oh no, I know myself too well."

"Well, any other notable failures among illustrious Australians?" he continued.

"I suppose I could mention John Monash, an Australian of German Jewish descent."

"Ah, one of those. What did he do?"

"He got in the way of the Germans in France in World War I."

"Plenty did that. Is that all?"

"No, he planned the battle for Le Hamel on the Somme to last exactly ninety minutes but it took ninety-three. He was quite disappointed about that."

"Oh, very good, Griffith," the Captain said, laughing.

They chatted on for a while longer. Griff and Roh were both keen to know how many people had survived and how the rest of the world was coping with the inundation of refugees. The Captain said he wasn't familiar with the scene apart from Australia, but there it seemed to be going reasonably well. Refugees were confined to the camps in the north of the nation until they could be slowly absorbed into the more populated south. Eventually, Captain Scott suggested they should vacate the room so the next group of diners could have their breakfast.

As they rose and walked out, the Captain remarked that he understood the victory at Le Hamel to have been the turning point of the Great War.

"Some historians have said that," Griff said, as the media people swarmed in with greetings and smiles.

The Captain leaned his head toward Griff and said: "Don't think too badly of him. He's not a bad fellow. It's just that his mouth gets the better of him at times."

"Doesn't it happen to us all, Captain, except the rare ones like you. And Roh, of course. She keeps well-buttoned." They all had a chuckle at that and agreed to assemble on deck in an hour for the media session.

Griff and Roh headed back to their cabin to get their snow gear. They agreed it would be best to put it on upstairs on the deck in case that is what the TV people wanted. Griff and Roh and their group gathered on the aft deck of the vessel and chatted while they waited for the media to assemble. Commodore Awati arrived in his helicopter and joined the group briefly before going off to see the Captain. The media arrived in dribs and drabs with their cameras and set them up and shortly after the Captain and the Commodore appeared. When the media indicated they were ready, Commodore Awati spoke to the survivors.

"Well, this is a moment we have all been looking forward to. We have seen some of the photos that Dr Dupre took of you in India at the time you were discovered in your epic trek and we are now keen to see you put your gear on and to watch you move about, so go to it, please."

The group unzipped their bags and pulled on their leggings and car tyre boots, their heavy coats, blanket ponchos, rubber sleeves and hand guards, gloves, sheepskin muffs, the snow glasses made from truck-tube rubber, their sheepskin hats and lower face scarves. Fully clad they looked almost as wide as they were tall. They looked a wild and ferocious group. Like a cross between stone-age mammoth hunters and medieval knights. They trundled around the deck, gave victory waves and then answered calls to put their snowshoes on too. Griff was reminded of how difficult it was to move quickly and fluidly with all that gear on and marvelled for a moment at how much work they got through out in the snow encumbered like that. After five minutes he lowered his face-mask and called to the media.

"Okay, folks, hope you've got enough, because we're reaching melting point. We are going to have to stop now."

The media people responded that they had plenty, but could they now have interviews.

The group stripped down to pants and shirts sat on the chairs brought out for them by sailors.

"Sorry, but we'll have to have some water too," Roh told them.

The Captain and Commodore joined them and they sipped cold water and got their breath back. Commodore Awati said he would like to get photos of each of the items of their snow gear and a brief description of the materials which they could put in a survival manual for instruction in the navy. Griff said he would be happy to do the notes. He also asked Rohini if she would do notes for them on the foods they had survived on. She was happy to oblige, she said.

The media people were now clamouring for interviews and the group sat ready for questions.

"Apart from the difficulties in coping with the sudden cold and the need for innovative responses, your survival seems to have gone pretty smoothly, Griffith. Were there no desperate life and death moments during your months trapped in the snow bound house?" was the first question.

"I guessed you would start wanting to dig into things like that. Yes, there were some desperate moments but as you can see, we survived them."

"Won't you tell us a little about those moments?"

"Well, they are still very fresh and painful for all of us and I would like to avoid the gruesome detail, but I suppose I can say that the house was attacked and taken over by four men with guns and there was a subsequent attack by another man causing one death. We were eventually able to overcome the attackers. In that struggle, three of them died and we captured two men. We eventually allowed two of the attackers to stay with us. Sadly, two of our men were killed during that prolonged struggle."

The media group was stunned into silence for a few seconds before it broke into a frenzy of shouted questions.

"We can't hear what you are saying when you all shout like that so you will have to take it in turns. I'll give the nod to each questioner," Griff said.

Rohini interrupted at that point.

"Just before then, I should say there is a crucial matter that Griffith didn't mention. He was forced out into the snow almost naked to die by the men who invaded our house and it was only due to his skill and courage that he was able to survive for three days and come back to rescue us," Rohini said.

The media erupted into another frenzy of questions and Griff waved them down.

Then, from behind, Subhash in halting English called out.

"They very bad man. They kill people, they rape Madam. We all very frighten. Saheb save us. He kill them all."

The media pack charged the group at that point with microphones held out in front like bayonets. Rohini turned to Griff and said: "Let's finish this now. It's getting out of hand. I'll tell the group to say nothing more."

Griff caught Commodore Awati's eye and gave him a "shut down" wave. His voice boomed out over the media questions.

"Alright, ladies and gentlemen. That's enough for now. We are taking the survivors off for morning tea and perhaps there will be a possibility to ask more questions later. We'll see. The Captain will let you know."

Chapter 8: Ship to Singapore

Griff and Roh pushed through the melee to join the Commodore and the Captain and they went inside and headed for the wardroom. Once inside, in the relative quiet, Commodore Awati put his arm around Roh's shoulder and gave her a squeeze.

"We hadn't realised that you'd had such a tough time. Sorry to hear that. You are alright, I hope. We have a doctor on the ship and you can have a medical check-up if you wish."

"No, I'm fine thanks Commodore," she said, with a rueful shake of her head. "I took precautions at the time and I didn't get beaten. Plenty of water has passed under the bridge since then, other adventures, you might say. So it is fading into the background now."

"You are a very tough woman with a lot of character, which both of you have, and my men and I admire you immensely. If there is anything you want to tell us or that you need to unburden yourself of, please let us know."

"Thanks, Commodore, you have all been very kind and considerate. We couldn't have asked for more. I think we realised deep in our guts that all the messy bits and pieces that make up survival in difficult circumstances where others are also struggling for survival would eventually come out. We just hadn't talked among ourselves about the best way to handle it, if, in fact, that sort of thing can be handled. Believe me, there is plenty more we haven't mentioned," Griff added.

Commodore Awati said he was curious about Griff's mention of the two attackers who were not killed.

"Who are the two you allowed to join the group, can I ask?"

"Yes, that is Deepak Godse. He is in fact the son of the man we initially turned free. It was a mistake to have turned him free and later we had another life and death struggle before Godse senior took his life after being wounded during our attack on his house. The other person is Shakunt. He is a fine man who was misled by Godse senior into making an attack on us that killed one of our group. After I captured him he realised he had been duped by Godse senior, who was his uncle, and he came over to our side," Griff said.

"My god, it is messy, isn't it," the Captain said. "And I can't see the media letting up until they get the whole story, now that they have had a sniff of it."

"Yes, and it could be written to reflect badly upon us. Griff has mentioned that he thought we should select a reliable agency such as ABC-TV and tell the whole story to them," Rohini said. "They will report it fairly straight."

"That sounds like a good idea," the Captain said. "You will, of course, be inundated with lucrative offers from the commercial TV channels to sell your story to them exclusively. They will give you no peace."

"Yes, we were aware of that," Griff and Roh said together.

"Anyway, if you like, Roh and I will sit down with you, Captain and Commodore Awati, this afternoon and tell you the whole story, blow by blow. But we would like you to keep it to yourselves for the time being, if you wouldn't mind." Griff said.

That afternoon, the four of them sat in the Captain's suite and went through their experiences in detail. They described how they set up the house with livestock, their scavenging forays including finding the bodies, the money and gold in the stranded vehicles, the scrounging for food and equipment in the village, the house invasion and rapes, Griff's exile into the snow and the subsequent killing of the two attackers, the trial and release of Godse, the attack by Godse's nephew and how he had become a loyal member of the group, their bomb attack on Godse and his dying gift of money to his son and to them. Finally, they went through their preparations for the trek to Pune and how they had become stranded at the tunnel. They also mentioned Ulhas, the engineering student and his suitcase of gold.

The Commodore and the Captain had sat silently throughout. When Griff and Roh had finished, Commodore Awati and the Captain looked as though they had come through a battle.

Eventually Commodore Awati croaked: "That is a harrowing, but extraordinary story. I have been in battles that were not half as demanding as that."

"Yes," the Captain added. "The media will go mad with it. How is the attitude of Godse's son towards you?"

"Not too good. We don't know how trustworthy he is," Rohini said. "But Griff has kept a detailed diary of all these events."

"That's good. You may well need it," the Captain added. "You had better keep that very secure. You wouldn't want it stolen. You can put it in my personal safe in my cabin if you wish, until we get to Singapore."

The Captain reiterated that he thought they would be bombarded with cash offers from the various networks to sell exclusive rights to them. The thwarted ones could get very sneaky in trying to outwit each other and to get the story.

"We are not hungry for money. We would rather have the story told properly than in a garbled and sensational form," Rohini said.

Griff lifted his shirt, pulled out the diary that was tucked into his belt and handed it to the Captain.

"I wondered how you managed to keep such a flat stomach," the Captain remarked.

"Oh, it is as flat as a plank anyway," Rohini said laughing.

They watched as the Captain locked the diary in his safe and then went back to their cabin. Once inside with the door closed, Roh flopped on her bunk and asked how Griff planned to deal with the media.

"I think we should speak to the Australian Broadcasting Corporation journalists now and ask them if they are interested in getting the detailed story. If so, they can get things set up in Singapore and we will do it there soon after out arrival. What do you think?"

"Yes, that seems to me to be the best way to handle it."

"Then we will say as little as possible to the other channels, since the whole story will be out in the open," Griff added.

They made a coffee and were sitting drinking it when there was a quiet knock on their door. Rohini opened it. It was a journalist asking if she could talk to them privately. They invited her in and offered her a coffee.

"My channel, as you would know, is a leading commercial broadcaster in Australia. We think you have a great inspirational story to tell the Australian people and we are willing to offer $750,000 for the exclusive rights. I have a contract with me now."

"Thanks for you kind offer," Rohini said. "We are still undecided about what to do, but if you give us your card we will get in touch with you, if we decide to accept your offer."

"Oh, have you had other offers better than that?"

"No, you are the first to approach us."

"We could increase that offer if you get others making bids."

"Thanks, we appreciate that, but just at the moment we are not concerned about making money out of our ordeal, so let's leave it at that for the time being, shall we?" Rohini added and opened the cabin door.

Another Australian journalist was waiting at the door and had probably been trying to listen to their conversation. Over the next hour before lunch they had approaches and offers from another Australian broadcaster, two from the US, one from Canada, one from Germany and two from the UK. The offers climbed over the million dollar mark. Griff and Roh treated them all courteously, but declined their offers. On the way to lunch they sought out the ABC team and laid out their suggestion for a full coverage for the ABC alone after arrival in Singapore. The ABC crew were delighted.

"What do you expect for that?" they asked.

"Nothing but an unvarnished account of our time during the crisis," Rohini said. The ABC crew agreed to set up the interview in Singapore and to get back to them with the day and time.

"Don't say anything to the other crews about this please, as we are already being badgered to sell exclusive rights. I am not promising you sole and exclusive rights but you have got the first crack at it and you will get the detail that so far hasn't come out. Are you happy with that?" Griff asked.

"Oh, yes. We are delighted. Thank you," they said.

Griff and Roh got their group together, told them what they were planning for Singapore and suggested that they should all be present for that series of interviews. They mentioned that there would almost certainly be offers made to them to talk to channels for money and they thought it best to say no more than what they would say at the Singapore interview with ABC-TV. The group agreed, with the exception of Deepak Godse who remained silent.

After lunch Roh and Griff returned to their cabin. From the state of their bags, it seemed clear that someone had been in the cabin rooting through their few belongings, but nothing had been taken. There were also a couple of notes on the cabin floor that had been pushed under the door. They contained requests for one-on-one interviews and more offers of money.

"The sooner we get to Singapore and get this interview with the ABC done and it hits the airwaves, the better it will be. Hopefully the frenzy will go out of it then," Griff said.

They locked the door and lying on one of the bunks snuggled up for a nap.

"I'm worried about Godse," Griff said. "He could give a twisted version of events that might create a lot of trouble for us."

"Don't worry now. We'll handle it if and when it occurs," Roh replied

"Yes, not much else we can do, is there?"

They drifted off to sleep and were woken an hour or so later by a steward with a note from the Captain saying they expected to dock in Singapore in an hour and a half. It also asked them to join the Captain in the wardroom for afternoon coffee. They freshened up and went to the wardroom where most of the officers were gathered.

"As you know we will be docking soon and there will be Customs and UN officials, as well as Australian High Commission staff waiting to meet you. The High Commissioner has asked us to let you know she would like you to stay with her in the residence while you are waiting for your plane to take you to Australia. If you are agreeable to that, I shall send word back to her now."

"Please say we are very grateful for her gesture and happily accept it," Griff said.

"There is some other information that has just come to hand that you will find interesting. The fellow you had saved from the tunnel who had the suitcase full of gold. It seems he had talked the Customs official into sharing the loot and they went out in the helicopter to return to the tunnel. The story is a bit confused but it looks as though the engineering student took off with the helicopter, abandoning the pilot and the Customs man at the tunnel, after loading it with whatever they had gathered. He tried to fly the chopper to Sri Lanka probably. On the way it may have run out of fuel and crashed. It's not known if the hijacker is dead or alive. Pune base have another chopper out looking for the chopper. They have picked up the pilot and the Customs man and they are safe, but of course they have a few questions to answer. The Customs man is almost certainly in a lot of trouble. It's likely the pilot was only acting under the Customs officer's orders."

"That certainly is interesting. We never trusted that bloke and he seemed bound for a sticky end," Griff said.

"Well, I'd like to say on behalf of Commodore Awati and my crew that it has been a pleasure and a privilege to have had your company on this vessel and that we hope life in Australia will prove to be safe and rewarding for you after the terrible ordeal you have been through. Be warned that the media frenzy will continue when you arrive," the Captain said, with a smile.

"We have spoken to the ABC crew and they are set to get our story as soon as possible after our arrival and we hope that as soon as that becomes known and the program is broadcast, things will ease on that front," Griff said.

"Let's hope so," the Captain said with a faint, perhaps disbelieving, smile.

They helped themselves to coffee and cakes and chatted with crew members.

"We didn't have a cake or a biscuit for three months," Rohini said. "So I hope you won't think us greedy if we have a couple now."

"Did you ever go hungry or lose weight during the spell in the snow?" they were asked.

"No, if anything we may have put on a kilo. We usually do a lot of walking and since we couldn't do that, we had to jog up and down the stairs to the third floor if we weren't outside doing hard work," Roh said.

The crew told them that most of the Indian cricket team had arrived in Australia at the outset of the polar shift, so it didn't look as though the loss of the subcontinent would lead to any let up of pressure on the Australian cricket team. The Indian team would continue to play as India in Exile. But other Indian athletes hoped eventually to compete for Australia because it enabled them to move out of the refugee camps and into the community.

"Well, Australia beats India in most sports including our much loved hockey, so it is only fair that we beat Australia in cricket, isn't it?" Roh asked.

Most of the officers were English so it was only natural that they agreed.

"Eminently fair," they said, almost in unison. "Wouldn't you agree, Griffith?"

"I can't see the logic in it, but there's no escaping the reality of it," Griff replied, laughing.

Roh and Griff went back to their cabin, gathered their gear, collected the diary from the Captain's safe and went on deck to get their group together. As the ship nosed into her berth they could see a large throng of people and a huge media pack with cameras rolling. Customs and other officials came on board along with the Australian High Commissioner and another person who said she was the Singapore representative of the Indian Government in Exile. The Captain introduced them and after farewelling him and thanking him for his great hospitality, they were led off the ship and into the Customs hall for processing. Waiting outside the Customs counters, the media formed a solid wall blocking the exit. Some were already shouting to draw their attention. Griff told the High Commissioner that they had already arranged to tell their story to ABC-TV. The High Commissioner said the ABC had been in touch with her and that she had offered her residence as the site for the interview. They happily accepted that and the High Commissioner said if it suited Roh and

Griff, the session could be held the next morning. They said that was fine with them, but they would have to give a general media session as soon as they were cleared through Customs. The High Commissioner said that a large VIP reception room had been arranged for that.

She went on to say she knew that Rohini and Griffith were the only two with passports and that she had had received copies of the lists of their group from Pune and the ship and asked for their papers. Rohini also handed to her the various ID documents she had been able to collect from some of the members of the group and the High Commissioner had one of her staff present them to the Singapore Customs. Twenty minutes later they were given transit visas that enabled them to stay thirty-six hours before departure to Australia. The High Commissioner led the group to the VIP reception area and handed over papers giving Rohini residence status in Australia and the rest of the group refugee status in Australia.

Griff told the High Commissioner that he and Rohini would stay in Darwin initially to see their group settled into the camp and then he and Rohini would travel to Perth to arrange a more permanent set up for them all on a farm there. The High Commissioner explained that refugees who did not have Australian citizenship or residency entitlement had to remain in the camps in the north of Australia until they could be taken into an Australian home or had the wherewithal to buy a house in the south. Griff said that Rohini and he planned to buy a small property just south of Perth and set up a cooperative farm with the rest of their group, or at least with those who wished to stay with them. The High Commissioner said that the rest of the group should be able to join Rohini and Griffith, as soon as the farm was able to accommodate them.

"When you are ready to face the media, let me know and I'll call them in," the High Commissioner said.

"We are ready when you are," Griff responded.

"Alright, perhaps you could sit in those chairs that have been arranged there and we can get on with it."

Roh got the group together and they sat while the High Commissioner had her staff open the doors to invite the media throng in.

"Some of you already know the group, but for those who don't, I will ask Mr Bolton and Dr Sane to introduce themselves and the group, and then you can proceed from there," the High Commissioner told the asembled media.

Griff introduced himself and said he would ask Rohini to introduce herself and the other members because most of them had only a brief grasp of English and then they would answer questions. He said he wanted to make it clear that they would not be giving any one-on-one interviews at this stage and they were not open to any offers of exclusive rights to their story. They had already had a number of lucrative offers which they had rejected. They were not interested in receiving any more. They would tell their story in detail shortly to one Australian broadcaster. He called on Rohini and she introduced the other members.

Griff then called for questions.

"Is the reason you are not interested in offers to sell your story because you brought out millions of dollars' worth of loot with you from India?" an American voice asked.

"No, that is not the reason," Griff replied.

"Well, what is the reason?"

"We would like the full and correct story told and we don't want to get into a bidding war."

"Did you bring millions of dollars out with you?"

"No, Dr Sane and I brought out about $1million US dollars."

"Did you get that from looting the dead?"

"No. It was given to us by a man who was dying. Well, he was dead in fact by the time we got to him. "

"Did you kill him?"

"We had wounded him and he could see he was going to be captured. He shot himself."

"Why were you attacking him?"

"He had staged a number of deadly attacks on us with the intention of killing us and had killed two members of our group and tried to kill me."

"Why would a person who had attacked you and whom you were trying to kill give you a million dollars?"

"It's a complicated story, but he had a lot of bad things to answer for that must have been on his mind. We were caring for his son in spite of that."

"What bad things had he done?"

"Well, apart from the deadly attacks on us, his invasion of our house resulted in his two brothers being killed, he had driven me out into the snow with only a t-shirt, and sexually assaulted Dr Sane and encouraged his two brothers to do the same. He also made subsequent deadly attacks on us after we caught him and later let him go with a warning to leave us be."

"Where is his son now?"

"He is still with our group. Give them a wave, Deepak." Deepak gave a sickly smile and fluttered his hand.

"How did you come to kill his uncles?"

"I killed them in the process of recapturing the house to rescue Dr Sane and the other members of our group."

"How do you feel about that?"

"No sane, reasonable person could feel anything but reluctance and shock about killing another person, but in the circumstances it was necessary. They were armed, had killed one of ours and had showed themselves ready to kill me."

"How does Deepak feel about the death of his uncles?"

"I don't know. You can ask him."

"What do you say Deepak?" Deepak merely shrugged.

"You don't want to talk about it?"

"Yes, I don't want to talk about it now."

Just then Subash interjected. "We all there when these thing happen. Griff Saheb good man saved us. Deepak father and uncles bad, bad men. Killing them was right thing."

"What are you planning to do in Australia?"

"When the group is settled into a camp, Dr Sane and I will go to Perth to see my family. We plan to buy a small farm and operate it as a cooperative. Dr Sane is qualified as a medical doctor and a vet and we will try to get over the trauma of the past three months. Perhaps we might wind it up now. You have had a good session," Griff said, glancing at the High Commissioner. She took the cue and said the group needed to get to their accommodation.

"Just a final question before you go, Mr Bolton," one journalist called.

"Yes, fire away."

"If Deepak's father was dead when you got to him, how did he give you the million dollars?"

"You'll just have to take my word that he did. Alright, I think we would like to leave it at that for the time being. Thanks for your interest. We would like to go now," Griff said.

The High Commissioner led the group out to waiting cars and a small bus. She explained that rooms had been booked in a hotel for the group for one night so that they could be present for the interview with the ABC team next morning. Then they would be taken by bus to the camp. Griff and Roh were to stay at her residence but she was not able to accommodate the whole group. They all went to the hotel and High Commission staff helped them to check in, after agreeing to meet Roh and Griff the next morning at the High Commission for the full session with the ABC-TV team. The High Commissioner, Roh and Griff then left for the High Commissioner's residence.

"How are you feeling after that media session?" the High Commissioner asked.

"I'm okay. How are you, Roh? Teek hay?"

Roh smiled and nodded. "Teek hay. The sooner we get the full story out through the ABC the better. The piecemeal picking of bits out of it by others could result in misinterpretation of things, I suspect," she added.

"You're right. We'll sew it up tomorrow morning," Griff said.

"I am dying to hear about your epic but I won't bother you now. I would be honoured if you would let me and some of my senior staff sit in tomorrow when you give the story to the ABC-TV team."

'Of course," Roh said. "We are really grateful for the help and warmth you have shown us. It means a lot to us. We haven't seen family members for months and there were times when we doubted if we would survive or ever see them again."

"Yes, you've been great," Griff added.

170

At the residence they settled into comfortable chairs and stretched.

"What would you like to drink - tea, coffee, beer, wine or spirits? We can have a meal shortly, if you like. It is ready when you are," the High Commissioner said. "And please call me Lucy," she added. They had a pleasant dinner and retired.

At 6.30 in the morning there was a rap on their door. It was the High Commissioner.

"Sorry to disturb you but there has been a rather nasty development that you will want to look at. It's all over the morning papers and no doubt on the TV news too. Young Deepak Godse has been making some allegations."

Chapter 9: Accusations of murder and theft

Roh and Griff showered, dressed and went downstairs. The High Commissioner gave them the local papers. "SURVIVAL HERO, KILLER, LOOTER," was one headline. There was a TV set in the room and Deepak Godse was performing, wiping the tears away as he gave his story.

Griff and Roh sat with the High Commissioner and read the lead story in one of the papers:

"One of the members of the group of survivors from India who arrived in Singapore yesterday evening said that Griffith Bolton, the so-called hero who saved them all, was a brutal murderer who had stolen a large part of his family's money.

"He said most of the story that Bolton had told about the alleged house invasion was untrue and Bolton had no reason to kill his uncles or his father. He said it was a lie that his father and uncles had raped Dr Sane. She was a willing participant. He said he had even had sex with her himself. She had lured him into having sex with her.

"Mr Godse, an innocent boy of only seventeen, said his father was a government officer who was making an official inspection of Dr Sane's house to see who was there and what food supplies and other resources they had. Bolton had refused to open the house to let them in and had fired a gun, trying to kill them. His father and uncles who were running low on supplies had then offered to go away if Dr Sane and Bolton would take Depak in and look after him. Later, when they were desperate to survive, they had returned to Sane's house and he had let them in. At the same time, Bolton ran out of the house. Later Bolton returned and killed his two uncles and had forced him and his father out into the blizzard.

"His father had gone to a nearby house. Bolton pursued him there and killed him and stole two suitcases of his father's money which belonged to him now, as the only son. Bolton had later given him half of the money.

"The boy, who said he was still in shock and severe grief from the loss of his father and uncles, had been held against his will by Bolton and Sane and told he was not to say anything to the media. He asked for protection from them and said he no longer wished to have anything to do with them. He was frightened that Bolton might try to kill him if he got the opportunity.

"The boy became very emotional when he described his father as a kind and gentle man, a generous member of the community who had helped many people and a dedicated government official who was trying to do his duty even during the great natural disaster that had struck India.

"A leader of the Indian community said these were very serious allegations and should be investigated by the international authorities handling the refugee program and, if need be, referred to the police."

Roh sat shaking her head in disbelief. "What a despicable, treacherous and ungrateful little wretch. We took him in and cared for him. He wouldn't have survived if we hadn't done that. His father was an unprincipled and corrupt official of the worst type, who was preventing his country from moving forward the way it should have, by enriching himself at the expense of others."

"What do you say, Griffith?" the High Commissioner asked.

"What Roh said is correct. What Deepak said is all a damned lie. I will be very happy to appear before a tribunal in Australia and we can rebut everything he has said. I have proof of the crucial points, apart from the evidence that Rohini and the other group members will give."

"Yes, I felt sure you would be able to set things straight. Let us have breakfast and get ready for the TV crew. I have just had a look out the front. There is a huge flock of media people out there shouting for you. What do you want to do about them?"

"Nothing for the time being, apart from giving them a wave. We will give the story to the ABC crew. They can extract footage from that for their news bulletins which will answer the allegations made by Godse. As soon as we have finished with the ABC team, I would like

173

us to move on to Australia. I really don't want to get tied up here in some tribunal hearing if we can avoid that. I'll be very happy to go before a tribunal in Australia," Griff said.

"I agree with you," the High Commissioner responded. "I will work to see that you get back to Australia promptly and that you will be pleased to attend a hearing there, if that is desired."

While they were talking, the survivor group arrived from the hotel. Deepak Godse was not with them. The last time the group had seen him was when they got back to the hotel the previous evening, they said. Media people were waiting there and they had asked for Godse.

The ABC crew arrived at 9.45 am and were let in. Other members of the big group at the gate tried to push in too. Guards blocked them. Griff told them he had nothing to say to them at the moment apart from the fact that Deepak Godse had lied to them and they would get the full correct story shortly. The crew set up in the main reception room of the residence and the interview began.

Griff told the story from the very beginning. He called on Rohini to tell her part. She also spoke about what sort of a person Deepak Godse's father was and previous dealings she'd had with him that indicated what a crook he was. The other members of the group backed up everything. Shakunt, Godse's nephew, told how he had been hoodwinked by his uncle and sent to try to kill off the group in the house. In the course of that, he had killed one of the group before Griff had captured him and taken him into the house where he learnt the true situation. He had then willingly joined them because he could see that they were good people. He also told how well Griff and Roh had treated Godse junior. They broke for a light lunch and drinks and then pressed on. It was late afternoon by the time they finished.

One thing Griff and Roh had not mentioned was that Griff had kept a daily diary of events and that he had the letter from Godse senior saying that he and Roh were to keep one suitcase of money and give the other to his son. Griff wanted no-one to know about that and the diary until they were called before any tribunal where they could clear the record for good. He knew that Deepak Godse did not know of the letter's existence and once it was revealed it would blow Godse's story completely away. He had also had Godse's signatures on his notes of the hearing that they had held before putting Godse senior out of their house. If people apart from Roh and him knew about those documents they might make strenuous, even violent efforts to steal them.

While they were having coffee after the session, the High Commissioner told them she was deeply moved by the account of their struggles and their will to survive against the odds. She said she already had arrangements in hand for them to fly to Darwin that night. The group would be processed in Darwin and Rohini and Griffith would have tickets to proceed on to Perth when they were ready. The ABC interviewer also told them it was a great story. He felt it rebutted completely what Godse had alleged. When it was shown, he believed they would get full recognition in Australia and from the world media for a really heroic effort. The rest of the crew clustered around and asked for autographs.

As the TV crew packed their gear, the High Commissioner returned to tell them that tickets had been arranged for a flight later that evening and they would arrive in Darwin in the early morning. They would leave for the airport shortly after dinner. She would provide a light buffet meal at the residence so perhaps the group could go back to the hotel now, get their bags and return.

"What are we going to do about Godse?" Griff asked the High Commissioner.

"I have a contact who is a leading figure in the Indian community here. I will have my staff call him to see if he knows anything," she said, and left to get that organised.

Griff and Roh went to their room, got their gear together and then flung themselves down on the bed. An hour or so later there was a call on their phone. It was the High Commissioner.

"If you would like to come down for a pre-dinner drink I'll fill you in on Godse," she said.

They went down.

"We spoke to our contact in the Indian community. It seems they want to take Godse under their wing. They say Godse doesn't want to be with your group any more and that the Indian community in

Darwin will take care of him, providing him with accommodation and all his needs. He will travel separately to Australia with some members of the Indian community. In fact, he is leaving on a flight within the hour. How do you feel about that?"

"Glad to be rid of the wretch," Griff said.

"Yes, we will be a happier lot without him and I don't think his lies can do any more damage than they have so far. Hopefully our story will negate everything he has said," Roh added.

They arrived in Darwin next morning to be greeted by UN refugee officials, Federal and Northern Territory police and two screaming mobs. One mob was the media, the other a sizeable chunk of the Indian community. The latter were waving placards saying: BOLTON KILLER LOOTER; BOLTON KILLER, SANE SEX DOLL; BOLTON SHOULD BE TRIED; BOLTON SANE LIARS THIEVES; BOLTON KILLER SANE HOOKER; RETURN GODSE'S MONEY, GAOL BOLTON SANE and such like. The UN refugee people and police said that there had been a request by the Indian Government in Exile for an inquiry into Godse's allegations. Bolton and Sane were to be confined to Darwin until the tribunal was appointed to deal with the matter and they had to surrender their passports and the suitcase of money until the matter was resolved. They had to report to the police each day in person. It was expected that the tribunal would be set up within a week or two. The rest of the group would be allocated tents in a camp one hour's drive from Darwin. They would be able to stay together in adjoining tents.

Griff and Roh told the group they would visit them within a day or so to bring them mobile phones and see that they were settling in. They asked police to drop them at a hotel and Griff used his credit card to draw funds for living. Having checked in at the hotel they set out to buy a second-hand SUV. There were plenty in the car yards and prices were cheap. Griff bought a four-year-old turbo-cooler diesel Pajero that had only sixty thousand kilometres on the clock. He guessed it was a town car from that mileage, unless the clock had been wound back. From the condition of it, he didn't think so. It went well. He had it registered and insured by mid-afternoon. When they got back to the hotel they found that the media and the screaming mob of placard-wielding Indians were camped outside.

They had coffee and a sandwich and then set out for the town centre to buy mobile phones for the group in the camp. When they got to the vehicle behind the hotel they noticed some kind person had let one of the tyres down and while Griff was changing the wheel, several members of the media turned up. No surprise.

"Any comments to make, Mr Bolton, Dr Sane?"

"Kind of you to ask. What media outlets do you work for?" Griff said. They told him they worked for Sydney and Melbourne radio stations.

"Well, my comment is this. Some moron has let one of my tyres down and it seems an extraordinary coincidence that you should turn up while I am changing the wheel. If it happens again, I'll assume it was you three and lodge an harassment complaint with the police. I might even ask for a restraining order preventing you from coming within one hundred metres of us. You may find that a bit deflating."

"Oh, is that a threat?"

"Whatever pleases you."

They drove to a nearby service station, left the wheel to be checked for a puncture and to be pumped up and then walked to the CBD looking for a phone shop, with directions given by the service station bloke. They bought two phones for the group as well as one each for themselves.

Back at the hotel, Rohini put a call through to her parents in the US and Griff rang his brother Dave and his parents in Perth to explain the situation. They told him Deepak Godse had been all over the commercial TV news with his sensational allegations about the killing of his father and uncles and the theft of the suitcases of money as well as Roh being sexually available to whoever wanted her. The Indian community had mobs outside the Parliament in Perth and in Canberra calling for Griff and Roh to be charged, tried and gaoled. His brother told him that Griff and Roh's story was being run in four parts on ABC-TV. The first part had been aired the previous night and there would be three more half-hour segments to be shown consecutively.

They were powerful and everyone he had spoken to, said the first episode had been moving, convincing and inspirational.

Griff told him not to worry. He said there would be a preliminary hearing by a tribunal within a week or so and that he would be able to rebut Godse's allegations.

Next morning they went to the Refugee Processing Centre Office of the UN High Commissioner for Refugees and spoke to the Director. They asked if a message could be sent to the Captain of the ship that had taken them to Singapore and to the Commodore of the Sri Lanka naval station, asking them to send copies of their reports to him for use in the upcoming hearing.

"We already have them," the Director said, "but although they help to provide proof of your bona fides, they are not factual. They are merely your side of the story."

"Yes, that is true, but they will help to provide background to the Tribunal during the hearing and that may save time for us all," Griff said. He added that he would be pleased if they would give him a copy of the reports and the Director did so.

Griff and Roh thanked the Director and left to check in at the police station. Next stop was a supermarket where they bought tea, sugar, coffee, powdered milk and biscuits for the group at the camp. At a newsagency next to the supermarket they bought newspapers that were full of stories and speculation about them and their group and Godse's allegations, which had a new twist. Someone had asked Godse if he thought Griff and Roh's group had indulged in cannibalism after Godse had told them that his uncles' bodies had disappeared after Griff had killed them. Godse had said people like Griff and Roh could do anything. The media had built that into a screaming headline: SURVIVOR GROUP MAY BE CANNIBALS. They also starred on the cover of *Time* magazine with photos and a heading: SURVIVORS – HEROES OR HORRORS.

Griff and Roh drove south-west out of Darwin towards the camp. Topping a slight rise a couple of kilometres before they got there they could see the camp stretching away in the distance to the east, west and south. It was vast. A sea of tents and corrugated iron sheds. They checked in at the office at the front gate. No cars were allowed in apart from official vehicles. The camp was well laid out in a grid with the rows of tents separated by two-lane graded dirt roads. Every couple of blocks there was a huge galvanised iron shed. Here and there trees that had been planted after the first tents had been erected were starting to rise above the tent roofs and provide some greenery and shelter. They would provide some shade in the summer but they wouldn't do anything for the humidity which was savage. Everyone wore shorts, light cotton shirts and hats, but the shirts were damp with sweat. At the office their bags were checked to see that they were not taking in banned goods. Staff told them that a bus would run them out to their friends. It ran every half hour and it was due to leave in ten minutes.

Roh and Griff were standing at the bus stop, batting the flies away and cursing the humidity when a shadow fell over Griff and a huge pair of arms locked themselves around him from behind and nearly squeezed the air from his lungs. Roh jumped back with a look of horror on her face.

"Griffith Bolton, you old bastard," boomed out from near Griff's left ear and he recognised the voice with its German accent as an old friend from Canberra days, Karl Strauch.

"Okay, you can put me down now so I can breathe and talk again, you great hairy galoot."

Karl dropped him and Griff turned and grasped him in a bear hug. "What brings you here, you broken-down adventurer?" Karl combined electrical contracting with hunting and buying secondhand cars in Canberra, but had often spoken of the lure of the wild country in the far north. He used to speak of crocodile and wild buffalo hunting. It was inevitable, Griff realised, that Karl would finish up somewhere around here.

"Money. Lots of money," Karl boomed. "I've got the contract to do the electrical wiring for the camp. I have five men here working twelve-hour days taking wiring into the tents and other buildings and maintaining it all. But I see you are in the news, you silly bastard, after your adventures. I wish I had been there."

"Yeah, I wish you had been too. We could have used you to throw trucks and cars around."

Karl was just under two metres but he was a cricket bat's length across the shoulders and had huge arms and massive legs. He was a one-man, bearded horde. Griff had met him in Canberra when they were fishing and picnicking on the shores of Lake Burley Griffin. Karl and his wife and daughter were newly arrived from Germany and their English was limited and rough. Griff had offered to teach them and they had become good friends. They used to go camping, fishing and rabbit shooting together. They had parted when Griff had left to go to India and lost contact when Karl moved up north.

"Let me introduce my wife Rohini, the light of my life."

"Ah yes, a beautiful lady. I have seen you on television. Dr Sane isn't it?"

"Yes and it is lovely to meet you, Karl. Griff had mentioned you a few times but the reality is bigger than the myth."

"Good German sausage, black bread, cabbage rolls and lots of beer. That is the recipe for big muscles."

"Yes, but not so good for building brains," Griff said, stepping back smartly, in case Karl gave him an affectionate swipe which might break an arm or at least knock him over.

"Ah, so why are you here?" Karl asked. Griff explained.

"I will take you there. Follow me." They walked through the gates to Karl's van and he headed for the address they gave him. On the way Griff told him about the threatening mob hanging about outside the hotel.

"You can stay at my place in Darwin. It's empty. I live here at the camp for the time being and my house is empty. I'd be pleased to have someone in it. Here are the keys. You'll need the security code. Treat it like your own home. Just make sure you bring the keys to me here before you leave." Karl gave them the address and his telephone number and told them to call him if they had any trouble with protesters. He said the house had a two-metre fence and gate and if they parked their SUV in the carport it would be out of sight from the road.

There were lots of people on the camp roads, walking, standing and talking. Karl drew up outside the first tent number given to him at the office and Griff gave him his and Roh's phone numbers. Karl said he'd call to see them in a day or two and they could have a meal together. He wanted to hear the whole story from them because he knew that a lot of what was being printed in the media and said on TV was rubbish. People stood around in groups watching them as they alighted.

"I'll wait till you make contact with your friends. This can be a bad place at times. There is a lot of theft and even daylight robbery. There are things for them to do, but a lot choose not to do them. They just hang around talking," Karl said.

Roh went to the first tent and called out in Marathi. Subhash threw the tent flap open and beamed as he saw it was Roh and Griff, who gave Karl the thumbs up sign. He took off. They all went back into the tent which was even hotter and more humid than outside, though it didn't seem to bother Subhash. He told them to sit on the metal army beds while he got the other members of the group. The tent was roomy - they could stand in it. It had a raised wooden floor, a lockable steel cupboard, a fluorescent tube light in the middle and a rack for hanging clothes and towels. The rest of the group flocked in. They were happy in the camp, they said. They had made some friends already.

The food was okay. Not good but just alright. Lots of rice and vegetables and roti flat bread. They were not allowed to cook in the tents or in the area around the tents. All the meals were served in the big corrugated iron sheds. The sheds also had TVs and table tennis tables, a shop where one could buy chocolates and biscuits and toiletry things. The showers and lavatories and laundries were also there along with a first aid centre. There was a temporary hospital near the front gate. Next to the sheds were playing fields for soccer and volley ball. And there was a camp officer, a security officer and two nurses in each shed to manage operations, answer questions and pass on messages.

"Plenty of chors (thieves) here, Bhai, Saheb," Shakunt said. "We go in twos to have shower, otherwise people steal our clothes or things from our clothes. One has shower while other one guards clothing and then other person showers. We don't mind. We can do easily. Women do same."

"What about your share of the money and gold from India? Is that safe?" Roh asked.

"We lock in our steel cupboard. No-one knows we have anything. They think we just poor farmers. But lot of stealing from tents. People can get cupboards open with big screwdriver. What can we do?" Subhash asked.

"Well, you can give it to Saheb and me for safekeeping if you wish. We will be staying in a private house in Darwin and it should be safe there until you need it," Roh said.

Roh handed over the phones to Subhash and Shakunt and told them she had put Griff's and her phone numbers on the phone for them. They should ring straight away any time of day or night if there were any problems.

"We can go walk to block shed for cup of tea, if you are wanting," Subhash offered.

As they walked, a truck passed spraying water to settle the dust on the roads. Shakunt told them that the water was coming from bore wells and being treated by big filtering systems. He said he had lived in a lot of army camps and this was better run than any he had ever seen. People were saying there would be a swimming pool built next to the playing fields soon. He was going to join the block soccer team that played in a competition on Saturday afternoons. He might join the volley ball team too. It played in the evenings. He would put his name down for the cricket team too when the dry season came. People were saying it would soon begin raining heavily nearly every day, like the monsoon season in India.

At the block shed, Griff and Roh were stunned at the size of it. It seemed to be as big as a city shopping mall, but nothing like as glamorous. Just a concrete floor with corridors running off the huge canteen area and signs directing people to the various offices and facilities. Shakunt and Subhash organised the tea and while they were sipping it, a fellow came over and introduced himself to Roh and Griff as the Manager. He said he recognised them from the television reports. It was an honour to have them visit, he said. He wished them well for the forthcoming Tribunal hearing. Everyone he had spoken to, he said, had said it was an extraordinary feat to have survived the cataclysm and get their group to safety and grossly unfair that they now had to deal with the allegations by Godse. "Why do you think he has made these allegations?" he asked.

"Probably three reasons," Roh said. "Guilt about the attack on our group and the part he played in it and fear that we might take action against him over that. Greed for the money that his father gave us, and people in the Indian community urging him on, in the hope of getting their hands on some of the money."

"Yeah, that sounds about right," the Manager replied. "Well, best of luck. Do you know when the Tribunal hearing is on?"

"Probably next week," Griff said.

Roh introduced the Manager to the members of the group. He said he was delighted to have them in his block. He would keep an eye on them. Griff complimented him on the set-up of the camp. It was really excellent, but he wondered how the tent city would handle the monsoon rain. The Manager admitted that the heavy rain could create problems. It would be very muddy. However, each tent was standing on a fifteen-centimetre high concrete slab with thirty-centimetre high wooden floor on top of that. There were big underground agricultural drains running along each row of tents so perhaps it would be alright and, hopefully, there would be no flooding. Contractors were working on the edges of the camp laying fresh slabs, digging the drains, fitting the wooden floors and putting in the electrical wiring. This camp held one hundred thousand and was being doubled to two hundred thousand. The problem with the roads, the Manager said, was that the flood of refugees had come so suddenly and in such great numbers that there was not the time nor the resources to lay properly-built metal roads. The first shelters were made up from anything that could be found, from shipping containers to water tanks to old army tents, family camping tents, garage sheds, garden sheds, old buses, trucks, and train carriages. Some were just three sides with a roof. Now they were getting organised and factories were making the sheds, tents and floors to specifications.

They left the block centre and walked back to the tents. Shakunt and Wasanta went to collect the valuables from the other tents. They sat in Subhash's tent and it was clear from some of the items on the shelves that he was sharing the tent with Jyoti.

"Who is sharing with whom?" Roh asked Jyoti. Sonba and Laxmi were in the next tent, Seema and Suman in the third one and Wasanta and Shakunt in the last one, she told them.

"Sonba and Laxmi want to be marry," Jyoti said with a smile.

"And what about you and Subhash?" Roh asked.

"Yes, we are wanting too," she said, flushing red and looking away.

"No need to hurry and whatever you do, don't get pregnant. You are far too young. Have you got condoms?"

"Yes, Bai. We are using. Subhash doesn't like, but I make him use."

"Good girl. When we get you out of the camp and settled in Perth, you can get married. We'll have a fine wedding," Roh told her.

Shakunt and Wasanta returned to the tent and Subhash gave them their money and jewellery to put in the haversack. Roh told them she learnt that the group would be able to exchange their Indian rupees for Australian dollars in a new federal government agency established in Darwin. The government had realised that most of the refugees were carrying foreign currency and the best way to help the refugees to be self-sufficient was to change it into Australian dollars. Roh told them it would be possible also for them to sell their gold jewellery for cash through the same agency.

"Have you been told anything about English lessons?" Roh asked.

"Yes. English lessons every morning one hour coming soon, they say," Subhash said.

"Good, make sure you all go and study hard. You must learn English now. There is no going back to India. This is your new life. You have to learn English, even Suman has to learn - everyone," Griff said. They all nodded.

"Shakunt and Subhash, you have the best English in the group. You must help the others and when we get together as a group again in Perth, Rohini and I will help you too," Griff added.

"Yes, Saheb, we know. We will help."

"Okay, we will go now but we will come back in a few days. Call us on the phone if you have any problems and if you can't get us, see the Block Manager. He says he will help you," Griff said, hoisting the haversack onto his left shoulder.

They walked down to the main crossroad and waited for the bus back to the gate. Shakunt, Wasanta and Subhash walked with them.

Driving back to Darwin, Griff said he thought they should get a bank deposit box for the haversack and also for his diary and the letter from Godse senior. If the diary and letter were stolen they could be in real trouble. Roh agreed. They stopped at a city branch of Griff's bank, arranged the safety deposit box and put the haversack and Griff's diary and the letter in it. They asked then for directions on how to get to Karl's street. It was close to the town centre. Only five to seven minutes' drive, the bank people said.

"If we lose the money, what have we got left?" Roh asked, as they drove back to the hotel to check out. "You know I have nothing except a few thousand rupees," she added. She had lost everything. Her farm, her investments, her veterinary equipment.

"Don't worry, my love. We are alright. I have $160,000 or so in shares and $50,000 in cash in an interest-bearing account with my bank, plus the hobby farm near Canberra. I can sell the farm for at least $600,000, and we can use that as a big payment on a small property south of Perth. Even if we lose the Godse money, we will still be able to get established and you will be able to set up your veterinary business." Roh squeezed his arm and kissed his shoulder.

They stopped at a petrol station to top up the fuel tank and buy a city map. After checking out of the hotel, Roh navigated and they arrived about ten minutes later at Karl's house. It was surrounded by a two-metre sheet-metal fence and gate. The front yard was a jungle of fan palms, bananas, bauhinias, bougainvillea and other tropical shrubbery. Griff used the remote control on the key ring to open the gates. Only the upper floor of the house was partly visible. The driveway curved around to the left into a large carport and the house, like the fence and the carport, was built of corrugated steel sheeting on steel pillars and girders. Most of the lower floor, which was set on a thirty-centimetre high concrete slab, was half walled in corrugated steel sheet with timber lattice work on the upper half. The top part of the house was similarly done with verandas and lattice work all around.

"The house is lovely," Roh said, "but why are the houses here nearly all made of steel sheet?"

"Well, you'll notice that there is some glass too. Steel and glass are about the only two things that termites won't or can't eat. They probably try though." They chuckled at that.

"Termites are bad here then?"

"So bad that if you stand still for ten minutes on the dirt they will eat the shoes off your feet."

"Oh, Griff, they can't be that bad."

"Don't put it to the test, is all I'll say."

They walked under the house with their bags to the door and opened it. Griff called the security alarm code to Roh and she keyed it in. They locked the door and had a quick look around. The lower floor had a small kitchen with fridge and cupboards, bathroom and lavatory, storeroom and one empty room. The lower floor was gloomy but cool. They moved upstairs and into a large open, airy room with kitchen on the east side, bathroom and lavatory on the west side, along with three bedrooms that opened on to the veranda. The gabled ceiling was high and lined with polished timber. The lower inside walls were clad with polished timber. The upper halves were glassed with cottage windows which allowed in lots of light. The end at which they had entered was a big comfortable sitting room. They opened several windows and a cool breeze blew in from the ocean which they could see several hundred yards away between trees.

"This is an expensive house. Karl must be doing very well to be able to build or buy a place like this," Griff said.

He went over to the fridge and opened it. Not much food. Some eggs, stale milk, a carton of German beer. In the freezer there were steaks, fish fillets, frozen peas, beans, broccoli, sprouts and sweetcorn. Griff pulled out two small bottles of beer and opened them, found a couple of beer mugs in one of the cupboards and poured a bottle into each. He took them over to Roh and sat next to her.

"Here's luck, my love," he said. She leaned over and kissed him on the lips. They sipped their beers. "We should go out and buy some

186

food. We'll need quite a lot. Karl has some stuff in his freezer but we shouldn't use that. He probably crashes home here late at night, exhausted and needs to cook up something quickly."

They sat side by side in contemplation until Griff felt Roh's hand sliding softly from his thigh to his crotch. He had forgotten about sex for a few hours but it came back with a rush as she deftly undid his belt. He rose up with such a rush that he could feel his cock straining against the restriction of the clothing. He stood up, slipped off his sandals, pants and undies, and lay on the floor on his back.

"Good dog, you know your tricks, don't you," Roh said.

"Woof, woof," he said and hung his tongue out like a contented dog. His rigid penis wagged slightly as he woofed. She watched it steadily as though it might somehow get away while quickly shucking her clothes. She straddled him and used the moisture from her loins to moisten the tip of his penis before guiding it into her. She leant forward and lay flat on his chest with a gentle sigh while he stroked her back and buttocks and neck. She rose a little, kissed him hard on the lips and a disengaged look came into her eyes as if she were focused on something a long way off. She raised herself up on her arms and began to slide up and down. He fondled her breasts rubbing his thumbs across her nipples. The tempo of her thrusting increased to a near frenzy and she began to moan until she fell forward on to his chest again. He could feel the pulsing of her orgasm on the head of his penis. A film of sweat glued them together. When she had rested and got her breath back Griff gently rolled her over and lay above her, supporting himself on his arms so that the only points of contact were their lips and their loins. His thrusts were slow and deep until he felt his climax approaching and the strokes became shallow and rapid. His release came with a primal groan and their lips met again, barely touching.

They dozed for a while until the sweat dried and Griff rolled to the side. "Always a joy to take the sacrament with you, my beloved," he said.

"Why do you call it the sacrament?" Roh asked.

"In the Roman Catholic faith, physical love is deemed to be one of sacred things given to mankind by god, so long as it is committed for

187

the purposes of procreation between a man and a woman properly married to each other in the Catholic faith."

"Yes, but we are not Catholics, we are atheists and we were not doing it for the purposes of procreation."

"No, what we were doing was merely sinful fornication. But it feels just the same as a sacrament to me."

"Yes, to me too."

"Let us try out Karl's shower shall we?"

"Couldn't we go for a swim?" Roh asked.

"Not unless you want to risk being eaten or killed?

"What do you mean?"

"That water out there has estuarine crocodiles in it, five metres or more long."

"Really?"

"Truly. You can't swim in the ocean here. It is full of deadly things."

"What else apart from crocodiles?"

"Box jellyfish, stingrays, sharks. All of them can kill you in minutes. Faster than snake poison. Then there are stone fish and cone shells. They can cause you so much pain you'd wish you had died quickly."

"So it is not like the beaches in Perth."

"No, it's a different kettle of fish."

She laughed and asked what stone fish and cone shells were.

"Stone fish are ugly things that look like a stone with seaweed growing on it. They sit on the bottom and have sharp upward pointing spines. When you stand on them they pump poison into you. Cone shells are sea snails with attractive black and brown patterned shells. They have a spike that is normally hidden but they push it out when attacked or picked up. It injects deadly poison."

"Well, that's handy to know. Let's shower. Anything dangerous in the water?"

"Probably, but it will kill you more slowly. You can probably drink it, but do it only in moderation."

"Right, Saheb. But I recall you saying once that moderation in all things leads to a dull life."

188

"Yes, but I haven't departed from that principle in everything. Only for Darwin water with which I am not so familiar."

"Of course. Just checking."

They took cold showers and felt briefly refreshed from the humidity which hung like a wet warm blanket over the city. It was nearly always like that and merely more so in the run-up to the rainy season.

They went shopping to stock Karl's fridge and cupboards. They bought barramundi steaks as well as lean Northern Territory beef, papaya, mango and bananas and lots of salad veggies as well as wholemeal bread, Italian coffee and Queensland tea, some boutique brewery beer from Perth and half a dozen bottles of sauvignon blanc from Margaret River. Next door they got clothes: several pairs of cotton shorts and short sleeved shirts, broad-brimmed cotton hats and sunglasses and swimmers. The next stop was at a shoe shop to buy sandals. Two pairs each. Then to a bookshop where Griff got a copy of *Capricornia* by Xavier Herbert and gave it to Roh.

"You need to read this. It's a novel that gives you the history of the Northern Territory in a very readable way. You'll love it."

For himself, Griff bought a copy of Patrick White's *The Tree of Man*. He had read it several times over the years back but felt an urge to read it again. It would help to reset his mind; get him back into the Australian ethos and cultural heritage that he loved. He realised now that he had been missing that spacious and peaceful life, in the frenzy and struggle of India's multitudes scrabbling to stay alive and make a living. He also realised that he had been missing his favourite music. Finally, they went to a music shop where Griff bought CDs of Handel, Bach, Mozart, Beethoven, Kathleen Ferrier singing Brahms' Alto Rhapsody, Purcell, Faure, Schubert and Ravi Shankar. That would do for a start, he told Roh. They would come back for more later, he added.

"We are now fully rigged for Darwin," Griff said, as they loaded the stuff into their vehicle. "Perhaps we should call the UNHCR office and the police station and let them know where we are staying, Roh."

She called and gave them the address and their new phone numbers, as Griff drove back to Karl's. The UNHCR office told her the hearing would be next Monday at the UNHCR office at 10 am.

They unpacked into the fridge and cupboards and then stripped to wash their dirty clothes and the new gear and put it all to dry on a line on one of the verandas.

"Let me cook you an Australian treat for dinner, Roh, my love. Grilled barramundi with salad."

"Sounds lovely," she said. "I am making a coffee for us. We haven't had a decent one today and you must be craving one as badly as I." There was a table on the veranda through the French windows on the ocean side from where a gentle breeze was blowing. They sat and sipped their coffee.

"I've been thinking about what we might do when we get to Perth. I reckon we should look for a small piece of land, say five hectares on the highway with an old house close to the road. You can set up your veterinary practice there, run sheep and goats and I will set up a small shopfront."

"You are joking, aren't you? What will you sell?"

"Grandpa's home-made muesli, Anzac biscuits, small quiches and good coffee."

"Where will we get a grandpa to do all that?"

"I will be Grandpa."

"Oh, dear old Grandpa Griff." She threw her head back and chortled at the image of a snowy-bearded Griff in an apron, trying to look homely and domestic. "Tell me more," she said, when she had recovered from her fit of laughter.

"I'm serious. I can cook. The trick is to keep it simple. We will pre-pack the muesli and biscuits and pre-cook and freeze the quiche. We'll reheat the quiche to meet demand. We have to have good signs, a pleasant shop front with seating under a wide veranda or pergola and a drive-in parking area. Once the word gets around, business will pick up."

"Well, no harm in trying, Griff. The idea could work."

"Yes, and perhaps when you have your clinic set up you could start making goat and sheep milk cheeses. We will sell stuff by the package. No mucking around with menus trying to cater to the whims of food and wine poseurs."

"It could work. Clever boy."

"It's something to think about anyway and we could set it up with the money from the sale of my ACT property, at a pinch. Later, when business is booming we can think about a larger property," Griff added. "But I must get back to my house-husbandly work right now, madam."

He took the coffee mugs, kissed her gently and went back to the kitchen. Roh joined him soon after.

"See if you can find a tablecloth and a couple of wine glasses, Roh. There are big plates in that cupboard and cutlery in the drawer above it."

Griff finished the salad, tossed it with olive oil and balsamic vinegar and put the barramundi steaks on the heated sandwich maker to grill. Roh set the table, polished the glasses, opened the bottle of chilled dry white and carried out the salad.

They sat at the table and ate their meal slowly.

"Oh my, Griff, this fish really is wonderful isn't it?"

"Yes. I remember the first time I ate barramundi at a barbecue at a hotel in Kununurra. I had never eaten fish that was so succulent. I made a bit of a pig of myself by going back twice. The trick is to cook it slowly."

After dinner they read their books and then slept under the mosquito net in the spare bedroom with the windows open to the veranda. They didn't need clothes or bedclothes. Next morning early, they put on shorts, t-shirts and sandals and went for a walk and jog through the streets for an hour before returning home for breakfast. It was Friday. They went to the police station to report, had a coffee and lay about reading until lunch time. In the afternoon they visited the museum which was nearby. There were fine displays of Aboriginal culture and the natural history of the land of the Northern Territory and its rivers and ocean.

Chapter 10:   The Tribunal hearing

On the way to the UNHCR office they stopped at Griff's bank and collected his diary and letter and photocopied the latter. He realised he might have to copy the diary later too. He didn't have time before the hearing. Griff and Roh led their group, who had been bussed to Darwin with a camp official and a security officer, into the office and asked for directions to the room where the hearing was to be held. It was a large conference room of laminex and stainless steel, with cheap hard-wearing carcinogenic carpet and fluorescent lighting hidden behind plastic panels. A hateful but necessary air-conditioner hummed as it poured out excessive amounts of cold air. Drapes with rubberised backing blocked the windows, no doubt to prevent people from becoming preoccupied with the activities of birds, trees and scenery in the freedom outside. There was a table at the far end set up for the Tribunal members and several rows of chairs for the group and various minor officials, Griff guessed. The chairs were separated by a central aisle and Griff and Roh and their group sat on one side, taking the first two rows. There were a couple of chairs set up in front of the Tribunal's bench, a table and chairs on each side of them. On one of them, recording equipment was laid out. There were earphones on all the tables and also on the chairs on which Griff and Roh and their group sat. Officials walked in and out. Shortly before 10 am, Deepak Godse came in accompanied by a smooth-looking Indian aged around forty years, with a practised superior and penetrating look. They sat in the front chairs on the other side of the aisle without looking at Griff and Roh. A couple of minutes later a small flock of Indians walked in and sat behind Godse and the other fellow. Officials occupied the tables to the right and left and more seemed to sit behind Griff and Roh's group, along with several Northern Territory police, two men and two women. At 10 am, a bell rang and three people emerged from a door behind the Tribunal bench, filed in and sat there.

The one in the middle checked the microphone and then spoke declaring the hearing open. He asked if all the members of the survivor group were present and if there were any others present, apart from invited officials and police.

The person accompanying Godse spoke at that point.

"Your honour, I am here to look after the interests of Mr Godse who is only a young defenceless boy as you can see and who has reason to fear further danger to his interests from Mr Bolton and Dr Sane and their group." He gave his name as Sumit Mukherjee from a legal firm well-known for urging people who had done stupid and injurious things, such as diving into the shallow ends of swimming pools, to claim excessive amounts of compensation.

"Well, sir, no need to address me as your honour. I am merely the President of this Tribunal and this is not a court hearing. It is a hearing to establish whether we might recommend that the police make further investigations. Mr Godse has nothing to fear, real or imagined in this room and I have to tell you that we will not be allowing legal representation on behalf of anyone, so you will have to leave."

"But, honourable President, he is only a child."

"No buts, sir, I have given you my ruling. Please leave now. I now ask, who are the people sitting to the rear of Mr Godse?"

One beefy man with dyed hair and a moustache stood and spoke.

"We are members of the Indian community who have come to protect and support the boy Godse."

"I can assure you that the Tribunal is here to safeguard Mr Godse's interests as much as anyone's and I must now ask you to wait outside."

"This is not justice. It is racial discrimination," one shouted. Court attendants moved towards them.

Grumbling and muttering, Godse's supporters got up and filed out.

"Thank you. I should introduce the Tribunal members as well as myself. I am a judge appointed by the UNHCR office to conduct this hearing to investigate whether certain allegations that have been aired have any basis. On my right is the senior UNHCR official in Australia and on my left a senior officer of the Australian Federal Police. We have a Marathi language interpreter here and if any of you are in doubt about your ability to understand what is being said, you should put the earphones on now."

Roh turned and spoke quickly and quietly to the group to tell them to put on the earphones, which they did.

"The first thing I would like to clarify, in the light of Mr Mukherjee's contention, is the age of Mr Godse. Please come forward and take the chair in the middle facing us, Mr Godse, and speak up so everyone can hear you. How old are you Mr Godse?"

"I am eighteen years. I got eighteen years last week."

"Thank you. In this country the law states that a person of eighteen years is an adult and deemed to be a fully responsible and independent person. Do you understand that?"

"Yes, sir."

"I understand that the events about which you have made allegations took place while you were under the age of eighteen, but they were in fact only several months back. I believe that makes little difference now that you are in a position to make any allegations as an adult person if you wish to repeat those allegations. Do you wish to make any allegations or claims about Mr Bolton, Dr Sane or any members of that group whom you accompanied from India?"

"Yes. I am saying money they say my father gave them belongs to me. They have lied about that. He would never give them any money. Bolton is a foreigner and Sane is no good. My father didn't like her. She is bad person for living with foreigner Bolton. She doesn't have a god and she is not married to Bolton. She is just sex woman."

"Anything else?"

"Yes, Bolton kill my two uncles and father to get hold of his money. My father was government official and Bolton kill him."

"I see. Do you have any documentation or can you call any witness who can verify what you have said? I understand your cousin, Mr Shakunt Godse, is present as a member of the survivor group. Do you wish to call on him to support you?"

"No, he is traitor and liar who says what Bolton tells him. There is nobody else. I need lawyer."

"Mr Shakunt, do you wish to say anything on the matter?"

"Yes."

"Mr Godse, you can return to your seat. Mr Shakunt Godse, please come forward and sit. Please go ahead, Mr Shakunt."

"I do not support what my cousin say. His father, my uncle was bad man who convince me Mr Bolton had murder my father and uncle without any reason and that I should kill Mr Bolton and Dr Sane and others living in Dr Sane house because they bad people. I was upset and angry about my father's death then. I did go to Dr Sane house and kill a person. I go another time to try to kill more people, but Mr Bolton grab me and take me into their house. They tell me true story about what happen. How my father and uncles had kill Mr Namji their watchman and make Mr Bolton go out into snow without clothes to die and how they rape Dr Sane and then Mr Bolton come back into the house and kill my father and one uncle. I say what Mr Bolton did was right. I was soldier and would have done what Mr Bolton do. They had guns and had kill Namji. Mr Bolton and Dr Sane very good people. They could have kill me but they look after me, fix my wound and take me into their house and trust me even when I had try to kill Mr Bolton. I would have kill him before I heard true story."

"Have you read the report that was given by Commodore Awati and Captain Scott of what they say Mr Bolton told them?"

"Yes, that is true story."

"And were you present with Mr Bolton when Mr Godse senior was found in his house?

"Yes, I am there."

"And was there anything with Mr Godse?"

"Yes, there were guns and bullets and two cases of American dollar."

"You say you were a soldier. Have you had any experience of seeing dead bodies?"

"Yes."

"Did you reach any conclusion about how Mr Godse had died?"

"Yes. It look like he shoot himself in head."

"Any other wounds?"

"Yes, lot of small wounds from bombs we throw. Shrapnel."

"Anything else."

195

"Yes, I think Mr Bolton get letter with suitcases of money, but I am not reading it. Mr Bolton keep it secret."

"What did Mr Bolton do with the cases of money?"

"He keep one and give one for Mr Deepak and tell him his father say one case for him and one for Bolton Saheb and Rohini Bai."

"Do you have any information on how Mr Godse senior would have obtained that money?"

"He was government official and make much money from that. Millions. And he also have many business and benami farms."

"What are benami farms?"

"They are farms he own but put in other family person names. It is not proper legal but he do it lots."

"Thank you, you may go back to your seat now."

"Mr Bolton, we have read the reports provided by Commodore Awati and Captain Scott of what you told them of your encounters with Mr Godse senior and his brothers and son. I understand that you have been given copies. Is that so and have you read them?"

"Yes, sir, I have read them."

"Are they a true record of what you said?"

Yes, they are a true record, so far as they go. They lack some crucial details."

"Would you care to elaborate?"

"Yes. I have with me now the letter that Godse senior left for me with the two suitcases of money. I have a photo copy for you. Shall I pass it to you? You are welcome to see the original but I would like to have it back, unless it is deemed to be so vital that it has to be seized immediately as evidence. If that is the case, I would like to have the copy."

"If you let us have both now for verification I will return the original to you."

Griff handed both to a clerk who came to him for them. The President and his two bench members examined them, muttered inaudible comments and the President handed the original back to Griff.

"We would be grateful if you would read the letter, Mr Bolton." Griff did so.

As he finished, Deepak Godse shouted: "I do not know about that letter. It must be forgery. I must see it."

"Please settle down, Mr Godse. You can see it by all means." The President handed the copy to the clerk who took it to Godse.

"Are you able to tell whether or not that is your father's writing, Mr Godse?"

"Doesn't look like to me. My father very neat man. This letter is rough writing."

"Mr President, may I offer a suggestion on that point?" Griff interjected.

"Yes, please do."

"I would think that this letter was written in a hurry by a man who was already wounded in many places, suffering from loss of blood and in a fragile and anguished mental state. It is understandable that his writing might be a little less precise than usual but perhaps Shakunt Godse may be able to give an opinion on whether the writing is his uncle's hand."

"I can only agree, Mr Bolton. Would you show the letter to Mr Shakunt Godse."

Griff passed it along to Shakunt who scanned it for a few seconds before looking up. "This is signature of my uncle and writing his too. I am sure. I see his writing many times."

"Good. Thank you. Now, Mr Bolton is there anything you wish to say about Mr Deepak Godse's allegations?"

"Well, I have with me now the diary that I kept of all the events that happened from the beginning of the natural disaster, including the hearing that we held after I recaptured the house from Mr Godse senior and his brothers. It includes the statements of Mr Godse senior and junior and other conversations that I had with Mr Godse junior about why his father and uncles and he tried to take over our house. It also covers the other attacks on us and our house by Godse senior or at his instigation. I am happy to hand the diary over now or for copies to be made for your use but, like the letter, I would like the original to be given back to me today."

"That will be very useful, Mr Bolton. Thank you. If you will give it to the clerk we can get copies made straight away. Perhaps we can have an adjournment for tea and coffee now while copies are being made and resume at 11.30 am."

Griff and Roh and the group walked out into the corridor and from there they could hear shouting from the street. Outside the building, a crowd of at least thirty, perhaps fifty people of Indian appearance had gathered, shouting slogans. At their head was the fellow who had spoken in the hearing, saying that they had come to protect Deepak Godse and his lawyer. The others had rough, hastily scrawled posters reading OZZIE LAW UNFAIR; GODSE DENIED JUSTICE; DOWN WITH RACIST LAW; RETURN GODSE'S MONEY; RETURN STOLEN MONEY; GIVE BACK INDIA'S MONEY and were chanting more of the earlier smears about Griff and Roh as murderers and looters and sex dolls. Deepak Godse joined them with hands raised above his head in a victory celebration. Mukherjee the lawyer drew him immediately into conversation. Griff and Roh and their group turned to walk by to a coffee lounge down the road. Shouts of murderer, looter and sex doll followed them. The media were there with cameras rolling and a flock of a dozen or so reporters mobbed them, asking what had happened and for comments.

"It is not for us while the hearing is still going to say anything," Griff said.

"The President of the Tribunal would be a more appropriate person to make a comment than anyone at the moment, if he wished to do so," Griff said, as they walked down to the coffee house. He held Roh tightly to his side with a hand around her waist as the mob increased its shouting to a higher level and pursued them down the street. They walked on at a steady pace as the reporter flock peeled off, leaving the television camera people to stumble along backwards in front of them filming as though they expected Griff or Roh to start doing something abominable at any second. Griff and Roh smiled for the cameras. Just as they turned into the coffee lounge, one cameraman fell over backwards and Griff helped him to his feet and gave him his camera which had been jolted from his hands.

The group was quiet and pensive as they sipped their coffees. "How long do you think this hearing will last, Griff?" Roh asked.

"I think it might finish this afternoon and the Tribunal will retire for a couple of days to consider the information and do a report."

"That's good. I don't like this scene much, do you?"

"No, it is bloody hateful, but it shows how easily malicious or stupid people can stir up trouble. We'll be out of it soon and make a peaceful life with the magpies singing to us in the mornings." She smiled at that.

They headed back to the hearing room with the crowd of protesters serenading them along the street. As they turned to go into the building someone shouted something in Marathi, too quick for Griff to pick up the meaning. Rohini stopped and turned around facing the person most likely to have uttered the statement and replied to him in a quiet even voice.

"What was that about?" Griff asked.

"He said 'killers, prostitutes, you will go to hell' and I said that if we were to go to hell we would certainly meet him and his friends there because they were a disgrace to humankind."

"You're a feisty devil, aren't you," he said, raising her hand to his lips and kissing it. "He looked quite shocked that you spoke to him," he added.

"So he should be. They are horrible people and I feel ashamed that they are Indians behaving like this," she replied.

In the hearing room, they took the places they'd had before and minutes later the Tribunal members and officials came in. The President said he would read the diary out loud and it would be simultaneously translated into Marathi. If any person objected to any statement contained in the diary or wished to expand on any points, they should raise their hand and note would be taken of their point. The Tribunal members might also ask for elaboration of aspects. Was there any objection to that, he asked. There was none, so he proceeded to read the diary. The reading went on to the lunch break without interruption. At lunch the group adjourned to the coffee lounge for sandwiches and then returned to the hearing where the reading resumed. Godse objected to nothing. He looked rather crestfallen, as though the revelation of the diary and its detailed notes of everything that had had happened came as a surprise to him. On completion, shortly after the post-lunch resumption, the President said that he wished each person in the survivor group to state whether or not they considered it to be a true statement of what took place.

"We will start with you, Mr Bolton. Any additions or amendments you would like to make?"

"There is a matter that is not covered by the diary but I believe it would be worthwhile for the Tribunal to consider and that is that Dr Sane has lost virtually everything but what she stands up in and her skills and good health. She has lost two valuable farms with equipment, vehicles and livestock, her investments, books, paintings and family relics and now there are even people who are trying to take her good name as well. Dr Sane has qualifications in medicine and veterinary science from Australia and Britain that are recognised internationally. She could have left India many years ago to settle in a developed country to live a life of relative luxury as a wealthy professional. However, she, like most of her family, had a patriotic devotion that impelled her to stay to work for India's development and for the uplift of its impoverished rural people. She does not deserve the baseless and disgraceful slurs that have been made against her, particularly by Deepak Godse, whom she has never harmed and whom she tried to help and protect. That is all I wish to say, for the time being at least."

"Dr Sane, is there anything you wish to add or to say about Mr Bolton's record of events."

"Yes. I would like to say that every word of it is true and correct and I would like to add that all of us in our group, including Mr Deepak Godse, owe our lives to Mr Bolton. We would not have survived without him. His quick thinking and ability to improvise and to look ahead and foresee possible dangers, as well as his ability to keep us all hopeful and occupied during the worst times of the crisis, were what enabled us to survive virtually unscathed. No-one suffered frostbite or snow blindness or hunger or injury because of his leadership, and the only hardship and suffering we sustained, which was tragic, the needless deaths of two of our group and the attempted killing of Mr Bolton, was caused by Godse senior's malicious and unjustifiable attacks."

The President thanked Dr Sane and questioned each member of the group. All of them endorsed the diary record. Finally the President spoke to Deepak Godse. "Do you wish to add or question any aspect of Mr Bolton's record of events, Mr Godse?"

"Yes, she say she is raped by my father and uncles and by me but she never fight or struggle and my father told me she agree to have sex with them. When my father told me to have sex with her because I was now a man, she agree and put condom on me and help me. She is not rape."

"Do you wish to say anything to that, Dr Sane?"

"Yes. Godse senior and his two brothers were both bigger and stronger than me physically and they threatened me with guns. If I had fought them they would have beaten me and I would have been raped anyway. I told them that if they were going to insist on having sex with me it would be rape but if they would use condoms I wouldn't fight them. I would have lost any fight with them, of course, but I would have been able to hurt them before they overpowered me. I needed to be fit and able to help Mr Bolton, if and when he was able to get back into the house and overpower the Godses. So far as the son is concerned, his father brought him to my room and told me to have sex with him. I could see that he was frightened. So much so, in fact, that he wet his pants. I made the father go out of the room and I tried to behave in a friendly way to help the boy. I put the condom on him and encouraged him to get it over with as quickly as possible. He rushed out of the room straight away after the deed, forgetting his clothes which I then threw down the stairs after him."

"Is that correct, Mr Godse?" the President asked Godse, who was scarlet with embarrassment and looking at the floor. He shrugged his shoulders but said nothing.

"You need to answer, Mr Godse, so that your response can be heard and noted."

"Yes, is true but she didn't fight. Good Indian woman and wife always fight for family honour."

"Well, it seems to me, Mr Godse, that she was fighting for survival and doing it peacefully and intelligently," the President added. Godse shrugged again.

"Well, I think that brings this hearing to an end. The Tribunal will consider the information gathered and will do a report for the UNHCR, the Australian Federal Police and the Northern Territory Police, as well as the Australian Government and the Indian Government in Exile who asked to be kept informed. We will reconvene here in several days. You may not leave Darwin and must continue to report to the police and UNHCR office daily. Thank you all for your cooperation and I am sorry that your group, Mr Bolton, had to suffer the indignities of that mob outside."

The Tribunal members stood and left through their rear door. A clerk returned Griff's diary and notes and Griff and Roh and their group filed out into the building foyer from where they could see that several Northern Territory police had moved the protesters to the other side of the road. A bus was waiting to take group members back to the camp. Godse came out and walked across the road to the protesters where he was cheered. After a few more half-hearted shouts towards Griff and Roh, the mob began to disperse. Griff and Roh walked to their car in the carpark and drove back to Karl's.

"Don't know about you, my love, but I could do a lot of damage to a cold beer right now."

"Me too," Roh replied, and headed to the fridge to get the stubbies and a couple of glasses. "How do you think that went, Griff?"

"Better than I expected. I got a strong feeling that the Tribunal members, well, the President at least, think we have told the truth and acted with good intent in difficult circumstances. What about you?"

"Same as you. But I will be glad when it is over. I don't care if we lose all the money so long as we are cleared of these absurd allegations and are left alone to get on with our lives."

"You're right, my love." He put his arm around her and kissed her. He could taste salty tears on her lips. "Another week or less and we will be on our way to Perth, free of all this crap."

"If they rule in favour of us, what will they do about Godse?" she asked.

"Nothing, I imagine. He will be left to fade away into the obscurity that he deserves, amongst those who have supported his ridiculous claims, but frankly I don't give a damn what he does or what happens to him. I'd just like to give him a farewell kick in the crutch for being such a treacherous little grasping ingrate."

Next morning's *Territory News* had Godse on the front page saying that he had been humiliated and embarrassed in the Tribunal hearing. It was clearly biased against him, he claimed, and showed favouritism towards Bolton and Sane. He believed it was racially prejudiced against Indians. There were no Indians on the Tribunal and he was not allowed to have an Indian lawyer to protect his rights and interests. Roh read it out loud as they ate breakfast.

"He really is a stupid bastard," Griff said.

"I hope he goes swimming and a crocodile eats him," Roh said and they guffawed like jackasses.

They passed a couple of days reading, lying about, taking long walks, making love and cooking some old favourites, like onion rissoles with peas and mashed potatoes, spaghetti bolognaise, seafood risotto, potato fritters with grilled tomatoes and broccoli and vegetable meatloaf interspersed with stir fried vegetables and seafood. They made another visit to the bookshop and a music shop to get some Bach, Beethoven, Purcell and Handel. Karl didn't seem to have any baroque music, only country and western. Karl rang and invited them to his girlfriend's place for dinner on Friday night. She would make his favourite meal of German potato salad, coleslaw and cabbage rolls. They noted the address. Only ten minutes' drive from Karl's place, he said. He told them there were a couple of good push-bikes in his workshop which they could use. That afternoon they went for a long ride and checked out the girlfriend's house. They used the bikes after that to do their check-ins at the police and UNHCR offices. Friday afternoon they got a message that the Tribunal wanted them back at the same location, same time Monday. The UNHCR office told them they had notified the group at the camp and the bus would bring them to the hearing.

Karl's girlfriend turned out to be a friendly and very attractive woman about Roh's age and of similar complexion. She called herself Rosie. She was tall and slim with creamy smooth honey-coloured skin and hair and brown eyes. She was a mixture of many races, she said. Part Aboriginal, part Japanese, part Malay, part European. There were many like her in northern Australia, descended from pearlers and adventurers. It had been a multicultural mixture up there for more than a hundred years. She had her own clothing shop in the city area and her own house.

They had been going out together for a couple of years. Karl was in a jolly mood and got more boisterous as he downed more beers.

"No marriage and no living together in my house. We spend nights together, here or at my house, but we don't stay. I have been fucked by two women already. Not just shagged, you know, completely fucked. Took my house and left me nothing but a car and my tools and clothes. No woman gonna get another dollar out of me. I have clawed my way back and I own that house you are staying in and no woman, no matter how lovely, is gonna get that one. Rosie can cook great cabbage rolls like a German hausfrau but no marriage." He banged the table so hard with his fist that the cutlery and glasses jumped.

Rosie just laughed and said: "Who cares about your house, you old dope. I don't need your house. I have my own and who cares about marriage these days. I'd rather not be married to a noisy rowdy fella like you." Karl tried to grab her arm but she spun away and laughed at him again.

They had a fine night. The cabbage rolls were delicious and the coleslaw too. Griff and Roh were not so keen on the potato salad but Karl ate their share of that. They made more of a hole in the apfel strudel and cream dessert. The conversation got around eventually to the refugees and they asked Karl what he thought would happen with all the people in the camps.

"They won't be allowed to go south of the tropic of Capricorn for ten years unless they have accommodation and a job to go to. ID cards were about to be issued to enable the various authorities to keep track of all refugees. The cards would be linked to the basic allowance the authorities would provide and to healthcare services. They wouldn't be able to access those services without disclosing their location. The Federal, State and Territory Governments are going to pass legislation on that and also cooperate to set up new industries and farming enterprises here. They will be large scale and need lots of employees.

Dam building, canals, plantations of fruits and nuts, new roads, new towns. Developments like the Ord River Scheme. Big fish farms. Industries to make housing materials and tourism too. Boat building, expansion of the renewable energy industries. They will use a lot more manual labour than in the past to provide occupation and wages for the refugees. Lots of schools and training centres to be built and hotels."

"Sounds like lots of work for you, Karl," Roh said. "You'll get rich. You might even be able to afford a new wife." They laughed at that.

"No more wives for me, especially if I get rich," he said.

It was late, close to midnight, when they rode their bikes carefully back to the house.

Saturday afternoon they did another trip to the camp to catch up with the group. They were all going well they said. The camp had offered work to anyone who wanted it at the huge vegetable gardens it was establishing near the camp and at an orchard of tropical fruits that was being laid in. They had all gone working and enjoyed it. English lessons were held early in the morning straight after breakfast and soldiers took them in army trucks to the work sites at 10 am. They worked until 4 pm, then went back to camp to shower ,have a tea and sports, like volley ball, basketball, soccer and ping pong before dinner. After dinner they could watch TV and films in the canteen. There were big screens. They had Hindi films from Bollywood as well as other countries. Most of the people in that camp were Indians, Pakistanis and Bangladeshis, so there weren't too many language problems. Shakunt could speak Hindi and Urdu as well as Marathi and he was happy to translate when needed.

Sunday they washed clothes and lazed about. Griff found a lawnmower in the workshop and mowed the front and back yards. In the afternoon they went for a long bike ride. Monday morning they had breakfast early and ironed clothes and left in time to reach the UNHCR office fifteen minutes before the hearing was due to start. The group from the camp were already in the room when they walked in. Godse came in shortly after and sat on the other side of the aisle. As before, the Tribunal members entered from the rear and took their places.

"It looks as though we are all here so I shall proceed," the President said. "Before I hand down the Tribunal's findings and recommendations I have an announcement to make relating to the two suitcases of money brought in to Darwin from India by Mr Godse and Dr Sane. The Indian Government in Exile, which as you know is based in New York, has stated that the money is to be seized as Indian Government property. The IGIE has stated that Mr Godse senior, the father of Mr Deepak Godse, was a government official and that the immense sum of money accumulated by him could only have been earned by illegal activities and is therefore forfeit to the IGIE. The Australian Government has no option but to accede to the wishes of the IGIE. However, the IGIE has stated that, in view of Dr Sane's loss of property and investments and in recognition of the work she did in helping the survival of the group who accompanied her to safety, it proposes to make an ex-gratia payment of $500,000 as compensation. It has also announced an ex-gratia payment of $100,000 as compensation to Mr Deepak Godse for the loss of his family and his inheritance."

At that moment Godse sprang to his feet and shouted that that was unjust and unfair. "I protest against this theft of my father's money. He was very hard-working official. He look after many people and help them. Why they give all that money to Sane and nearly nothing to me."

"Please resume your seat and calm down. It is not this Tribunal that has made the order about the money. It is the Indian Government in Exile. If its decision is not acceptable to you, you will have to take the matter up with them. However, from the conclusion of this hearing today, you will be able to collect $100,000 and Dr Sane will be able to collect the sum granted to her. The payments will be by bank cheque. That concludes that matter. Now we must proceed to the Tribunal's findings relating to the events that took place during the period in India after the beginning of the natural disaster. We have concluded that Mr Bolton and Dr Sane did not act improperly in any way. The opposite in fact is true, that they made strenuous efforts to save the lives of their farm and household staff and to care for them through exceedingly difficult times. If they had not made that effort it is quite

206

likely that all of them, except Mr Bolton and Dr Sane, would have perished along with virtually everyone else from that remote rural area of India. We do not believe there was any truth in Mr Godse senior's claim that he was on government business when he initially approached Dr Sane's house and demanded entry. That was simply a ruse to gain entry and to take over the house and its people and resources. We have also concluded that he and his brothers behaved brutishly towards the residents in Dr Sane's house and acted criminally towards Dr Sane and her employee whom they killed. Were they still alive, they would be liable to criminal prosecution. We believe that Mr Bolton acted with legitimate force in retaking control of the house and killing the two brothers and subsequently expelling Godse senior and junior. We conclude that Godse senior committed further criminal acts in misleading his nephew about the intentions of the Sane household and inciting him to murder another member of the Sane household and to try to kill Mr Bolton and all of the others.

"It seems clear to us that Mr Bolton and Dr Sane acted with fairness and compassion to Godse senior's nephew and also to Godse junior in taking him back into their household, even though he had betrayed them previously in a way that led to his father taking over the house and committing criminal acts. The Tribunal has been impressed by the courage, innovation and dedication shown by Mr Bolton and Dr Sane in keeping this group of people alive and guiding them to safety when millions had perished around them. We are grateful for the documented information about their experiences and have no reason to doubt the authenticity of the facts. We believe they acted with honesty and fairness at all times. We are sorry that Mr Bolton and Dr Sane have had to suffer slurs to their names after the turmoil and struggle they put into guiding this group of survivors to safety and, on behalf of the Tribunal, I wish to record our admiration and our thanks for their courage and what they achieved. It's a pity that there were not more people in India and China and neighbouring countries who were able to achieve what they did. They remained human and compassionate when others lost their heads. You are now free to get on with your lives. Mr Bolton and Dr Sane may leave Darwin whenever wish and the rest of their group will have to return to the camp to meet their obligations there. Mr Godse may return to those he is proposing to live with in Perth. Printed copies of our report are available to the public from the Court office. Thank you."

The Tribunal members stepped down from their bench to the body of the Court and moved to Griff and Roh to shake their hands. Deepak Godse had risen and rushed from the room as soon as the Tribunal President had finished speaking. Griff and Roh walked from the Courtroom to the foyer and from there they could see the crowd of placard-waving people, ninety-five per cent of whom were of Indian appearance, crowding around Godse junior and the lawyer of superior aspect. Some were looking serious or even glum and others were mouthing and shaking fists at the Courthouse.

The media formed a separate but smaller crowd closer to the Courthouse doors. Griff and Roh collected a copy of the Tribunal report and then pushed out through the doors. The heat, glare and humidity hit them at the same time as the questions flying at them from the charging media pack.

"Whaddaya think about the Tribunal findings, Mr Bolton, Dr Sane?"

"We are very relieved that the Tribunal vindicated our actions, recognised our struggle to help and to defend our group. They made the right decision and we wish now just to get on with our lives in Perth," Roh said.

"What about you, Mr Bolton?"

"Couldn't have said it better than Dr Sane and I hope you will give the Tribunal President's summing-up prominence equal to that which you gave to the baseless and false allegations by Deepak Godse and others."

"Nothing else?"

"Just goodbye and good luck." He gave them a beaming smile. There were a few smiles and sniggers from the ABC TV crew and a few of the saner members of the pack, as Griff and Roh turned to talk with their group and then walk with them to their waiting bus. They promised to call out to the camp the next day to have a talk about the future and make some plans before heading south. Griff and Roh waved them off and then went back into the Courthouse for Roh to collect her cheque. The clerk was all smiles and congratulations on the Tribunal outcome.

"We were all behind you here and glad that the Tribunal laid those lousy allegations to rest."

"Thanks, mate, it's good to have it over and to know that a lot of people weren't taken in by the slander. We took care of that sod and he turned out to be a wretched ingrate. We could have left him to perish. Still, he's been sorted out now and hopefully that is the end of all this nonsense."

Roh led him away out of the Courthouse down to their car. "Let's go the bank so I can get this cheque in and then let's celebrate with a drink or a coffee and a cream cake or both."

"Yep, let's go." He raised her hand to his lips and gave a lingering kiss to the smooth, golden skin.

When they got back to the house, Griff called Karl and asked him to come over for the evening meal and a drink with his girlfriend. They told them about the outcome of the hearing and Griff said they planned to head south in a day or two to set up base near Perth. He thought Pinjarra might be a good spot.

Chapter 11: The last attack

Next morning they set out after breakfast for the camp to hand over the keys to the safety deposit box, brief the survivor group on how to get their satchel from the bank when they needed it, and how they planned to get them down south to join them, as soon as they had bought a property near Perth. As they drove out of the driveway from Karl's house, Griff noted a four-wheel-drive vehicle that had been sitting up the road a bit take off and follow them. He did a few twists and turns that he wouldn't usually do to get to the highway south, while keeping an eye on the rear vision mirror. The vehicle kept after them.

"There's an SUV keeping tabs on us. Don't look back, just check it out in the rear vision," Griff said. "You'd better get your seatbelt really firm in case of funny business," he added.

About ten kilometres after they left the outskirts of the city on a long straight stretch where there were no cars following and none ahead, the vehicle following made a charge and drew level with them. Griff saw them coming and as they pulled alongside he saw that the passenger had hoisted a sawn-off shotgun onto the window sill. He looked Indian, as did the driver. Without thinking, Griff flung his left arm out to hold Roh in her seat and hit the brakes hard. The other SUV flew ahead, then braked and swung across in front of them. The one shot fired by the shooter passed in front of Griff and Roh's SUV, taking a streak of paint off the bonnet as it went. The gun holder, who wasn't wearing a seatbelt, had to drop his arm down the side of the door to stop himself from flying across on to the driver. The shotgun was out of sight. Griff dropped down two gears and then pressing Roh back into her seat, accelerated hard at the SUV before it had fully come to a stop. His bullbar hit the shooter's arm and crushed it against the door. Griff heard no sound but the crunch and thump of clashing metal, but the look of shock on the shooter's face as he realised his arm was hanging by a shred told him that the shooter wouldn't be picking his nose with his left hand for a long, long time if ever and he definitely wouldn't be bothering them again that day. The other SUV rose slowly into the air under the impact and then toppled on to its side. Griff reversed, drove around the SUV, stopped briefly to check that there was no movement and then headed off fast down the road towards the camp. The whole operation had taken only seconds.

"How's your blood pressure, sweetheart?" Griff said, turning to look at Roh. She was sitting rigid with her back pressed against the seat, staring dead ahead and holding on to the roof handle.

"Don't think I've got any. My heart stopped." She gave a weak but gritty smile. "That was pretty slick, Griff. They might have killed us."

"I was lucky. When they swung across in front of us, I had them. If they hadn't done that they could easily have finished us with the shotgun. It looked like a nine-shot automatic. They must have been amateurs."

"You'll have to let me save you sometime. I owe you a couple of lives now."

"If I lost you, I'd lose everything, Roh. I need you." He touched her cheek. She smiled and squeezed his hand.

"That may be so, Griff, but I certainly need you. Who do you think would want to kill us?"

"No-one but our little friend Godse, I imagine."

"Yes, it could only be him. He must have used some of his Tribunal payout money to hire a couple of killers. There must be plenty around who will do anything for money in this chaotic situation with the refugees flooding in."

They reported the accident to the police station at the camp and gave statements. The police called Darwin police to go to the accident site. Griff and Roh were allowed to go to see their group on the condition that they returned to the police station before leaving the camp. Over coffee and tea at the block centre they told the group about the attack and that they should be alert to any possible harm. The group assured them that they had a lot of support in the camp and people would be on the lookout for their interests. Griff told them to spread the word through the camp about the attempted shotgun killing and how they had dealt with the killers. They would deal with any others who thought to embark on a similar adventure with equal ruthlessness. Roh told the group they would be wise to leave their haversack in the bank until they were ready to leave to join them down south. Perth would be the best place to convert their gold jewellery into cash when they eventually wanted to do that. That done, they farewelled them and headed back to the police station where they were told they must report to the Darwin police station as soon as they got back to the city. Driving back to Darwin they didn't see the crashed SUV. It had been towed away, probably as a crime exhibit. There was just a heap of dust and baked mud on the road shaken from the vehicles by the impact to show where it had happened.

At the police sationdetectives asked them to repeat their version of what had happened. They were questioned separately and then brought together.

"Your stories match exactly in every detail, so that looks good. The problem is there was no sign of the two men at the crash site. They must have phoned someone to pick them up or hitched a ride. If what you say is correct, the shooter would be in a bad way and would have need to have urgent medical attention. We've alerted the hospitals and doctors and we'll get that fellow if he seeks help anywhere in Darwin," the senior detective told them, and then asked their plans for the near future. They told him they wanted to head south to Perth to catch up with family and look around for a small property within a couple of days.

"That'll be okay, but come and see us before you leave, if we don't get in touch with you before then," the detective added. "And before you leave now we will take a few photos of your vehicle."

The photographs done, Griff and Roh drove off to the house. Roh padlocked the front gate while Griff parked the SUV. Inside, Griff poured a glass of light dry white each, put on Handel and sat down to knit up the ravelled sleeve.

"Jesus, I hope I don't have many more days like that for some time," Griff said. "It must be prematurely ageing. There's a memorable line that comes to mind from a Harrison Ford movie, I think – it's not the years that count, it's the mileage. He was right."

"Another glass of wine and a shower and you'll be rejuvenated. I'll probably be fighting you off."

"Not tonight, Josephine. You can bathe. I'll just inject some of this wine straight into my carotid artery."

Roh noticed that he was asleep on the couch when she came out of the shower and she went to the kitchen to cook stir-fried veg with prawns. Griff woke to the clashing of the pots in the galley and went for a shower. Refreshed and in clean khaki shorts and a check shirt, Griff arrived in the kitchen as Roh was serving the dinner. He set places on the veranda table looking out to the ocean and put on the overhead fan to give the mosquitoes something to dance to. There was no breeze. Over the meal they talked about heading south. Griff thought they could hold on to the Pajero rather than sell it and drive south, stopping for a couple of days to enjoy a little relaxed high living at the Cable Beach Hotel. They could buy a sturdy trailer and a decent tent and some camping gear and call in at the regular beach holiday and camp sites where the grey nomads frittered away their declining decades in fishing and sitting around yarning over cold beers with their mates and neighbours. Griff and Roh weren't anything like grey nomads although they could mix happily with almost anyone, but it was the nomads who knew where the good spots were. Roh thought it was a great idea.

Next day they hit the car yards looking for a good trailer and had one by late morning. Next stop was the camping store where they got a roomy canvas tent with a strong floor and a mosquito and snake proof annexe along with other bits and pieces including a camp oven, fishing rods, primus stove, solar lanterns, shovels and axes, a couple of lockable steel chests and some large plastic tarps, jerry cans for extra fuel and water. Griff wanted a shotgun too, ostensibly for rabbits, but in the back of his mind was the worry of another bit of funny business from Godse. And you never knew what ratbag or desperado you might meet out in the wilds of the Kimberley between Darwin, Kununurra and Broome. They checked at the police station to let them know they were still in town and to get a licence for the shotgun. Griff

213

went back to the camping store and got a Browning automatic nine-shot and a couple of boxes of duck shot, one of buckshot and one of solid head, in case of unwanted pestering from a croc, feral pigs, feral bulls or feral humans.

"What do you think about us getting a dog, Roh?" Griff asked, as they left the camping store.

"I'd love it, but what did you have in mind, a pup?"

"No, I thought we could pay a visit to the dog pound and see if we can pick up a young Blue Heeler. They're smart dogs and gritty and I'll feel more comfortable camping in the bush with a good dog for early warning signals and general deterrence."

"Okay, let's try it."

They went back to the camping store and asked for the location of the pound. Twenty minutes later they were at the pound and talking to the office staff. The staff recognised them and were friendly, congratulated them on their epic survival and the Tribunal finding and showed them the newspaper. There was a report on the front page about the attack the previous day. The police had issued a release saying what had happened and asking for public cooperation in finding the attackers. Griff explained to the pound staff that they would be travelling south, camping, and would like to get a youngish friendly Blue Heeler.

"You're in luck. We have one who is two years old. He was a family pet but the family had to move overseas and they couldn't take the dog. He is house-trained and well looked after. Most of the dogs we get here are lost or abandoned cattle dogs. They can be a bit wild and touchy, but this little fella is a beauty," the Manager said.

"Sounds perfect," Roh said.

"What's his name?" Griff asked.

"Bluey."

Bluey was a classic Blue Heeler cattle dog. They abounded in northern Australia, where they helped with the huge cattle herds. They reckoned up there that a good Blue Heeler was worth six blokes on horse. They were more than a match for any bull and kept them moving by nipping at heels of the cattle, hence the name. Blue Heelers were supposed to be a mix of kelpie, sheep dog and dingo.

They walked out the back to the pens and the dogs set up a racket as soon as they saw them, calling for attention. There were quite a few Blue Heelers and some Red Clouds, same shape as Blue Heelers but with reddish colouring. In the last pen of the row there was a solitary dog, looking at them intently through the chain mesh with a big grin and his tongue hanging out. As they looked at him he gave a little yip, as if to say, "Go on, tell the Manager I'm the one".

"This is the young fella," the Manager said.

"Oh, he is lovely," Roh said. "Can he come out?"

"Yes, but I'll have to put a leash on him first."

"He's not a big dog, is he Griff?"

"No, Heelers aren't big in the body. They're big in heart. They're middle-sized, but built very solid, very stocky and they can run all day. Probably bred small, so that a stockman could carry one sitting on his horse behind him or on the saddle in front."

The Manager came out with the dog and Roh and Griff made a fuss of him with lots of pats and kind words. He soaked it all up.

"Okay, we'll take him, shall we, Roh?"

"Yes, let's. He's part of the family already."

The Manager handed the leash to Roh and they strolled back to the office to fix up the paper work with Bluey loping along like he'd been with them since a pup. All the other dogs that had been clamouring for attention suddenly fell quiet.

"This always reduces me to a blubbering mess, when the dogs fall quiet," Griff said.

Dog pounds were a new experience for Roh. "Why do they make such a row and then fall quiet like that?" she asked.

"They know they haven't made the team," Griff said.

"Yeah, it's sad," the Manager said, "particularly because we eventually have to put down the dogs that nobody wants."

"Oh yes, that is awful," Roh said. "It must be upsetting for you?"

"You never get used to it," the Manager said.

Out at the car Griff opened the back door and Bluey jumped and sat in the corner looking out the window like a very good boy. He had done it all before. They called at a butcher shop on the way back to the house and bought some liver, heart and rib bones which the butcher chopped for them. At the supermarket they got some worm pills and tick repellent. At home they sat on the veranda with a drink and made a list of the supplies they would need for the trip. Bluey ate his dinner on the floor beside them.

Later that night they got a call from the detectives. They had picked up a bloke who'd sought treatment from a doctor for a badly infected left arm that had been amputated just below the elbow. They were asked to go in next morning to the hospital to identify the fellow. They went to the police station at 9 am and one of the detectives took them to the hospital. The fellow they had picked up was unconscious, following an early morning operation to take off the remnant of the arm to the elbow. Roh and Griff recognised him as the shooter. Back at the station they made statements confirming that and the detectives told them they were free to leave Darwin. They would keep looking for the other bloke. Griff and Roh said they had only got the merest glimpse of him. Barely enough to see that he looked South Asian. They wouldn't be able to identify him. They provided their intended temporary address in Perth and telephone numbers and then went to the supermarket to buy supplies for the trip. Griff realised then he would need a car fridge, an esky and a couple of large food storage bins for the dry food: the oats and rice and pasta and protein biscuits. They went back to the camping store and got the fridge fitted. They were able to get an extension to plug the fridge into the cigarette lighter socket, then headed back to Karl's house to make final preparations for departure. They packed the rear of the Pajero and the trailer and cleaned the house. They took the sheets off the bed and left new ones in their packets for Karl, gave him a call to thank him, invited him south to stay and told him they were off early next morning and would leave the keys in the key strongbox.

They were up at five next morning, had breakfast and fed Bluey and headed away at six. They checked the rear vision mirrors regularly but nothing was following and they were soon heading south-west at a good pace. The trailer, which was a four-wheeler, rode steadily with its solid load. By mid-morning when they stopped to cook up a pot of coffee and scoff a banana, they'd covered three hundred and thirty kilometres, with another five hundred to go. All going well, they'd be in Kununurra for afternoon coffee rolling along at about ninety kilometres an hour. They would camp just outside Kununurra and then strike out next day for the exotic Bungle Bungles, the cone-shaped hills of striated stone.

Roh was feeling a bit nostalgic and teary as she looked at the Kimberley hills and countryside that had a remarkable resemblance to the hills around Maharashtra where her beloved farmhouse was now disappearing for eons probably, under an ice sheet.

"When I look around at this and see how similar it is to the hills near the farm, I can't believe that it has all gone, all gone. It's unreal. A dream. I feel sure I will wake up and be back on the farm with life going on as usual," she said.

"Yeah, it's tough. It will take a while to get used to an idea like that. A massive shift in the usual way of life, like the sudden change from peace time to war. But the good thing about this tragedy is that we are on the winning side. We've got away from the battle and we're in safe territory. We'll make a good new life, my love." He reached out and caressed her cheek. She turned and gave him a teary smile.

"Yes, I know you are right, but for me it's like losing a close member of my family. I will be grieving for years I think. I can't help it. I hope you can understand that and be patient with me."

"I do understand. I'm still coming to grips with it myself because the place got into my blood too. Take as much time as you need, Roh. Lean on me as long and as often as you like."

She patted his leg. "Thanks, Griff." She gave Bluey a big hug. He was so pleased that his tongue hung an extra couple of inches out of his mouth.

"Sing us a song, Roh."

She sang a whole lot of songs and that cheered them all up. They followed that with some Purcell and Handel CDs and then followed that with some Beethoven, Bach and Vivaldi. After that they played the haunting songs of Jagjit Singh. They told Bluey that he would become a very cultured and worldly dog if he stuck around them. The length of tongue he hung out and the amount of saliva he generated seemed to indicate he agreed it was a good prospect.

They rolled into Kununurra singing some Australian folk-songs and ready to eat raw the bum out of some old road kill. Luckily, they found a cafe and had a coffee and a steak sandwich and then went looking for a camp site. They found a good spot overlooking Lake Argyle, the Ord River Dam, put the tent up and cracked a coldie from the car fridge while Bluey checked the environs. They agreed a good walk before preparing the evening meal was needed to get the sludge moving through the body after so long in the car.

They locked up all their small gear and set off to walk along the ridge overlooking the lake. They got back to the camp after a good hour's hike. As they walked toward the campsite they noticed a young dark-skinned man sitting in one of the two folding chairs they had left out. He sprang to his feet as he saw them walking towards him and Bluey started to give a low growl. He was a nice-looking young bloke with a broad smile and dimples and a tall, rangy figure wearing jeans, boots and a khaki shirt.

"Hope ya didn't mind me sittin' in ya chair, boss. I was guardin' the place for ya. I saw ya settin'off for ya hike and I wanted to talk to ya so I thought I just wait."

"That's okay, mate. How can we help you?"

"I was wonderin' if ya might be going to Broome. I come up here from down south 'bout a year ago to visit me 'lations and work as a station hand but I've had enough of it now. They're all drinkin' and fightin'. I'm sick of it. I bin working hard, getting wages, and me relations are bludging off me. It's too bloody dangerous."

"How is it dangerous?"

"They go mad with the grog, boss, do anything, throw shovels and hatchets. I'm not use to that sort of muckin' about. Scared the wits outa me."

"What's your name, mate?"

"Charlie, boss."

"And where are you from?"

"Narrogin, boss."

"And you want to go back there?"

"Yeah, boss. I wanna go back there to me family. I gotta mother and father and brothers and sisters. They're all hard-working people, boss. We gotta nice house. "

"Okay, Charlie, we are going to Broome and you can come with us. We will be going south to Perth after a couple of days in Broome and if you are a good travelling companion on the way to Broome you can come down to Perth with us."

"Gee, boss, that's real kind of ya. I got some money and I can pay ya for food and help with petrol."

"No need for that, Charlie, but thanks. You hold on to that money. Just pitch in and help with setting up and taking down camp and getting firewood and you'll be right. This is my missus, her name's Rohini."

"Righto, boss. That'll do me. Please to meet ya, missus. Can I get some firewood for ya now?"

"Yeah that'd be great Charlie," Roh said. "By the way, do you have a bag, Charlie?"

"Yeah, just a small one. It's over there beside the truck." He ran over and got it and showed it to them. It was a sturdy overnight bag with a canvas bedroll. "I'll get some wood now," he said, and loped off towards the scrub nearby.

"He seems a nice young fellow," Roh said.

"Yeah, he does. Has an honest face, but just keep a sharp eye on him for a few days. I think he'll be fine."

They got three steaks out of the freezer and some frozen veg and gathered some large rocks for the fireplace and some kindling from nearby. Charlie came back dragging a dead tree and started ripping it apart with his hands and boots. Griff gave him the axe and he had the tree cut to fireplace size in ten minutes, then set off to get another.

By the time the sun dipped below the far ranges, the dinner was cooking and Griff and Roh were sipping a glass of shiraz. Charlie declined the offer of a glass of wine. He said he only drank light ale and little of it.

"Could you handle a Cooper's Light, Charlie?" Griff asked.

"I reckon I could, boss," he said.

They were cooking the meal in a large heavy frying pan and a steamer saucepan with the vegetables, sitting on a piece of three-eighth steel sheet, about sixty centimetres by thirty centimetres. As soon as the steaks were done on one side Griff cracked three eggs into the pan.

Roh had set up a folding table with the plates and cutlery, mustard and pepper, a bowl with some fruit and three glasses of water in stainless steel cups.

"Gee, you do this campin' thing pretty flash, missus," Charlie said. "It's bettern' some hotels I been in."

"Stick with us, Charlie, and you'll be right."

"I reckon."

Roh took two plates over to the fire and Griff served up the meal. She went back to the table and gave one to Charlie and kept the other and took the third plate to Griff for his meal. They sat and ate.

"I'm real grateful for this, boss. You can trust me. I'll do the right thing by ya. You're real decent people. I'll do the dishes and the pots after dinner if ya like."

"That's nice, Charlie," Roh said. "But I'll do them. You did a great job with the firewood. I'll show you how we do the pots and then you'll know for later."

After the main meal and a piece of fruit each, Roh made a pot of tea the old way in a billy, with tea leaves and some grated ginger to give it a tang. After the dishes and pots were done and the gear locked away, they sat around the fire and had another glass of red and yarned. Charlie told them about his work on the station and the trips into Darwin with his workmates that turned into wild and usually bloody bouts.

Charlie asked about them and how they came to be travelling through. He didn't know who they were. He hadn't seen much TV since he left Perth, he said, but he knew about the polar shift and the cataclysmic events that followed it. The massive in-rush of refugees. When they told him about what had happened to them in India and their struggle to survive and get to safety, he was dumbfounded.

They all went different ways into the dark for a late night pee and then bunked down. They made up a shelter between the four-wheel

220

drive and the trailer with a big plastic tarp and Charlie slept under that with his drover's sleeping roll. Bluey was in the tent with them. Griff and Roh woke in the morning at sun-up to the sound of Charlie whistling while he chopped firewood. Bluey wanted to get out. They rolled out of bed, had a quick armpits and crutch wash with a bucket of water from the lake and made a breakfast of rolled oats with yoghurt and chopped fruit and a mug of tea. They hit the road before 7 am.

On the way Charlie told them about his family in Narrogin. His father was a fencing contractor and his brothers worked for him. They all played footie with the town's first eighteen and cricket in the summer. Charlie had only been to Perth a couple of times. He didn't like cities. Too many buildings and people, not enough trees and grass and animals. Roh told him about their plans to get a small property somewhere south of Perth and set up a veterinary clinic and do some hobby farming. She told him they planned to reach the Bungle Bungles by lunchtime, set up camp there and spend the afternoon and night there before heading for Broome next morning. Charlie told them he had been to the Bungles and knew a good place to camp where there was water and he could show them some of the gorges near there.

As they drove, Roh looked through a tourist guide for the area.

"Here's some info about the Bungle Bungle Ranges. They rise to about three hundred metres above the plain, have a diameter of seven kilometres, are three hundred and seventy million years old and are formed by the erosion of sedimentary layers which give them that striped effect. You're not allowed to call them the Bungle Bungles. It's either the Bungle Bungle Ranges or the Bungles. And the most fascinating thing is that they weren't discovered until 1983, when a film group stumbled upon them."

"Yeah, well, I reckon the local Noongars knew about 'em a bit before 1983 and the cattle station owners too," Charlie said.

"I reckon you might be right there, Charlie," Griff added.

"Yes, well, we Indians are used to that. The British claimed to have discovered all sorts of things in India, like the Ajanta and Ellora Caves and Vijayanagar and a thousand other places that Indians built and lived in and then moved away for one reason or another. I don't know why they don't say 'rediscovered'."

"You're right, missus. Us darkies gotta stand up 'gainst all that whiteman crap about discovering the whole damn world. They used to reckon 'Straya was an empty continent. Noongars didn't count."

"You two better be careful if you don't want to be walking. This is a white man's car," Griff said, with a laugh.

"Did you know, Charlie, that a lot of anthropologists think some of the Australian Aborigines came to Australia from India? There are people in India who look very much like Aborigines," Roh said.

"Go on, missus, I didn't know that but it musta been a long time ago. They say the Noongars have been here for more'n forty thousand years."

"Yes, well, they say there was a land bridge all the way to India then and they were able to walk."

"Could be, missus. Noongars really like walking. They're pretty good at it, so I can believe that."

"Well, here is something else to think about, Charlie. A lot of Indians, mainly those who call themselves Hindus, arose from Europeans who walked into northern India from around 1500 BC. They were more advanced than the Indian Aborigines and were able to dominate them, enslave them and keep them on the outer of their society. They developed a caste system and the Aborigines were kept outside the system. They were outcasts, you might say, and have been kept that way for three thousand years. It's only in the last fifty or sixty years that they have been able to begin to rise up. Most of them, millions of them, are in a much worse state than Australian Aborigines."

"Jeez, missus, I didn't know that."

"It's a fact, Charlie. Australian Aborigines have had some tough times but they are already a lot better off than most of the Aboriginal people in other parts of the world in only two hundred years. An Indian Dalit would swap places with an Australian Aborigine any day of the week."

"Well, I'll be damned. I oughta go to India and have a look."

"It would certainly be educational, Charlie."

"Tell me, Charlie, what do you think about these millions of refugees flooding into Australia now?" Griff asked.

"Well, there's not much any of us can do about it, I s'pose. The poor buggers gotta go somewhere if they've lost their whole country, but I reckon it'll probably be a bit like what it was when you white fellas decided to come here and take over."

"What do you reckon that was like, Charlie?" Griff asked.

"A lot of fighting, killing, strife and disease, but I s'pose it'll settle down after a while."

"Yeah, that's the way of the world, Charlie. It's been going on for thousands of years. There'd be some good in it if we all finish up about the same colour."

"Yep, that would be something, but the silly buggers would find something else to fight about then, eh, boss?"

'I think you are right, Charlie. We've still got a way to go."

"Okay you bros, that looks to me like the Bungles rising above the horizon ahead. What do you reckon?

"Yeah, looks like it to me," Charlie said.

They reached the camp site by 12.30, paid their park entry fee, put up the tent, made sandwiches for lunch and then followed Charlie into the narrow lanes between the huge conical rock formations.

"You could get lost in here if ya weren't careful," Charlie told them. Roh and Griff agreed. The place had a magical, out of this world feel about it. Charlie's family had always lived in the south of the State, he said, and he didn't know much about the culture in the Kimberley, but he told them stories about the Dreamtime.

"I dunno much about the old Koori culture, missus. My family been livin' in Narrogin for more'n a hundred years. We're town people now, I guess," he said. "Not city people. But we still love the country and wanna work there."

Next morning they were up early, had breakfast in the dark and set off at sunrise with a nine-hour drive ahead of them to reach Broome. Griff wanted to get there before dark.

"I bin thinkin' boss, I might stay in Broome for a few days and let you go on south by yerselves. Would that be okay? You was kind to offer to take me all the way, but I got some friends here I wanna visit."

223

"Don't give it a second thought, Charlie. It's been a pleasure having you and we're happy for you to get out whenever it suits you," Griff said.

"Thanks, boss. I'll give ya some money fer tucker an' petrol."

"No need for that, Charlie. We took your country from you, so a ride of a few hundred kilometres and a few meals hardly seems like compensation. Look us up when you get down to Perth."

They drove on for hours through the red pindan dirt and mesas, stopped to make lunch and a coffee, topped up the fuel from the jerry cans they carried in the trailer and surged on. They had to dodge a couple of kangaroos, but finally their luck ran out and they whacked one with the bull bar. Luckily they only clipped it with the side of the bullbar and it flew out to the edge of the road rather than coming over the bonnet and wiping out the windscreen and possibly them too.

"Lotta blokes been killed by kangaroos coming through the windscreen," Charlie said. "I know one fella got killed when a car hit a roo and threw it into the air and the car behind got it through the windscreen. Broke the fella's neck. Ya gotta have bullbars up here. Ya gotta have 'em down south now as well. Roos everywhere. More'n we've ever known. They reckon clearing of the land for pasture made it good for kangaroos. They're breeding like rabbits now."

"Yes and I hear the Americans are protesting because Australians cull them and eat the meat and export it. They say it's cruel and they are being wiped out. They don't see anything wrong with shooting deer and eating them," Roh said.

"I don't think we'll be exporting too much roo meat for some time now. We'll be needing it all here with the hundreds of thousands of refugees flooding in. We might be facing some hard times for a few years while we get on top of this," Griff said.

"Do you think so, Griff?" Roh asked.

"I reckon so, but it gives me an idea. There will be a growing market for meat. If we can get a hundred acres or more quickly, before the price of land goes through the roof, we could make a profitable business raising beef cattle."

"I think it might be better to raise Boer goats, Griff. They grow more quickly than beef and they're easier to handle. They don't need as much space as cattle and a lot of these refugees prefer goat meat to beef. In fact a lot of them won't eat beef, as you well know."

"I can't argue with that. It's a Boer goat farm. Tagasaste grows like a weed on the sandy soils around Perth and that will provide the goats with the browsing they need."

They talked on about setting up the farm throughout the rest of the drive to Broome. Roh would run her vet clinic from the farmhouse and Griff would run the goats. There would be plenty of work for the other members of the survivor group who decided to join them. The time passed quickly and they started to feel a sense of excitement about the new life down south.

They dropped Charlie off at a house in the town after telling him how he could get in touch with them in Perth and then drove on south for fifty or sixty kilometres to a beach resort. Roh had booked a chalet there and they would be able to have Bluey there without problems, as long as he was kept chained or on a leash. They checked in late afternoon and went for a walk along the beach and a swim. The place had a pool but they eschewed that in favour of the briny. Bluey enjoyed it as much as they did. They showered, gave Bluey his dinner from the supplies they carried in the car fridge and then went to the main part of the hotel for their own meal. Barramundi with salad and a bottle of sav blanc to wash it down. Over dinner they talked about the farm again. They would look for a block near Pinjarra at the foot of the Darling Ranges. They would have an orchard with stone fruit and a big vegetable garden.

"I think I've had enough holiday. I reckon we ought to head off early tomorrow morning for the south and look for our land," Griff said, as they savoured the last of their wine.

"I'll drink to that," Roh said. They clinked glasses.

Now that you have finished reading *The Bird of Time*, we would appreciate your feedback. There is a Reader's Comments page for this book on the Valentine Press website: **http://valentinepress.com.au/?page_id=1439**

www.ingramcontent.com/pod-product-compliance
Lightning Source LLC
Chambersburg PA
CBHW020626110726
47899CB00002B/669